TRANSLATED BY
NANDINI KRISHNAN

ESTUARY

PERUMAL MURUGAN

eka

eka

First published in Tamil in 2018 as *Kazhimugam* by Kalachuvadu Publications Private Limited

First published in English in hardback as *Estuary* in 2020 by Eka, an imprint of Westland Publications Private Limited

Published in paperback in 2023 by Eka, an imprint of Westland Books, a division of Nasadiya Technologies Private Limited

No. 269/2B, First Floor, 'Irai Arul', Vimalraj Street, Nethaji Nagar, Alapakkam Main Road, Maduravoyal, Chennai 600095

ISBN: 9789357764797

10 9 8 7 6 5 4 3

Typeset by Jojy Philip, New Delhi

Printed at Manipal Technologies Limited, Manipal

ESTUARY

Perumal Murugan is the author of eleven novels, five collections of short stories, five anthologies of poetry and a collection of personal essays in Tamil. Three of his novels translated into English—*Poonachi, Or the Story of a Goat, Trial by Silence* and *A Lonely Harvest*—were shortlisted for the JCB Prize for Literature in 2018 and 2019. His other novels translated into English include *Seasons of the Palm,* shortlisted for the Kiriyama Prize in 2005, *Pyre,* longlisted for the International Booker Prize 2023, *Current Show* and *One Part Woman*. His first non-fiction book, *Amma,* was translated and published in 2019.

Nandini Krishnan was shortlisted for the PEN Presents translation prize 2022 and the Ali Jawad Zaidi Memorial Prize for translation from Urdu 2022. She is an alumna of the Writer's Bloc playwrights' workshop by the Royal Court Theatre, London. Her novel-in-manuscript was a winner of the Caravan Writers of India Festival contest and showcased at the Writers of the World Festival, Paris, 2014. She has translated *Four Strokes of Luck* by Perumal Murugan and is currently working on a new translation of *Ponniyin Selvan* by Kalki.

Praise for the Author

'His stories were well received and established him as an important new voice in the Tamil literary milieu. ... Versatile, sensitive to history and conscious of his responsibilities as a writer, Murugan is considered to be the most accomplished of his generation of Tamil writers. Apart from his profound engagement with Kongunadu and its people, he is also a writer of great linguistic skill, being one of very few contemporary Tamil writers who have formally studied the language up to the post-graduate level.'

—*The Caravan*

'One of India's most well-known literary writers. ... His novel is no less than the narrative of all humanity.'

—*Columbia Journal*

'Iconic Tamil writer'

—*Deccan Herald*

'Murugan's unsurpassed ability to capture Tamil speech lays bare the complex organism of the society he adeptly portrays.'

—*The Guardian*

'Murugan's style is conversational and the prose is funny, ironical and poignant.'

—*The Hindu*

'Murugan allows his words and landscapes to speak for his characters. With his lexical precision, he conjures a dizzying array of moods.'

—*Mint*

'There is a touching simplicity to Murugan's words and yet, make no mistake this is writing at its most profound, layered, and heart-breaking.'

—*The New Indian Express*

'Murugan is nothing if not a chronicler of the ordinary. ... It is rare to come across a writer who enjoys such intimacy with not just the land but also the customs that govern the lives of the people who live on it.'

—*The New Yorker*

'Murugan's extensive body of work has always been inspired by social issues in his community. ... I'm hoping for a whole shelf of books from this writer.'

—*The New York Times*

'Murugan has redefined literary resistance with the way he fought the censorship imposed upon him.'

—T.M. Krishna to *BBC*

To my dear friend Anand,
who turns conversation into an art form
and art into medicine

Translator's Dedication

For my Tamil teachers Mrs Usha Subramanian and Mrs Chitra Raghavan, who nurtured my love of a language that was not spoken at home and its rich literature through eleven years in school

FOREWORD

The Story of the Novel's Fateful Progress

All that I have written and all that I write is fictional. Not a word is truth. I would go so far as to say there is no such thing as truth. There are things that appear true. What appears true one moment takes on fictional tones the next. Therefore, everything is fictional. One has to work rather hard to give fiction the appearance of truth. I have worked hard for years to achieve this. I understand from experience that this did not go in vain. However, I cannot continue to work as hard anymore. And therefore, I wrote this novel after deciding I would give fiction the appearance of fiction rather than of truth.

Birth, coming of age, food, growth, family, joy and death are aspects of the lives all humans lead, and they live these lives to the fullest extent. Humans have no problems, internal or external. Those who live in bliss in Devalokam may face crises, but everything is smooth sailing for earthlings. In a world where everything is straightforward and where perfection prevails, what work does the writer have? It is the world where ugly habits prevail, where rules are broken, a world with no values, a world of greed and desire and cruelty, a world that has rotted from all these that best lends itself to fiction, and this world is that of asuras, Asuralokam.

Therefore, I have set this novel in Asuralokam, and my characters are asuras. Asura names and practices may strike the readers as strange. But one will get used to these. A few pages in, one will find not just the names but everything about this world endearing. And if not, it will, at the least, whet one's appetite for novelty.

I have not described the characters' physiognomy. They are all asuras. I believe each person has his or her own image of an asura. The reader will not be hard put to fit the characters into this mould and imagine their height, breadth, mien and so on. I have not dwelt much on the setting either. The reader must make an effort to conjure this world in his or her head. It isn't particularly difficult to imagine roads broad enough for asuras to walk on and buildings tall enough for them to live in. Many, many films have shown asuras as humans. They are just supersized humans, aren't they?

In this novel, I have abandoned the compactness and intensity and nuance for which my writing has been praised earlier, and have given my hands the freedom to write. There were no restrictions. My hands turned into the hands of fate, and kept writing. In several places, the smart aleck in me keeps poking my brain with his index finger to point out that my hands have spoken too much and much of what I have written may be shortened. I believe I've been successful in my attempt to twist that finger and drive him away.

I have come across lists of ten things one must keep in mind while writing, such as conciseness and precision, and ten errors that one must avoid, such as expansive description or vagueness in writing. It has occurred to me that, whether or not I write a novel with all ten positive aspects, I must write one with all ten negatives. In this book, I have intentionally included several of these errors, such as repetition and long description. For some reason, they seemed suited to the subject of this novel. And it does give me some excitement to make these errors. One could call it deviant to be excited by errors. Deviance has been the starting point for various arts. I cannot decide whether here, this has stopped with deviance or turned into art. I leave that decision to the readers.

1

The call of Yama is certain.

A call from one's son is an event.

This had been Kumarasurar's philosophy until the previous night.

His son Meghas had finished a semester of his engineering degree. Having written his exams, he had spent his holidays sleeping at home, and had just returned to college for the second semester. In the 180 days he had been away during the first term, he had never once called his father. But Kumarasurar had called him every evening, at eight. Meghas would have finished his dinner at the hostel mess. He would either be in his room or hanging out with his friends outside the hostel.

'Where are you, aiyya?' Kumarasurar had once asked.

'Where could I be? In the hostel!' Meghas had snapped.

Since then, Kumarasurar had stopped asking the question.

On answering the phone, Meghas would say, 'Solluppa'—tell me, Appa—his only word through the entire call. On some days, he said it fast; on others, he said it gently; on still others, he barked it out; and there were days when he seemed to speak it with hate and resentment. A single word could be a storehouse of emotions, each utterance stirring a different one. It could unleash a torrent, a flash flood, a stream, a wave. Kumarasurar would instantly guess

Meghas's mood from his intonation and fortify himself to counter it.

He would ask his questions, in this order:

'Are you well, aiyya?'

'Did you go to class, aiyya?'

'Have you eaten, aiyya?'

'Do you have enough money, aiyya?'

'Have you washed your clothes and hung them to dry, aiyya?'

'Are you studying, aiyya?'

'Shall I hang up, aiyya?'

Seven questions. The first and the last remained in their fixed spots. The number of questions was unvaried too. The other five questions might occasionally change seats. To each, Meghas offered a single, monosyllabic answer.

'Mm.'

That was it.

Some of his 'mm's were, in fact, demisyllabic. Some were even quarter-syllables that Kumarasurar's ears could barely register. Some 'mm's became 'mmm', and occasionally 'mmmm', venturing into a syllable and a half. The final 'mm' was the strongest of all, sometimes hitting a disyllabic count.

One day, Kumarasurar had told his friend about this pattern of conversation.

Kumarasurar had three friends—Kanakasurar, Thenasurar and Adhigasurar. Kanakasurar had been his classmate in school. Thenasurar was from his village, and so was a childhood friend of Kumarasurar's. They knew each other within an inch of their souls. Kumarasurar's acquaintance with Adhigasurar had begun later, and they had grown close over the years. Kanakasurar was the only one of the three who lived in the same town as Kumarasurar, and they met nearly every day. Thenasurar lived a few hours away and visited the town for weddings, temple festivals and other occasions. Adhigasurar lived in a far-off city, and they rarely met. They spoke over the phone every now and again. In this case, absence may have made the heart fonder.

There was a large open corporation ground in town, which the residents had appropriated for their morning walks. Enthusiasts would begin to trickle in by four in the morning. This would become a stream and then a current and then go into spate between five and seven, until the very earth began to quake under the thom-thom of asura feet. Middle-aged asuras with powerful bodies and prosperous stomachs stomped their feet, lifting their legs off the ground and even leaping for good effect.

Asuras had cordoned off areas for exercises and sports. The earth could soon be heard screaming for mercy under their ruthless soles. This was the secret behind all the children in the neighbourhood being early risers. The collateral effect pleased parents who had to send their wards off to school. They were spared the pain of having to shake the children awake. Parents with infants were less grateful.

Kumarasurar was fastidious about his morning walk. He woke up at five and set off for the corporation ground right after his morning ablutions. He slept in the sitting room of his house, and the bathroom and toilet were in the backyard. So his fitness routine didn't disturb his wife. Sometimes, Mangasuri would already be awake. On those days, he would hear sounds from the kitchen. But he wouldn't bother with telling her he was heading out. It was a habit that went back years. If she was asleep, he would open the door softly, lock it behind him, put the key safely in his pocket and set off.

The iron gate of his house opened on to a small street with only thirty houses. A couple of residents would be up and sweeping their courtyards as Kumarasurar walked past. They lived near the centre of town, and so the grounds were only a quarter of a mile away.

It was cool in the mornings, and he enjoyed his stroll to the grounds. As he approached, he would see heads bobbing over the walls. Motorcycles lined the streets.

Kumarasurar had a routine. His walk lasted about forty-five minutes. Once he began to perspire, he considered his work done.

Right outside the city corporation grounds were vendors who had targeted the fitness mania of the walkers and sold various health products—Bermuda grass juice, aloe vera squash, buffalo milk, peppermint infusion, essence of spinach, foxtail millet laddoos, kozhukattai, mung bean balls, mango rice cake, chickpea rolls, coconut flatbread and banana flower vadais. Each stall drew its faithful.

Kumarasurar was no patron of the stalls. He, along with others who dismissed these health foods as opportunistic businesses, gathered at Gluttony Vilas. The shack had no name board, but had been christened by its customers.

This was a favourite gossip spot. Asuras liked scheming while eating or drinking. Even if Kumarasurar secreted himself away in a corner, his fellow customers wouldn't leave him alone. Someone would approach him with a strangely authoritative request like, 'Sir, this gentleman is retiring from our office this week. We need a poem to felicitate him. Write one, won't you?'

Kumarasurar had a reputation as a poet. He took great pride in this, and never turned down such requests. He would write a short poem overnight and hand it over the very next day. His poetic style followed this pattern:

You tireless scion, bullion who was forged in a golden ore
Fearless lion who served the government with a mighty roar

As long as they could spot rhyme, people were happy to celebrate it as poetry. Some of his aficionados would return the next day with a ponnadai, the golden shawl that is ubiquitous at felicitation events in Asurapuri. They would present it grandly to Kumarasurar, saying, 'We want to honour the poet.'

He had collected several such shawls over the years, and his wife Mangasuri had found various uses for them. In her kitchen, the blender, grinder and refrigerator had each been endowed with a shawl. The cabinet wore a shawl. The television flaunted a shawl. Their home shimmered with shawls.

Kumarasurar had written poems for weddings, for ear-piercing ceremonies, for birthdays. Requests for ghostwriting came from anxious parents whose children wanted to participate in poetry contests, and he obliged. Some of these poems even won prizes. When he was informed of this, he would jump about as if it were he who had been honoured on stage. It delighted him that society could appreciate poetry. His penchant for poetry also ensured that he was treated to free vadais at Gluttony Vilas.

The shop would start making urad dal vadais early in the morning. These vadais, fried in an enormous pan, each had a hole in the middle that was just the right size to stick a finger through and hold the vadai up to one's mouth. The vadai was wrapped in paper that turned greasy from all the oil. Kumarasurar would squeeze out the oil from the vadais until they fluffed up like cotton balls, and then savour their flavour and texture. Each time he ate them, it struck him that Mangasuri's vadais were never quite like this. He couldn't stop with one. His tongue would beg him for just one more as soon as he was done with the first. And for just one more when he was done with the second. He would argue with his tongue every day at the shop. On most days, he managed to put in the enormous effort it took to silence the voice of his tongue. On the few days that his tongue assumed demonic proportions and refused to listen to him, he would bend his ear to it and accord it the respect its victory deserved. He would eat two vadais, drink a glass of tea and burp his satisfaction. And then his tongue would acquire a different voice.

'If you're going to gobble up vadais dripping with oil early in the morning, won't your cholesterol and blood pressure go up? And heaven knows what kind of oil it is, too. It must be old stock left over at a wholesale shop. Apparently, that's the sort of thing that leads to jaundice. So much for your morning walk. The calories in your vadai are far more than you burn.'

What could he say in response? The voice would nag him all day. The slightest burp made him think it was the vadai going about its insidious work. When he farted, he would panic. The aroma which had teased him into helpless temptation in the morning had morphed into a stink that taunted his nostrils. A spell of dizziness or heartburn or drowsiness conjured a gigantic finger that pointed right at the vadai.

I'm not the only one. There are hordes of customers at Gluttony Vilas. I'm not the worst, I stop with two. There are morning walkers who eat four or five vadais. Nothing happens to them, does it? So why are you tormenting me?

He would answer his conscience bravely. He would vow not to eat even a single vadai from the next day on. He would promise to avoid even looking at the delicious handfuls of flour mixture in the pan. The resolve would last until the next morning.

He and Kanakasurar often sat together and ate the vadais. Being friends from school, they used the familiar 'da' while speaking to each other. Kumarasurar made his friend privy to thoughts he didn't share with anyone else. But he did have to be careful. He was all too aware that, despite their deep bond, they belonged to different families and had different mindsets. 'Even a mother and son have different tongues and different stomachs,' goes an old proverb. If mother and son had to heed such warning, one couldn't afford to forget that friends shared a lot less than tongues and stomachs.

And there was another reason for Kumarasurar's cautiousness.

Kanakasurar had two daughters. He and his wife had been to various temples and immersed themselves in various bodies of purportedly holy water to appease the gods into providing them a son. But their wish had not been granted. When tests had revealed that his wife was pregnant with a girl for the third time, they had aborted the foetus six months in. It was a miracle that Druvasuri had survived the surgery. As she was convalescing in bed, her mother-in-law, Madyasuri, had arrived like a raging storm from their village, grabbed her by the hair and slapped her across the face. Pushing her to the ground, Madyasuri had screamed, 'Why does a creature like you, who can't even birth an heir for the family, deserve to wear a sari?' She had begun to strip Druvasuri of her clothes. The neighbours had had to intervene to save Druvasuri from her wrath.

Canals of blood had flowed from Druvasuri's body as she lay on the ground.

'I can't have any more children,' she had told Kanakasurar. 'I'm done. My daughters are enough. If you and your mother want a son, you can get married again. I'm through.' And she had registered for a family-planning surgery.

Kanakasurar had neither the courage nor the stamina to marry again. His mother and wife had not met since. Druvasuri would attend family functions only if she knew for certain that her mother-in-law was not coming. She often said, 'I won't even go to the crone's funeral.'

Kanakasurar's yearning for a son had become a permanent ache. He would stare greedily at every boy who crossed his path, as if he were drinking the child in with his eyes. The usual, placid charcoal of his eyeballs would turn into burning cinders. When the fire in them was spent, he would speak with venomous contempt for the boys.

'Look at their bodies, look at their faces,' he would begin. 'Built like bulls and feeding themselves like buffaloes. And their heads look like coconuts that have been chewed up by dogs.' Having thus described their physique, he would move on to their personalities. 'They're already on to cigarettes and booze and weed.'

His concern for the asura clan grew everyday. The very sight of youngsters drew a deep sigh from him. 'Poor things, what are they going to make of themselves? Their future is ruined. They won't have fresh water or air or food, and are going to waste away,' he would say, anxiously. 'You've got nothing to worry about, pa. You've got a sole heir. Both my children turned out to be girls. If only the first had been a boy, I would have stopped with one myself.' He had a tendency to overshare.

If Mangasuri came to know that Kanakasurar had chanced upon Meghas, she would do a ritual to remove the Evil Eye. 'Damned eye that feeds on the flesh of children, damned eye that stings the innocent,' she would mutter as she circled his face with a lit wick and made him spit on it.

If Meghas happened to be home when Kanakasurar came visiting, she would hustle her son into his room and draw the bolt. 'He's gone out,' she would say.

'Kids these days, they go out all the time and ruin their lives by getting into the wrong company,' Kanakasurar would begin. He would then launch into a detailed analysis of all the addictions to which they were exposed, all the tricks they would learn, and how these would be the undoing of them, their families, their society and the world.

If, in the hope of averting this, she said, 'He's gone to see a friend,' he would reply, 'They look like good chaps when you see them alone. But once they get into a gang, they're capable of murder. If Meghas hangs out with all sorts of boys, he'll come to nothing.'

So, Mangasuri had finally hit upon a solution. Whenever Kanakasurar asked about Meghas, she would say, 'He's studying for an exam.' One couldn't really fault a boy who always had his nose in a book. Kanakasurar was caught offguard the first time. 'Oh, let him study, let him study,' he had said.

Eventually, he had found a way around this ploy too. 'They'll fool you saying they're going to study. Either they're going to fall asleep or they're going to be looking at pictures in *that* kind of book. Where do boys these days bother with studies? It's always the girls who top the exams. They're the ones who pass in bigger numbers. Boys are good for nothing.'

Mangasuri was hard put to stop him from coming home, until a fateful series of events unfolded. Kanakasurar had a stentorian voice. If you heard him from a distance, you'd think a tree was being hacked with an electric saw. Each word he spoke echoed through the whole street. There was no way he could keep a secret. One day, he had launched a tirade against someone to Kumarasurar, who sat listening with his arms folded and lips sealed like an obedient schoolboy. Kanakasurar showed no sign of leaving. He probably had nothing to do. Or he had been swept away by his rant as by a tide. Whatever it was, it appeared Kanakasurar was there to stay.

Having exhausted the last reserves of her patience, Mangasuri intervened. 'Enga. The boy is studying. Do you have to scream your head off like this? This is just gossip after all. If you must indulge in it, can't you do it softly?'

No woman had ever confronted Kanakasurar in this manner. He was too shaken to reply. He gathered all of this ignominy into a single syllable—'Chhhi!'—and walked out of the house. Since then, he had not visited Kumarasurar's home. If he happened to see Mangasuri, he would not stop to speak to her and would turn his face away.

'He doesn't have to visit, and he doesn't have to talk to me. I'm finally at peace,' Mangasuri would say.

But Kumarasurar could not bear to lose a childhood friend.

'Let it go, that's how her brain works,' he had told Kanakasurar, by way of renewing their friendship over vadais at Gluttony Vilas.

Nonetheless, a vestige of fear remained. Kumarasurar was afraid that when the search for a bride for Meghas began, and prospective in-laws turned to family friends for discreet enquiries, Kanakasurar would say something along the lines of, 'The boy's a fine one. His mother is the problem.' Kanakasurar's resentment of boys had now extended to the mothers who had borne them. So, Kumarasurar was wary of speaking about his son.

There was a crisis in Asurapuri. It was hard to find a bride. When there was a drought of girls, it would not do for rumours about the character and eligibility of his son to spread. Kanakasurar was a long-time friend, but he did not have a son. He was not exempt from the asura clan's tendency to exaggerate the tiniest flaws and elevate them to eclipse all else. Besides, to speak about Meghas in public was to expose him to eavesdroppers, who would do the job even if Kanakasurar refrained.

However, that day, his heart was so heavy he couldn't stop himself from recounting his last conversation with Meghas. The moment he finished, Kanakasurar dug into his mouth to fish out the vadai he had popped in a while ago, held it safely in one hand and began to roar with laughter. He laughed and laughed, and wouldn't stop laughing. Tears of mirth rolled down his cheeks and glinted in the sun. He staggered to a shuttered shop nearby and collapsed in a heap, laughing. He held his sides and laughed so loudly that the people who were eating vadais outside the shop froze and stared. They wondered for a while whether the laughter therapy club which congregated in a corner of the grounds and made horrifying sounds of 'Hahahahahahahaha … Hihihihihihihihihihi' had now laid claim to the streets too. Then, figuring there wasn't much they could do about it, they turned their attention back to the vadais.

Kumarasurar was troubled. What had he said to provoke such a strange reaction from his friend? Had he tarnished the spotless image he had striven to create of his son? What if Kanakasurar went around saying, 'You know how his son talks to him on the phone?' and built a ridiculous story around the 'mm'? He wished he had not confided in his friend.

When Kanakasurar had finally overcome his laughing fit, he wiped his tears, drank some water, turned to Kumarasurar and said, 'What are you, a professor? You only seem to ask questions of your son?'

Kumarasurar was relieved that it was he, and not his son, that his friend had found risible.

'If you're going to ask questions that only merit "mm" for a reply, that's all you'll get,' Kanakasurar continued. 'You should speak about different subjects with a teenage son. Speak about the movies, speak about actors, speak about politics, speak about TV programmes, speak about Facebook and WhatsApp …' Having listed a few more prospective topics of conversation, he signed off with, 'Speak, speak, keep speaking. And then he will find something to say too.'

2

Kanakasurar's parting advice haunted Kumarasurar all day. Could he talk about the movies? It had been years since he'd last gone to the cinema. He hadn't seen any recent releases—or any, for that matter, from this era. Until recently, if a black-and-white film happened to be running on the television, he would watch it for a while. And then, he would begin to feel sleepy. When he woke, he would try to remember at which point in the story he had fallen asleep, but would not be able to recall the plot.

'The man says he wants to watch a film and sits himself down. And then he sleeps with his mouth open as wide as a bandicoot's burrow,' Mangasuri would say. He didn't like arguing with her. Why provoke her, he thought, and stopped watching the television too.

Of course, there were popular film songs. He didn't understand any of the new ones. They sounded to him like animal cries. If the music was bestial noise, the lyrics were worse—they only proved that language could be chewed and spat out like betel leaves. The lyrics of certain songs, and the scenes which accompanied them, threw him into panic.

He had once heard a song which went:

Oh, Cupid King, my Cupid King,
The fragrant rose is so alluring
Smell it, how intoxicating!

Two unidentifiable forms danced to the music. He rubbed his eyes and stared. They bore little resemblance to asuras. They danced like ravens that had got drenched in the rain and were trying to shake off the water. Their clothes left little to the imagination. The choreography appeared to simulate sexual intercourse. Each word of the lyrics was a double entendre. All the songs were the same, he thought.

And these were the songs his son hummed as he went about his day. He often watched foreign films, in languages Kumarasurar could not follow. These films were choreographed entirely around fight sequences. Someone was constantly destroying someone else. It appeared Asuralokam was surrounded by enemies waiting to close in. If Kumarasurar walked into the room when he was watching a film, Meghas would either pause it or change the channel, and head off to the toilet. If he wanted to figure out what Meghas liked, he would have to slink around like a cat and spy on him.

How, under these circumstances, could he talk about cinema with his son?

Could he talk politics? He was a civil servant. He was afraid to speak about the government, especially after what had happened to one of his colleagues.

That man had been so enthusiastic about things that as soon as each year ended, he would change calendars.

In the calendar provided by the government, the pages for the twelve months of the year featured pictures of the king in robes of different colours. It would take at least seven months for the new calendar to reach the office.

It was only after the turn of the year that the authorities began their annual deliberations on the calendar. A Calendar Committee would be set up, and it would take them four months to prepare a report. Their suggestions would have to be taken into consideration, executed and the costs calculated. The government's official printing press would have to be paid and the calendars checked. Once they were approved by the competent authorities, they would be sent to the head office and then distributed to each department. This was no easy task, and it was commendable that it was usually achieved under eight months. It took yet another month for each department to distribute it to its constituent branches.

So, the government's calendar did its job only for the last three months every year. Then how did the employees manage their schedules the first nine months?

Usually, a private concern would visit the office and provide two calendars to each civil servant as New Year gifts—one for the office, and one for home. The private company was driven by the altruism of serving the nation by serving government employees, so that civic work could be planned under the auspices of their logo. Some people requested a third calendar.

The year of the incident, Kumarasurar's colleague's promptness in serving the nation had cost him dearly. He had made one little mistake—rolling up the old calendar and its twelve pictures of the king, and chucking it into the bin. His reasoning could not be faulted: If each calendar sheet had been printed on one side, the paper would have come in handy. What could one do with a calendar that was glossily printed on both sides?

But an anonymous ill-wisher of his had taken a photograph of the king's pictures lying in the garbage and sent it along with an unsigned letter to the head office. The letter said Kumarasurar's colleague had not just thrown away the calendar with its pictures but had also stamped on it and driven it into the ground. The photograph did show a footprint on the king's face. Transfer orders were sent to the civil servant the next day. He rushed with the notice to the head office to plead his case, but no one would give him the time of day.

When he finally managed to meet the minister in charge of his department, the latter said, 'Follow the orders for now. We can figure this out later.'

The man had no choice. He moved cities. He said he had never, ever insulted the king and that he was a faithful citizen who believed in the monarchy. He wrote a letter citing several anecdotes to support his case—for instance, once, riding his motorcycle on the main street, he had happened to see the king's cavalcade; he had immediately got off his bike so he could bow low from the waist.

But he found no respite. He now lived in a far-off place, and his family stayed behind in their town in the hope that the transfer would be rescinded. He was forced to dip into his savings to grease the palms of various officials at the head office who'd hinted that they could be bribed into helping him out.

Kumarasurar exercised extreme caution in such matters. He often said that a government servant ought to follow this golden rule—never be the first to do anything; always make sure someone precedes you. The last person to finish a task never got into trouble.

Above Kumarasurar's desk, the previous year's calendar had pride of place five months into the next. He could get through a couple of months without keeping track of dates. He had made it a daily habit to look at the calendar at home and memorise the day, month and other details that might prove useful.

Once the new calendar was issued by the government, he planned to remove the previous one with veneration and accord it a place in the old iron cupboard where the office's obsolete files were stored. It already held several years' worth of calendars. If he were ever asked to prove his fidelity to the government, he could produce the evidence with the turn of a key. The calendars also served as a tab of the number of years he had spent in government service. Once he retired, he would hand over the calendars to his successor and ensure he had a signed receipt. Then, no one could declare him a traitor.

When such intense planning went into his interactions with the government, it wasn't a good idea to talk politics with his son.

Every topic Kanakasurar had suggested presented such problems. Perhaps he had tried to instigate Kumarasurar into digging his own grave, for his epicaricacious pleasure?

Having ruled out all other options, Kumarasurar decided that his conversation with his son had to remain restricted to the same seven questions.

But Mangasuri was different. She could talk to their son for hours. The moment Meghas called, she would take her phone into the kitchen. Kumarasurar would hear the sound of laughter, punctuated by disjointed phrases. He had tried eavesdropping, but he could barely follow the trajectory of the conversation. He didn't dare press his ear against the door—if Mangasuri happened to catch him red-handed, he wouldn't have an excuse. But until she hung up, he wouldn't be able to turn his mind to anything else. She spoke to Meghas for at least a quarter of an hour every day. Sometimes, she went on for half an hour.

Mangasuri rarely left the house. What could she be talking to their son about? If he asked her, she would demur.

'Could I possibly run out of conversation with my own son?' she would say, without letting him in on what they spoke about. Kumarasurar had driven himself crazy trying to figure out how she kept Meghas on the phone for so long.

'If you show him some affection, he will talk to you,' she said at times. 'All you have for him are instruction and interdiction. What can he say to those? You snap at him all the time.'

Did any of his seven questions sound snappy? On the nights when sleep played coy—which was most nights for Kumarasurar—he would analyse each of these seven questions.

'Are you well, aiyya?' was certainly not snappy. He did not even use 'da' with his son. He said 'aiyya'. One had to begin a conversation by asking if one's interlocutor was well. So, the first question could not be faulted.

'Did you go to class, aiyya?' was the next question. He only meant to ask whether Meghas had finished his work for the day. Perhaps Meghas thought this was a veiled suggestion that he was likely to play truant. So, this was a problematic question. He could consider changing it. How? 'Did you have college today?' This could imply that the college often went on strike. 'Did class go well today?' Wouldn't that mean class did not usually go well? Should he leave this question out and stick to six questions? He did not want to reduce the number of questions. Should he replace it with something else entirely? He couldn't think of an alternative at the moment. He would retain it as a placeholder till he could figure out a substitute.

'Have you eaten, aiyya?' was the third question. It was a standard enquiry. It was customary to ask this question to show one's concern for the other's well-being. Perhaps he should explore the follow-up questions for which this one offered scope: 'What did you eat?' 'What did you have for breakfast?' 'How about lunch?' 'Did you like the food today?' Meghas would be forced to articulate in more than a single, or demi, syllable. But this presented a dilemma. What if Meghas said he didn't like the food at the mess? The thought of his son eating unappetising food would torment him. Besides, Meghas might use this as a springboard to say he wanted to move out of the hostel and into paying-guest accommodation.

Kumarasurar had always been firm that Meghas should stay in the college hostel, which had regulations and curfews. If he stayed in private accommodation, no one would be able to keep tabs on what he did, where he went or how long he stayed out. He was at an impressionable age. If he chanced upon intoxicants, he would get addicted at once. As his parents, Kumarasurar and Mangasuri had to be careful. And Kumarasurar would have to be careful with his questions too. A qualitative question could have unforeseen ramifications. He decided to avoid these.

'Do you have enough money, aiyya?' was a question he asked because he worried for his son. A father could only prove his solicitude by offering money. He was the breadwinner and had to provide for his son. So this question could not be avoided.

The next question had its defects, Kumarasurar thought. 'Have you washed your clothes and hung them to dry, aiyya?' Meghas was an only child and had been adored all his life. For as long as he had lived at home, he had never had to lift a finger. His mother had taken care of all the chores at home and his father had run all the errands outside. Meghas had had little to do other than focus on his academics. He had not learnt how to wash his clothes or spread them out on a line to dry. He could not know how to fold them and stack them in a cupboard, or how to iron them before use. But washing one's clothes was important. It had to do with hygiene, and therefore with health.

Sometimes, Kumarasurar was tempted to add questions like, 'Have you bathed, aiyya?' 'Do you scrub your clothes while washing, aiyya?' 'Were your stools normal today, aiyya?' He had acted on this impulse a couple of times, only for Meghas to hang up on him. Since Kumarasurar was determined not to provoke Meghas, he had already decided to do away with follow-up questions to the fifth query. But even the main question suggested Kumarasurar did not place much faith in his son's sense of cleanliness. What could he do about this?

'Are you studying, aiyya?' could not be avoided. This wasn't a question which sought an elaborate reply. It was important to remind Meghas of his duties as a student of engineering. It was a father's responsibility to ensure that his son was constantly reminded of his duties. He would not shirk his paternal obligations, and those necessitated the sixth question.

The last question, 'Shall I hang up, aiyya?' could not be replaced with anything else. He did have to seek his son's permission to hang up. If he simply signed off with, 'I'll talk to you later,' he would worry that Meghas might have had something to say and that he had cut him off prematurely. He had to retain this one too.

So, his seven questions were unavoidable. He would have to ask them irrespective of whether Meghas chose to respond. His son was conditioned to expect these questions by now. Even if he resented them, these questions were designed to direct him towards a healthy, happy life. Kumarasurar had never shied away from his parental duties; he never would.

3

When Meghas needed something, he deputed his mother to speak to his father about it.

Mangasuri would open her oration with: 'Would you believe it? Your precious son wants a thousand rupees a month for pocket money!' or 'Your precious son has to buy some book for college; he needs two thousand rupees by tomorrow.'

Meghas became Kumarasurar's 'precious son' each time his mother conveyed a request. His appeals—for new clothes, for money to go hiking with his friends, for things he needed to buy on his professors' orders—were all filed through his mother. Kumarasurar did not like this. It rankled that Meghas felt the need for a conduit. Meghas had been tremendously attached to his father when he was a child. Often, Kumarasurar had felt so crowded by Meghas's constant neediness that he had found excuses to go out, just for a break from his son. Could this be the same boy?

His wife was indeed his son's mother. But all the same, she was a third person, wasn't she? Why did his son feel the need for a third person between the two of them? Did he have no love—or even affection—for his father? Then, Kumarasurar began to think about it from another perspective. If Meghas made a direct request, his father would not be able to deny him, even if it stretched his finances thin. When he was represented by his mother, Kumarasurar could rant about the boy to her, he could delay granting the request. Perhaps Meghas had decided that he shouldn't make things easy for himself at his father's expense. Not acceding to his request would force the boy to manage his pocket money carefully. Kumarasurar liked to think Meghas was too considerate for his own good.

This was how things had worked till the previous day.

Irrespective of whether he was sleepy, Kumarasurar always tucked himself into bed by ten. For a while, he would toss and turn, thinking of work he had to do in his office and around the house. After an hour or two, he would have exhausted his mind into sleep. He had scheduled his bedtime after accounting for the time that must be set aside for his thoughts and worries.

His son was an owl. No one—not even the boy himself—knew when he would go to bed or what he would occupy himself with through the night. If asked, he would say, 'I'll sleep when I feel sleepy.'

Kumarasurar couldn't fault the logic of that response. But the night was meant for sleep, wasn't it? Why did Meghas stay up all night and sleep at dawn? It didn't bode well to turn one's back on the rising sun. The birds that chirped themselves awake in the wee hours roosted by sunset and fell silent. But even after the lights were out, Meghas's mobile phone would cast a glow over his face and chirp all night. Kumarasurar could do little but make his annoyance known.

The previous night too, Kumarasurar had made his bed and tucked himself in. He was thinking about work. That morning, he had been told off by his boss for bringing a file half an hour late to his office. Kumarasurar had heard him out in silence, knowing that the man was keen to make his presence felt during his rare visits to the office. Now,

Kumarasurar conjured him in his head and started letting loose the retorts he had held back in real life.

Suddenly, his mobile phone began to ring. The video in Kumarasurar's head was automatically paused and the ringing of the phone took over.

No one called him at this hour. Everyone who knew him well was aware that he wouldn't answer his phone after ten. Even Adhigasurar, who lived so far away, never called him at an inconvenient time. If he had something important to say, he called Kumarasurar's wife. Mangasuri liked talking to Adhigasurar. She called him 'anna' and briefed him on all of his friend's shortcomings every time he called, to which Adhigasurar made appropriate noises of sympathy. Mangasuri would give her husband the low-down the next day. So this had to be a wrong number. Or one of those annoying telemarketing calls. It didn't make sense for him to get off the bed and check.

The phone stopped ringing, but started again immediately. If someone was calling incessantly late at night, it must be important; it could only be the dreaded call to announce the death of a relative. Who would it be? Kumarasurar leapt off the bed and reached for the phone.

Contrary to his expectations, the call was from his son. He had saved Meghas's number as 'A', giving him premium place in his phone directory, as in his life. He was paralysed with disbelief and stood staring at the ringing phone. He was so ecstatic that his son was calling that he felt himself floating off the ground. And then he came crashing back. Why was Meghas phoning him at this time? What emergency could it be? As Kumarasurar contemplated the less savoury prospects, the phone stopped ringing.

He wanted to tell Mangasuri right away that their son had spoken directly to him, for once. She would not have gone to sleep yet. She would do her washing and cleaning before she wound down for the night.

He left the room to seek her out, but changed his mind. What if she responded with, 'Oh, yeah, he called me before that. It was I who asked him to call you.' That would deflate his enthusiasm entirely. He would leave it till the morning. That way, he would have all night to hold on to the thrill of his son calling him. Would Meghas try to reach him again or wait for his father to call? The anticipation of finding out excited Kumarasurar. He placed the phone on the table and tucked himself back into bed. But his mind did not quieten. Why had Meghas called at this time? Could there be some trouble in the hostel?

There could have been a fight among the boys. This generation was warped. The smallest disagreements led to clashes. These were no small tiffs. They went at each other with murderous rage. Just last week, there had been a fight between rival gangs in a college hostel, and a number of students had been admitted to hospital with bloody wounds to the head and limbs. Some of the boys had been arrested. Apparently, a student had stepped on another's foot while travelling in a bus. The boy who had stepped on the foot was of a low caste. The boy whose foot had been stepped on was of a higher caste. A verbal altercation had snowballed into a violent caste clash. What if something like that had happened?

What if one of Meghas's friends had asked him to come out for a motorcycle ride, and they had got into an accident? These days, everyone had a vehicle as high as a horse. And a flying horse at that. No asura seemed to remember he was riding on the streets. It was as if they were sailing through the air. The fathers who allowed their sons these indulgences should be whipped. Every day, the newspaper carried reports of road accidents, most of which involved youngsters. Something he had read in the papers a couple of days earlier came to mind.

Two boys had been speeding on a motorcycle. They had had an accident and died on the spot. The parents of one of the boys had rushed to the site of the accident, drunk poison the moment they identified their child's body, and died on the same day. Had they taken the poison with them? Where and when had they bought it? What kind of poison could it have been? The office canteen had been buzzing with speculation. Kumarasurar had been listening silently. The boy had been an only child, like Meghas. If this had happened to their son, would he and Mangasuri have done as these parents had?

Kumarasurar began to panic now. He should have answered the phone at once. Meghas had not tried calling a third time. Should he call him? But if it had been urgent, Meghas would have called yet again, surely? It must be a minor matter. He should wait. Just a little longer. He would give it another quarter of an hour.

'I nodded off some time ago. I just woke up to go to the toilet. I checked my phone to see what time it was, and you seem to have called,' he could say, by way of explanation for returning his son's call late.

His ears perked up suddenly. No, he wasn't hearing things. His phone was indeed ringing for a third time. Afraid his son would give up, he jumped up and answered.

'Appa!' came his son's eager voice.

His tone indicated he was fine, and there was no cause for worry. What an immense relief.

'Tell me, pa,' Kumarasurar said.

'Appa, I need a new mobile phone.'

'Why, aiyya? What happened to the one you have?'

There was a moment's silence. Then, Meghas said, 'The other students tease me about it. They say things like, "You call this a phone?" I feel humiliated.'

'All right, aiyya. When you come home, we'll go to the store and buy a new phone.'

'No, Appa ... if we order it online, they'll send it home.'

'Is that so? How much will it cost?'

'I'm checking. I haven't decided which model I want. Whichever one I choose, it's going to cost more than fifty, Appa. I'll check, and let you know once I do.' And with that, the line went dead.

For a while, Kumarasurar's head swam. Had his son actually just said what he had heard? Was it really Meghas who had said the words? What had he said? That he wanted a phone. He'd also told him how much it would cost. 'More than fifty.' Fifty meant fifty thousand rupees, right? Could a phone really cost that much? He wasn't able to sit still. He tried to go back to sleep. He couldn't lie still either. His tongue went dry and he felt suffocated. What if he was going into cardiac distress? He had been to the doctor's the previous month and his parameters had been fine. But people who were otherwise perfectly fit could have sudden cardiac arrests. He got off the bed and glugged down some water. His palpitations seemed to stop.

He opened the door gently. The light was on in the kitchen, and he could hear vessels clinking. Should he tell Mangasuri about Meghas's call now? What would he say? He could barely process what his son had told him. He let himself out by the front door and climbed up to the terrace. It was a new moon's day. The stars twinkled feebly. They couldn't defeat the darkness of the night.

Kumarasurar sat heavily on a bench by the parapet. What had his son just said? He had asked for a mobile phone. What had he said it would cost? More than

50,000. What could 'more than 50,000' mean? 60? 70? 80? 90? It could be Rs 99,999. A rupee less than a lakh. This was how things were priced these days. Rs 99, Rs 199, Rs 999 ...

Why should a phone cost that much? He must tell his son right away that he could not buy such an expensive gadget. But he had left his mobile behind in the room. So what? He could fetch it at once, call his son and say, 'No way.' If he didn't object right away, his son would assume he had consented.

Something else occurred to Kumarasurar. His son was a teenager. His friends must have been speaking about the phone. Yes, that must be it—he had been egged on to ask for it. True, Meghas had been inconsiderate. But he would be hurt if his father snubbed him immediately. Kumarasurar would give his son the night to dream about the phone, and let him down gently the next day. Or he would visit him in college and speak to him in person. He was absolutely certain that he would not grant the boy's request this time. His quandary was simply this—how would he say, 'No'? As was typical of him, he decided, 'It's always a good idea to postpone something until one has had a good think about it.'

4

Kumarasurar was engulfed by anxiety. How had Meghas worked up the courage to ask for such an expensive phone? And to ask him directly? Could Mangasuri have known about this? Perhaps the boy had told her, and she'd been so shocked that she had refused to convey his request? Perhaps she'd said, 'I won't ask your father for such a thing. If you want it so badly, ask him yourself!' Meghas knew what his father's job was and how much he earned. How could he have found it in himself to make such a callous demand? He wasn't a child.

Just four more years. Meghas would have to score over 90 per cent in the examinations held by his university at the end of each semester, in order to qualify for interviews with the most prestigious companies during campus placement. Kumarasurar was certain he would score over 80 at the very least. Once he had received his degree, he would find a job. He would earn a respectable salary. If Kumarasurar and Mangasuri began to look for a bride as soon as he found a job, they could marry him off within a year. Marriage should not be postponed once one had a job and monthly income. Financial independence could make the mind wander. Also, Meghas might stop listening to his parents' advice once he had his own money. There was no shortage of waiting traps.

Kumarasurar had planned out Meghas's future, and new mobile phones did not feature in these plans. How was he to defeat this demon that had materialised from nowhere? Had this desire floated to the top of his son's mind like milk skin, or had it taken root in the boy's brain like cancer? If it was the former, it could be blown away. Or folded around a finger and thrown into the bin. But cancer could not be quite so easily destroyed. Its origins had to be found and the source removed. Even so, it might have already metastasised. How had this desire grown inside Meghas? Had his friends poked fun at the phone Kumarasurar had bought him? Yes, it must have been they who had caused the cancer to flare. There were rich brats in that college, who had no interest in their studies. They didn't need to study. Their fathers had made their millions, which these brats would inherit. Their pocket money flowed into shops. They needed excuses to indulge their materialism. How could he save his son from this influence?

Kumarasurar was so deep in thought that he did not hear the footsteps on the stairs.

'Are you not able to sleep today either? Which kingdom are you going to conquer that merits such intense introspection?' came Mangasuri's voice suddenly.

Kumarasurar wasn't sure whether he should share his worries with his wife. Meghas must have spoken to her already. Perhaps this was part of a conspiracy between mother and son. She was here to figure out which way he was leaning.

'Why are you silent? Are you counting the stars? Is your lifetime going to be enough to finish that task?' Mangasuri said with a smirk.

Kumarasurar decided to take the bull by the horns.

'Did your son call today?'

'Oh, yes, he did. Perhaps around nine. He had a lot to say. I believe they had kuzhipaniyaram at the college mess today. He said he had ten or fifteen of those. But even so, they weren't as good as mine, he said. I told my little boy to come home, I'll make paniyaram for him.'

'Was paniyaram all you spoke about? He had nothing else to say?'

'He didn't.'

'Really?'

'Really. Why, did he say anything to you? You seem to be driving at something. If he had anything important to say, wouldn't I tell you? And whom would I tell if not you? I only see the four walls of this house. Where would I go?'

'All right, all right, that's enough.'

'I can't get a sentence out before you snap at me. What did I say that was so offensive? Why did you bite my head off?'

'Your son called me out of the blue today. And after I spoke to him, I wished he hadn't called. You know the old saying about the baby whose parents ached to hear it speak, and when it did, its first words were, "Amma, when are you going to tear off your nuptial chain?" It's the same story.'

'So, I suppose he wanted money. What is it for?'

'Your son wants a new mobile phone. *New mobile phone*. And one that costs over fifty thousand.'

'Is that what he asked? A-ha, so you're trapped! Buy it for him, why don't you?'

Although he couldn't see his wife's face clearly in the dark, he could make out the mockery in her tone, the amusement in her voice. He felt a sudden impulse to punch her in the mouth. He restrained himself. He could think of nothing to say in response.

'Do you buy me anything I ask you for? Have you ever bought me a sari? Whenever I ask if we can buy something, you say you don't have money right now, we'll see later. Now, you have to fulfil your precious son's demands.'

His wife's glee irritated him further.

'Where have I fallen short? What are you ranting about?'

'What's ever been in abundance here? Everything falls short. All the jewellery I have is what I wore at our wedding. Have you ever bought me anything? When I ask you, you shut me up with, "Do we have a daughter for whose wedding we have to start collecting jewellery?" Clearly, I don't look like a woman to you.'

'Are you going to wear jewels all day like a doll in the showcase? And do you think I'm going to buy your son the phone he wants? Where do I have the money for it? I've spent everything on his education already.'

'That's your song for now. You'll give it a good think, turn your options over in your head and eventually buy him that phone. That's what you always do. Want to bet on it?'

'Yeah, right, that's all I need now.'

'Which phone did he want? Did he tell you what it's called?'

'No, he said he's looking. Do you know of any mobile phone brands?'

'Of course, I do. You're the only one who's clueless about everything. Let me ask him. Give me your phone.'

'I didn't bring it with me.'

His wife turned and rushed down the stairs. He could hear the eagerness in her feet. It hurt him that she had borne so much resentment against him all these years. His son was a child. One couldn't expect him to be pragmatic. But his wife? He was the tiniest cog in the government's machinery. However hard these little cogs worked, they had all the influence of a molar in one's mouth. It was one's front teeth that shone in photographs. They were the ones that got the attention, the ones that merited expenditure. All the molars got to do was grind against each other.

He had joined the service as a junior clerk. He worked in the Department of Statistics, with no scope for additional income. His job was to contact other departments and compile the statistics that the government demanded. He had to type and send letters every day. His office was tucked away at the far end of an alley that was barely noticeable between the enormous buildings of the district corporation. Flies and mosquitoes visited frequently. The department did not have a head. Directors of other departments had to supervise Statistics as an additional duty. They dropped in occasionally, and usually asked for files to be sent to their office for approval.

Kumarasurar had worked his way up to the position of supervisor over the years. Although he was given the dignity of a promotion, his work had not changed. The government had decided not to waste its resources by allocating more clerks to departments like Statistics, which did not play an active role in the running of the country. Kumarasurar was technically a supervisor, but his role was still that of a clerk. His salary hadn't increased much either. He was just about able to keep up with the inflation. He had taken a long-term loan from the bank to build their little house. He would only finish repaying it some years into his retirement. Giving his son a good education had further stretched his finances. How could Mangasuri expect him to fill her wardrobe with jewellery and saris? It was their frugality that had allowed them to give Meghas all that he needed. If his wife could not see this, how could he expect his son to?

He stood still as a statue, mulling over these things. Mangasuri climbed back up the stairs, having finished speaking to her son. She told him with great excitement all that Meghas had said. He had chosen the model he wanted. It hadn't yet hit the market. But its features had already been detailed online. It was sleek and attractive; it made one itch to hold it. It would have a limited release the next month. On the fifteenth of the month, a portal for orders would open at midnight. It would close after an hour. One had to place an order within those sixty minutes. The phones would be made to order. Their son was going to ensure he registered for the phone within that window. The phone cost Rs 74,999. Meghas had asked for the money to be transferred to his account.

His wife couldn't stop talking. She spoke so animatedly, one would think it was she who was ordering the phone. He could forgive her for not being daunted by the phone's price. But shouldn't a parent wonder why her son wanted this phone? Shouldn't a wife pity a husband who had been in severe shock since their son had called?

Once she was done with her speech, she said, 'You're staring like you're in severe shock. Go down and get some sleep. You can think about how to arrange for the money in the morning. Go on.' She seemed to have decided he would buy Meghas the phone. He was determined not to buy it. But how would he break the news to Meghas? He must change his wife's mind first. He could not deal with Meghas until that was out of the way. Now, he had not one problem but two.

5

Meghas was born four years into their marriage. They had longed for a child and lost hope after years of trying. He was an unexpected gift. Kumarasurar's parents wanted to name this precious grandson after their clan deity, the son of Ravana, Meghasura.

Earlier, the future grandparents had promised their demon-gods that if a child were born to the couple, they would have two maces made and sacrifice two male buffaloes to propitiate Meghasura. They had also prayed that they would name the child Meghasuran if he were a boy and Meghasuri if she were a girl. They had to cover all their bases.

When Mangasuri had finally conceived, Kumarasurar—ever the obedient son—had no thought of giving the child any name other than the one chosen by his parents, who had been alive back then.

How could one object when the patriarchs of the family wanted to name a child after the clan deity? But Mangasuri ventured to say hesitantly that the name sounded rather old-fashioned. Kumarasurar's spousal devotion was now in conflict with his filial obedience. His wife was the person who would carry the baby in her womb. She had a right to an opinion on the child's name. Kumarasurar began to consult others.

His friend from school, Poovasurar, now taught language. They ran into each other occasionally. The first time

Poovasurar had told him he was a teacher, Kumarasurar had found it hard to believe him. How could a teacher afford to be so well-dressed, and sport branded clothing? Kumarasurar asked him about his profession again a couple of times to ensure he hadn't misheard.

Once, he asked, 'So do you take part in debates?'

Poovasurar said, in an embarrassed tone, 'I'm not interested in those things.'

How could someone who was not interested in debates teach language?

Kumarasurar began to lose faith in Poovasurar's words. But he tried to give him a chance.

'Will you write songs for weddings?' he asked.

'I can't do that sort of thing,' said Poovasurar, seeming even more embarrassed.

'Then what on earth do you do?' Kumarasurar asked in frustration.

Poovasurar began to look guilty. At that moment, he must have decided not to tell anyone else he was a language teacher. He said, diffidently, 'If someone wants me to write a speech for their child to recite at a competition, I do. If someone wants options to name their children, I make a list of ten or twenty names.'

That was not too bad. Poovasurar seemed to meet two of the four criteria Kumarasurar believed a language teacher should.

In the months before Meghas was born, Kumarasurar considered asking Poovasurar for suggestions. But he had forgotten in which school his friend taught. When he walked about town, he would scan the crowd for Poovasurar's face. Had he been transferred to another city? He made enquiries. A friend's friend's friend's friend put him in touch with a clerk in the district education secretary's office, and Kumarasurar managed to trace Poovasurar through him.

On a government holiday, Kumarasurar went to his friend's house with a box of sweets, and told him about his wife being pregnant and the tensions at home over the naming of the child. Poovasurar did not seem to need time to think. He went into a room and came back with a sheet of paper titled, 'Boy Child Names'.

'Choose whichever one you like,' he said.

Kumarasurar folded the sheet and tucked it into his bag. He told Poovasurar about his parents' choice of name and about Mangasuri finding it old-fashioned.

Poovasurar looked amused. 'Meghasuran is an old-fashioned name, yes. But there's only one difference between the outdated and the modern. Old names have long tails. If you snip off the tail, it becomes trendy. Why don't you name the boy "Meghasur"?'

This struck Kumarasurar as genius. He was finally able to come to terms with Poovasurar being a language teacher.

He went back home and told Mangasuri, 'Let my parents think his name is "Meghasuran". We'll put his name down as "Meghasur" on official documents and call him "Megha" at home.'

She was glad her husband set store by her opinion. But she found 'Meghasur' rather outmoded too. And the 'surrrrr' sounded like an angry twist of the tongue. She mulled over this for a month and decided they would call the child 'Meghas'. Everyone agreed it was a beautiful name. The 'sssss' of the finish was reminiscent of a snake's hiss to Kumarasurar, but he held his peace. After all the months of unpleasantness, all he wanted was for a name to be agreed upon.

Meghas was such a precious child that even his name had undergone careful consideration and much scrutiny.

Even before marriage, Kumarasurar and Mangasuri had individually dreamt of raising their children to be doctors.

Once she became pregnant, it was determined that she was carrying a doctor. They decided they would have to start coaching the child right from birth. Every time they spoke to the infant, they would have to ensure they imparted some knowledge to him. Every time Meghas folded his fists and wailed, Mangasuri imagined he was practising how to hold a syringe before stabbing a patient with it. The baby's laugh had the restraint of a doctor's. He knitted his brows into a frown, like doctors did. Mangasuri dressed him in the clothes she thought doctors wore.

Kumarasurar was pleased with this. But he pretended he wasn't as zealous as his wife. The academic year began when Meghas was a year and nine months old. Kumarasurar had already found a reputed school and enrolled Meghas early so he would have a head start on his classmates. But the school, which had sounded like a hallowed institution on paper, now seemed unsatisfactory. Two-year-olds were not even taught the alphabet in its entirety! What kind of lackadaisical education did this school offer?

Kumarasurar couldn't wait for the academic year to end. The moment it did, he shifted Meghas to a different school. Although this school had a tiny campus and the students were crammed into small, stuffy rooms, it had a good reputation. But once Meghas joined, Kumarasurar was devastated to learn they did not work full days. Once the children had had their lunch, it was naptime. There was also a rumour that sleeping pills were mixed into the food of children who fussed about napping. It was only when the parents went to pick them up in the evening that most of the children woke from their siesta. Children could sleep at home. They didn't have to go to school to nap. Worse, having rested during the day, these children stayed up late and troubled their parents at night. Husbands who were longing for their children to sleep so they could have their wives to themselves began to despise the school. And so, once again, Kumarasurar looked for another school the next year.

Meghas studied in a different school each year. It appeared every school in town had the sole aim of preventing him from becoming a doctor. The eleventh year would culminate in the board examination. Kumarasurar and Mangasuri enrolled him in a famous school outside the town. Kumarasurar had to travel some distance to drop off his son and then come back to his office. This took a toll on him. But it was a crucial year. It helped that he worked in a government office, and in a department whose existence everyone seemed to have forgotten. No one kept tabs on the hours he clocked.

All of a sudden, a head was appointed to supervise the Department of Statistics. This man was resentful of his job. He figured his transfer to a department of no importance had been carried out with malicious intent, and showered his frustration on his subordinates. If someone was late by five minutes, he would glare at the offender. Each word he spoke seemed to have been marinated in venom. Kumarasurar was hard put to get through the year with his new boss. But he bore all the humiliation for his son.

Meghas, having completed fourteen years of education in fourteen different schools, did not let his parents down. He scored 780 marks out of a possible 800. He scored 99 per cent in mathematics. It troubled Mangasuri greatly that she couldn't flaunt a perfect score to the world.

Not a day went by when she didn't say, 'If only you had watched what you wrote, you wouldn't have let that one mark slip, my darling.'

One day, Meghas said, 'Whose answer sheet should I have watched?'

Another day, he said, 'But my friend didn't let me watch what he was writing.'

Yet another day, he said, 'I was in the first row. There was no one sitting before me.'

Meghas laughed it off. But Mangasuri would carry the burden of the one lost mark all her life.

But a bigger disaster was headed her way. Meghas had decided on the branch of study he wanted to pursue, and made the big revelation. He was not interested in medicine. He wanted to be an engineer, and had decided to go with computer science instead of biology for the final two years of his schooling.

His parents were in shock. They couldn't come to terms with their dream of a doctor-son evaporating. Mangasuri tried to play on her son's conscience by going on a hunger strike for two days. Meghas gave it right back. He refused to eat unless his parents agreed to let him choose the computer science stream. Kumarasurar consoled his wife—Meghas was their only child and they should let him live his life as he wished.

Mangasuri sobbed through the day. She tried cajoling her son. She tried begging him. She threatened to commit suicide. She got various relatives and friends to speak to him about a doctor's societal capital and financial prospects. Nothing worked. Kumarasurar did not help her. A boy who did not listen to his mother would not listen to his father, he said. 'Let him study what he wants to' became his mantra.

Meanwhile, another dilemma presented itself—which school would ensure he got a seat in a prestigious college? Meghas, tired of watching his mother blow her nose into her sari and hearing his father spout advice, made a request—seven hours away from their town was a city that only had schools, which trained their pupils to pass the medical and engineering entrance examinations; he wanted to finish his schooling there.

His parents now had a glimmer of hope. They would enrol him in a school of his choice, they said, as long as he chose medicine. He refused. While the standoff was on, he disappeared one evening. He had never left home without telling his parents where he was going. Kumarasurar and Mangasuri scoured the streets for him, but in vain. He strolled home after ten o'clock that night. He said he'd been to see a friend in the neighbouring town. They'd gone to watch a film. His parents had learnt their lesson. They would not stand in his way.

6

They went to the city of schools the day before the class eleven exam results were announced. The city had no native inhabitants. It had no fields. It was all dry desert. Neem and acacia trees, which could survive the harsh sun, made for spots of greenery. There were more schools than trees. Everywhere one looked, the emblem of a school stared back. A board at the entrance to the town read, 'School City'.

Academic and hostel buildings rose towards the sky and stretched across the earth. The schools were gender segregated. Three quarters of the city was dedicated to boys' schools and a quarter of the city to girls' schools.

One could not approach the girls' zone easily. A board marked it as 'Protected Area'. A wall, stacked as high as three or four grown asuras, ran around the girls' sector, and sharp shards of glass were embedded on top of the wall. A fence rose a further two feet above the wall.

The boundary walls of each school carried paeans to themselves: 'This wall cannot be mounted before finishing one's studies'; 'This wall cannot be mounted even by pole vault champions'; 'Our wall is our pride'; 'Studying behind a wall ensures success'.

Kumarasurar wondered where the staff quarters for each school were. He made enquiries and learnt that once a teacher was married, he or she was asked to resign from the school. Only sworn bachelors and spinsters, who had no intention of marrying, worked in the city. There were also some youngsters who wanted work experience before marriage. Those who were teachers by day turned hostel wardens after school hours. Students were expected to study in school all day long, and then in the common room once they returned to the hostel. They studied through the night as their teachers played monitors. Marriage was prohibited to ensure these night watchmen did not slip up or shirk their duties.

On the facade of each of the numerous schools in the city was a notice board. There were no words on them, just scores—800/800, 799/800, 798/800: the cut-offs for entry. Most schools had 800/800 as their cut-off. The parents were confused. Which of these schools should they choose? Did so many students really secure a perfect score in their class eleven exams that it could be a cut-off?

Someone knew the secret: 'They'll take in the students who have scored 800/800 first. Once that's done with, they'll change the board to read "799/800". And so the cut-off keeps reducing until they've filled their seats. So there's no real cut-off. As the marks reduce, the fees increase, that's all.'

They toured the schools all day. One couldn't fault a single school. They all provided meals to the visitors. They had equipped their auditoriums and grounds so parents and prospective students could stay the night. Some provided sleeping mats, others had bedding, others offered pillows.

When some parents said, 'Oh, how lovely, they've provided mats. This must be a good school,' another parent would rush over and say, 'That other school provides pillows too!' The parents made a beeline for the providers of pillows, and returned promptly. It turned out pillows were only provided to the first ten parents who chose the school. The lucky parents smirked at the latecomers as if the pillows were a ticket to heaven.

Word went around that one of the schools provided mattresses. The group that went and boomeranged back said dolefully that this was a rumour. Most parents spent the best part of the night running from school to school to ascertain what sleeping facilities were available, and eventually tired themselves out enough to flop down where they could and sleep on whatever surface they found. They were allowed to use the students' toilets and showers, which were open to the sky. Kumarasurar had never seen such a crowd in his life. Vehicles bearing parents arrived through the night.

'Do you think you'll score 800 out of 800? Shall we look for a school with that cut-off?' Kumarasurar asked Meghas.

Meghas looked dejected.

Parents swarmed around schools with the '800/800' cut-off. The sight was evidence of the hope and faith they had invested in their children. The children, though, were in a quandary. Not only were they unsure of what their scores would be but they also felt their self-confidence erode upon learning of the standards they were expected to meet.

Meghas made up his mind. 'Let's just stay in one place, Appa. Once my results are out in the morning, we'll figure out which school I should join based on my marks.'

Kumarasurar asked, with a tinge of longing, 'So you don't think you'll get a perfect score?'

Meghas pretended not to hear.

Each school had prepared a veritable feast for dinner. Sweets, payasam, vadai, two kinds of vegetables, and for the non-vegetarians, pieces of buffalo curry were served in eco-friendly areca cups. It was melt-in-the-mouth curry. The diners at each school were determined that they had had the best meal in town. Some hopped schools and tried the food at each. But it turned out all the schools offered exactly the same menu. The grains of rice shone like stars on a moonlit night. The aubergine in the sambar popped to the surface like slivers of crescent moon. Though there was no difference in the food, the school-hoppers critiqued each dish they had had at each place—too much salt, too little spice, too much water in the gravy.

Kumarasurar did want to sample the food in four, perhaps five, schools. But one look at Meghas convinced him he had no ally. They had dinner together, took their mats and spread them out on the grounds. Meghas fell asleep at once. Kumarasurar couldn't sleep a wink. He walked around for a while. Several parents were in the same situation. They formed little groups and spoke. It turned out they all wanted their sons to become doctors.

Soon after midnight, queues began to form outside the internet hubs nearby. It was crucial to be the first to note down one's marks and rush to register in a school. The moment the results were announced, there would be a surge of applicants. Several schools had advertised a tuition fee waiver for the first five or first ten students who came in with the highest marks. So the parents were further motivated to win the race to the hub. Although Kumarasurar joined a queue fairly early, hundreds of parents were ahead of him. Some tried to cut the line, and others objected. Some allowed friends to slip into the queue.

Meghas wasn't in a flutter like his father. He sat with the asceticism of a sage. Kumarasurar wondered at his composure. Every now and again, he had to call out to Meghas, because the boy would stroll off. Eventually, they learnt he had scored 780 out of 800 and chose a school that would admit him. As they were waiting to register, Mangasuri called and asked to speak to Meghas.

'Won't you choose biology so you can become a doctor?' she begged one last time. 'Listen to your mother, my darling, just this once. Do this one little thing for me. I will never, ever ask you for anything again. I'll let you do anything you want.'

But her pleas fell on deaf ears. Her son chose computer science, so that he could do a degree in engineering after graduating from school.

Their troubles did not end there. How could one live in peace when one's only child was studying three hundred miles away? Meghas would be away for two academic years. That was twenty-two months in a row. He was not allowed to leave campus in all that time. The students had no holidays, not for births or deaths or festivals. Parents were allowed to visit on the second Sunday of each month.

Kumarasurar and Mangasuri would board the train with Meghas's favourite food packed in a lunchbox. The school bus would receive them at the station and take them to the campus.

The first time they went, they saw parents and children huddled in small groups around the school playground near the hostel. All the boys had dark circles under their eyes. Meghas stared at the floor when his parents asked whether he slept well. At what time did he wake up, they asked. He continued to stare at the floor. Every question was met with silence. He only had one piece of information for them. All the boys had nicknames. Their class eleven exam scores had become their identities. A boy might be called, for instance, 'Dei, 780!' If more than one person had the same score, they were given the additional tag of '780-1', '780-2', '780-3', and so on. Their physics teacher had made a minor modification—'Dei, eater of 20 marks.'

'Don't tell anyone I told you this,' Meghas whispered. 'Here, the walls have ears.'

Meghas couldn't blame his parents because he had chosen the school himself. Two refrains echoed across the stadium.

'Study, pa, study. You have to buckle up and work yourself to the bone just these two years. And then you can relax all your life. Don't lose heart. Study, my boy.' That was the refrain of the parents.

The boys, for their part, offered a chorus of wails.

'Study, pa, study, pa,' bounced off the walls like a mantra.

The underlay to this mantra began as a whimper and rose to a caterwaul. When the parents had to leave in the afternoon, it was as if the city were drowning in tears. The flood of tears swallowed the syllables of the parents' mantra. Eyes shed tears. Hearts shed tears. Stones shed tears. The walls shed tears. The doors shed tears. The windows shed tears. The air was heavy with tears. Slowly, the wailing shrank into the schools, and the parents' silence filled the world outside. At night, owls and whimbrels and nighthawks circled the city.

It broke Kumarasurar's heart to see his son cry. He wished every day that he hadn't enrolled Meghas in that school. Through those twenty-two months, he didn't have a single night of peaceful sleep. He would lie in bed wondering what his son was up to. Had he eaten? Had he studied? Would he do well in his exams? Had he been caned? Did he get any sleep? Kumarasurar was haunted by the image of Meghas in tears. He could only imagine Meghas going about his day shedding tears over each task.

Once, in his office canteen, he overheard someone speaking about schoolboys crying.

'Boys should be disciplined in their adolescence. Or they'll waste their lives away. Let them cry. If they cry through these two years, they can laugh their way to the bank for the rest of their lives. Cry today, laugh tomorrow.'

This gave Kumarasurar great solace. Every time he thought of Meghas, he told himself, 'Cry today, laugh tomorrow; cry today, laugh tomorrow.'

He would later learn that this aphorism was, in fact, a mantra popularised by a self-styled godman. This godman had devoted his life to teaching people how to breathe and to spreading the message, 'Cry today, laugh tomorrow.' The mantra achieved national prominence after a movie star used it in a film. It appeared Kumarasurar was the last to learn a secret everyone knew—except Mangasuri. He imparted this knowledge to his wife. Whenever she saw him moping, she would whisper in his ear, 'Cry today, laugh tomorrow.' The mantra got them through the two years of separation from their son.

On the last day of Meghas's final exams, Kumarasurar went to fetch his son home. Cars lined the streets leading to the school, and parents waited for their children in the grounds. An announcement called out the names of parents of certain pupils. It turned out their children had taken ill during their course of study and had passed away; they had been buried in an impressively maintained cemetery attached to the school. The parents were ushered there with great ceremony.

Those who tried to fight with the authorities were shown the school's rulebook. The parents hadn't read the small print. The school had put in a note on the cemetery. Below a picture of beautifully manicured trees, in letters smaller than an ant's head, was printed: 'Curated cemetery'. A note below said students who committed suicide from fear of examinations or died from illness would be buried immediately so that their fellow pupils would not be affected.

The stomachs of the other parents churned. They were terrified their names would be called out next on the loudspeaker.

'Nothing would have happened to Meghas, he will be fine,' Kumarasurar repeated to himself, over and over again.

As soon as the final bell rang, a tsunami of students overran the grounds. Heads bobbed over a sea of uniforms.

Someone said the teachers had bolted themselves into their rooms. Apparently, those who hadn't escaped in time had been beaten black and blue, and lay bleeding over their own broken limbs. Parents stepped into the storm of uniforms, searching in vain for their sons, so that they could pull them out and take them home before there was a stampede. But all the faces looked alike. The parents ran helter-skelter, panicking about their sons. Kumarasurar stationed himself at the entrance to the hostel. Meghas would have to return to his room at some point.

Students ran past, laughing as they spoke about how some of the wardens had been locked into the toilets, and had had their heads banged against the walls and legs twisted. The boys broke glass windows, pulled doors off their hinges, threw chairs against the walls and ran around with weapons of destruction. Kumarasurar was terrified his son would be among the marauders. But he finally spotted him standing on the sidelines, watching with great enjoyment.

He hustled his son to his room to fetch his things. The room was a mess. His school uniforms and books lay in tatters, as if a thousand rats had ransacked the room and bitten through all his belongings. The mattress, bedspread, duvet ... nothing they had bought him had been spared. His bucket looked new. Kumarasurar reached for it, so they could use it at home. Meghas grabbed it from him and smashed it on the ground so it would break. It didn't quite split in half. Another student ran in, took it from him and threw it into the hallway. Kumarasurar watched in shock as several students hit the bucket and whacked it down from the second floor, as if they were showering flowers on the assembly below.

The satisfaction of having avenged two years of torment beamed on the boys' faces. Word went around that the school authorities had informed the government and that the armed forces were being sent to restore peace in the schools. Apparently, they had been issued orders to shoot at sight. Rumours spread about the number of people who had been wounded or shot dead in each school. Some of the boys insisted that the school authorities had started the rumour.

But Meghas was flustered.

'Come, Appa, let's go, let's go fast,' he said, dragging Kumarasurar by the arm.

Parents ran behind their children.

There was nothing Kumarasurar could salvage from his son's room. All he wanted was to take Meghas to safety.

When Meghas came out with only the clothes on his back, Kumarasurar asked, 'Don't you have anything else with you?'

'I don't want anything that reminds me of this school, Appa,' he said. 'Let it all go to hell. I want to forget I ever studied here.'

The moment they reached home, Meghas tore off his school uniform and set it on fire in the backyard. As he watched it burn, his face turned incandescent. Once the uniform was in ashes, he stomped on them. He ran after the ashes that flew in the air and stamped them into the ground. He was at this for a long time.

Mangasuri boiled vats of water and scrubbed down the son who had returned home after two years. She fed him buffalo curry and his favourite sambar. Meghas wolfed down his meal. Then, he settled down in front of the television and fell asleep within minutes.

The boy did not wake up all day. They decided to let him sleep. He did not wake up on the second day either. How could someone fall into such a deep sleep? He hadn't eaten in a whole day. They tried to wake him up on the second night. He muttered in his sleep, but would not open his eyes.

'Have a bite to eat and then you can go back to sleep,' begged his mother.

But he would not wake up. Mangasuri brought some fruit juice and tried feeding it to him. He let her, and then rolled his head back against the pillow. He slept for ten days in a row. All he had by way of nourishment was juice. He wet his bed in his sleep. Mangasuri cleaned him up and changed his sheets. She kept vigil by his bed. It seemed he was catching up on two years' worth of sleep.

On the third night, Kumarasurar had an epiphany. Their clan deity Meghasura's uncle Kumbhakarna slept six months of the year. Perhaps this was an inherited trait. He told his wife about the epiphany. This was of great comfort to her. She made for the puja room, and began to pray to the figurines of Meghasura and Kumbhakarna. She kept at her prayers until her son woke up. Their demon-gods had not failed them.

Meghas couldn't believe he had slept for ten days in a row. He wasn't convinced by the date on the calendar either. It was only after he went online and ascertained the date for himself that he conceded his parents were right. Neither Kumarasurar nor Mangasuri told him he had wet the bed.

They made arrangements for a grand puja on the day he woke up. Mangasuri had no doubt that it was her prayers that had saved her son.

It was then that she realised she didn't care whether he became a doctor; all she wanted was for him to be alive and well. She never again voiced her disappointment at Meghas's refusing to become a doctor.

The results of his final examinations would be announced after two months. They would have to look for a reputed engineering college after this. Until then, he was pampered at home as he had never been. Each meal was a feast. Mangasuri prepared dishes from various cuisines. It was during these two months that Kumarasurar realised his wife was a wonderful cook. Thanks to his son, he too was fed well.

7

During the three months Meghas spent at home, between the school final examinations and the start of the college term, a problem cropped up. The television wasn't enough entertainment.

First, Meghas asked for a computer. Kumarasurar couldn't fault his reasoning—he intended to study computer science engineering, so he did need a computer.

But once he went to college, he would need a laptop. Kumarasurar suggested they buy a laptop right away, so that they could avoid spending twice over. Meghas thought otherwise.

Several colleges insisted on students buying a particular brand of laptop. Some even bought the laptops for the students and billed them for it. Since the colleges placed bulk orders, these laptops were less expensive than they were in-store. Several colleges said the students didn't really need laptops until the second year. To Meghas, it made more sense to buy a desktop computer for use at home.

'But you'll go away to college in a couple of months, and then no one will use the computer,' Mangasuri said. 'Won't it begin to rust?'

Meghas rolled on the floor laughing. 'Ask Appa to use it so it doesn't rust,' he said, wiping the tears from his eyes.

Kumarasurar had his own troubles. More than a decade ago, the government had announced plans to computerise all its offices. His office had managed to escape the first net cast by the palace. The government had conducted workshops to train civil servants in basic computer science. His name had been on the list of eligible trainees, but he had had no wish to attend. On the first day of the training, he had called in sick and made use of his unclaimed medical leave.

It made him anxious to even look at computers. The wires that coiled around them like snakes made him tremble. He was certain that one could be electrocuted if one's arm or leg happened to graze these wires. He touched the keyboard with one hesitant finger and decided he was too old to learn how to type on this newfangled equipment.

Most government schemes did not see the light of day for about a quarter of a century after they were announced. Given that his department was one of the least important ones, it was likely that they could evade computerisation for half a century, well into Kumarasurar's retirement.

However, for once, the government was inconveniently efficient. Parcels from the palace, containing computers, were issued to every government office within a year and a half of the announcement. This upset all the officials who worked in the state's administrative department. Usually, once such a scheme was announced, a sum was set aside for the purchase of the product required. A committee would be formed under the chief administrative officer and tasked with buying the product. But this time around, the palace had cut out the middleman and explained that they were centralising the process.

The dreaded parcel arrived at Kumarasurar's office too. It was accompanied by an executive assigned by the manufacturer. This man opened the parcel, showed Kumarasurar each part of the computer and explained its specifications in great detail. Kumarasurar did not register any of the terms the executive used, but nodded wisely.

He was told he would have to sign for it. He counted the number of items in the parcel several times over and checked them off against a list. When he couldn't find something on the list in the parcel, the executive would patiently point it out. Even so, he refused to sign an acknowledgement of receipt.

Kumarasurar told the executive he could sign the document only after having received a signed list of parts from him. The man told him he would be back the next day for the signature, and set off. It surprised Kumarasurar that he had taken the risk of leaving without the acknowledgement.

Kumarasurar had to log information related to the receipt of the computer in ten different registers. It took him all day. When the executive returned the next day, Kumarasurar made him countersign each of these registers. Kumarasurar also read the acknowledgement he had to sign for the executive several times over.

Finally, he asked the man to return each part to its place in the box and seal the parcel again. The executive did as he was told. Kumarasurar then checked all the cupboards in the office to find one with a functioning lock. Several hours into his search, he settled on one and locked the parcel inside.

He was also tasked with compiling the statistics on the distribution of computers to all government agencies. He wrote to each department to confirm that a computer had reached the office. He then typed his notes on his trusted typewriter and posted it to the palace. Every now and again, he checked the parcel in the locked cupboard to ensure nothing was missing.

At the end of each financial year, an official from a different department would be sent to audit Kumarasurar's office. If the auditor were to ask about the computer, Kumarasurar planned to show him the parcel in the cupboard. But none of the auditors asked or even looked around the office.

'Where should I sign?' was their only query before they left.

Kumarasurar would not have to worry until the government insisted on computerisation. And if that were to occur, he could get one of his subordinates to learn to use the monstrosity. As one rose in the profession, one lost the need to learn. Everything could be delegated. The boss's main job was to find fault with the subordinate's work.

However, there was a minor problem. He had not been assigned a subordinate.

Kumarasurar wrote every week to the government, asking for an assistant. Each letter he wrote received the same reply: 'There is no junior clerk available at the moment.'

Eventually, several departments began to complain about vacancies, and the government was forced to hold a recruitment examination. The exam was held a year after it was announced. The results were announced a year after it was held.

Appointment orders were not sent to the successful candidates. Some of these candidates would reach retirement age within a year or two. They got together and sent the palace a request for the immediate issue of appointment orders. They started an organisation called 'Union of People Waiting for Appointment Orders'. They announced several protests on behalf of the organisation. They took out processions. They picketed offices. They went on hunger strikes. They took to the road with their families.

The king announced that protests against him would be countered by the armed forces.

'This is not a protest against the king. It is only against the government. We have great respect for the king,' the union announced hurriedly.

This warmed the king's heart.

The protesters then went on a fast unto death. Some fainted. They were admitted to the hospital. When it was announced that a few were in a critical state, the king paid the hospital a visit. The patients looked pitiful. It struck the king that even a death or two could place his government in jeopardy and ruin its track record. He held a press meet right on the hospital premises and announced that the appointment orders would be issued immediately.

An 'Appointment Order Issue Festival' was held, at which the king personally handed over envelopes containing appointment orders to some of the protesters.

Only after the king had made full use of the photo ops and left did his subjects think to open the sealed envelopes. The 'appointment orders' were blank sheets of paper.

The deception infuriated the recipients, and they began to create a ruckus. But a government official told them, 'The envelopes were for the photo op, but the appointment orders will be ready in a day or two. Please be patient.'

The protesters were afraid they would lose all chance of getting their orders if they spoke to the press about what had happened. They had come this far. A day or two didn't sound too bad. Three months after the promise, appointment orders were finally issued.

Yet, no one was sent to Kumarasurar's office. Everyone wanted to join a department which had prospects for additional income. There was stiff competition to join the Revenue Department, which carried out the government's welfare schemes. The Registration Department was fairly popular too. People were even willing to pay bribes to ensure they were assigned the department of their choice.

It was a while before the government found itself obliged to assign people to the Department of Statistics. One fine day, a youngster called Kumbhas joined Kumarasurar's office. This brought immense relief to Kumarasurar.

The very day he joined service, Kumbhas asked, 'Isn't there a computer in this office?'

'Of course,' replied Kumarasurar.

'Where?' asked Kumbhas.

'You'll see, you'll see,' Kumarasurar said vaguely.

They had this exchange every day for six months.

This became rather stressful for Kumbhas, who had been looking forward to using a computer and the free internet connection in office. He had searched every nook and cranny of the department in vain for the elusive computer.

Either he, or someone whom he had deputed, sent an anonymous letter to the palace.

'The computer supplied to the Department of Statistics is no longer in office. It is believed the department's supervisor, Kumarasurar, has sold the computer. Some say he has taken the government's computer to his house and is putting it to personal use. This is why he only writes typed letters. The government must initiate an inquiry and take suitable action immediately,' said the letter.

A photocopy of the letter was sent from the palace to Kumarasurar, along with a demand for an explanation.

Kumarasurar was furious. He sent for Kumbhas right away.

Waving the letter in his face, Kumarasurar demanded, 'What the hell is this?'

Kumbhas took the letter, read it calmly, handed it back and said, 'I have nothing to do with this.' But he did not stop there. 'If you haven't sold it, send them a reply with proof that the computer is in office, sir. Why are you asking me about this? You send typewritten letters to so many departments. Anyone in any of those departments could have got suspicious. Why are you snapping at me, sir? If you're not guilty, there's no reason to be afraid.'

It hadn't even been a year since Kumbhas had joined government service. Yet, he spoke with such audacity to a senior officer. This generation had no respect for its elders, thought Kumarasurar sadly.

They argued for a while. Kumarasurar brought it to a close by opening the cupboard and showing Kumbhas the brand new computer inside. He also pulled out the ten registers in which he had got the executive's counter-signature.

Kumarasurar then wrote a note that said, 'The items below have all been handed over to the junior clerk in the Department of Statistics, Mr Kumbhas,' and signed it. He then asked Kumbhas to sign a note which read, 'I hereby take on sole responsibility for all the items listed above.'

Kumarasurar cross-checked each item against the list. Kumbhas did not bother with this. He began to assemble the computer. He made several phone calls, to various people, when he had doubts. By the end of the day, the computer was in working order.

Now, the office computer was Kumbhas's responsibility. A burden had been lifted off Kumarasurar's shoulders. He began to delegate all his work to Kumbhas and spent long hours in the canteen.

Under these circumstances, it was terrifying to hear his son say, 'Ask Appa to use it so it doesn't rust.'

'What am I going to do with it?' he retorted. 'I barely have the time to use the one in office. You think I'm sitting around all day with nothing to do? Why would I go digging into these things?'

'Digging into it? Have you got it mixed up with your nose?' Meghas said, laughing.

8

Meghas was determined to buy a desktop. He enlisted the support of his mother. He told her one could watch all the films that had ever been made, from the Silent Era movies to the latest releases, at a time of one's choice.

'But I don't know how to go about that,' Mangasuri said.

'Oh, it's no big deal, Amma. There are four or five buttons. You just have to click an icon and the film will play. I'll teach you. Don't be scared of technology like Appa. It's just the same as watching television.' He also told her she could store all their photographs on the computer.

There was little Kumarasurar could do once his wife and son joined forces.

Meghas made enquiries, bought the computer in its constituent components and assembled them himself. Kumarasurar was reminded of the day the parcel had arrived at his office. What did Meghas know of these things? Where had he learnt to convert these boxes into a working whole?

When Meghas had arrived with the parts, Kumarasurar had assumed he would shut it into a cupboard as he himself had once done. Kumarasurar had decided he would have to document each component if Meghas did so. To this end, he had bought a register on his way home.

He was greeted by a house shuddering from the beats of a song whose lyrics made no sense at all. He dumped all his things in the sitting room and rushed into the room from which the noise emanated, worried that something was awfully wrong.

The computer screen glowed with scenes from a film song. The room echoed from the booming sounds. Meghas was throwing his limbs about in the air. Though she couldn't quite keep up with him, Mangasuri was trying to mimic his steps.

Was this really his home? Could a film be relived inside one of his own rooms? Kumarasurar stood with his mouth open from shock and horror. When he came to, he demanded in a stentorian voice that drowned out all other noise, 'What the hell is going on?'

Mangasuri was the first to react. Terrified by his tone, she ran into the kitchen and hid herself. Meghas was undaunted. Without breaking step, he danced to the door, shut it on his father's face and locked himself in.

Kumarasurar sank into the sofa in the living room. He stayed immobile. He wasn't sure what to do with the register he had just purchased with his hard-earned money. Could he bill it to his office? He could hear the strains of the song through a crack in the door.

It was three days and three nights before his wife could meet his eyes.

After the incident, Meghas didn't leave his room. Thanks to his mother, three plates of food and three mugs of tea made their way in and out at mealtimes. Mother often locked herself in with son. Kumarasurar heard them laughing together. When he was at home, songs were not played on the computer.

He did his accounts. The computer and the table had cost him nearly fifty thousand rupees. What had his family gained from such an extravagance? It made no sense to him. He often asked himself of what use the computer was. The question made its insidious way from his mind through his mouth and bounced off the walls of the house, breaking all the barriers he had placed in its way.

The question spread through the air as he strolled on the terrace by himself and as he watched television in the sitting room.

Meghas, who had initially ignored the question, wasn't able to avoid it when it began to echo through the rooms. 'Appa,' he said in a gentle voice one day, 'why don't you learn to type on the computer?'

Every time Kumarasurar spoke about the computer, Meghas would repeat this. Kumarasurar had nothing to offer in reply. Meghas's suggestion nudged the question out of the house.

It was only a few days before Meghas tired of the computer and parked himself in front of the television, where he would switch channels constantly. Both his parents began to look forward to his leaving for college. They could neither object to nor make peace with the way he had begun to intrude into every corner of the home they had made theirs in the years he had been away. He seemed to be changing the very vibe of the house to suit himself. The house began to look messy not just to Kumarasurar, but to Mangasuri too. They walked about the rooms that had once been theirs in irritation. Mangasuri spent the entire day tidying up the house, only to find a mess each time she returned to a room. She would start from scratch again. And again ... and again ... and ... several agains.

One fine day, Meghas said he needed a new mobile phone. Kumarasurar was determined not to be tricked as he had been with the computer.

A year ago, there had been a landline in the house, provided by a government-owned concern. Kumarasurar had also owned a mobile phone. The landline was often out of order, and each time, he had to go to the telephone exchange to register a complaint. It would take over a week for it to be processed. At the telephone exchange, he had to meet various levels of officials—the Assistant Executive Engineer, the Associate Executive Engineer, the Joint Executive Engineer, the Co-Executive Engineer, the Head Executive Engineer. These feats could not be accomplished in a single day. It was an unwritten rule that they could not all be available in office on the same day. Each had to be propitiated on a different visit. Each had his own moods. Kumarasurar coined names for each—Angry Engineer, Snappy Engineer, Grouchy Engineer, Lazy Engineer, Nasty Engineer and so on. It would take at least a month for the phone to be fixed.

Kumarasurar got so tired of this that he sent a request for the landline to be permanently disconnected. He bought Mangasuri a mobile phone for her use. It was a smarter phone than his own.

'I'm at home all day. Leave the old one here and take the new one with you,' she said.

He refused. 'Keep the one I bought you.'

Having a new model of mobile phone thrilled his wife. She did not know of the two reasons for Kumarasurar's generosity: one was that he had got used to his old phone; the other was that he was loath to adapt to a new phone.

Since his mother's phone was lying unattended all day, Meghas took over its ownership. It had few features of relevance to him. There were just two games, both designed for the entertainment of toddlers. His father's phone was a generation older.

'What on earth, this has nothing,' Meghas grumbled.

'What should it have? If you want to call someone, you should be able to dial. If someone calls, you should be able to pick up. It's got those two things, hasn't it?' Kumarasurar said.

Meghas looked at him strangely. Perhaps Meghas felt sorry for his father's innocence, so apparent on Kumarasurar's face. The boy did not pursue the conversation.

But his silence did not last. Within a day or two of this exchange, he began to pester Kumarasurar for a new phone. Why did he need a new one when there were two mobile phones at home? Who would call him? It could only be a friend who was as jobless as he. On the bus, Kumarasurar had seen some boys grinning into their phones and talking into headsets in voices they themselves could barely hear, clearly to their girlfriends. One couldn't discern a word even if one were seated right next to them. One could only see their lips move. Kumarasurar could not read lips. He wondered if the phones had sensors that could. Perhaps the phones were programmed to then convert the lip movements into words.

When Kumarasurar had to answer calls, he went to the terrace and yelled into his phone. He wasn't convinced people who lived far away could hear him if he didn't shout. There was another reason too: he was used to projecting his voice. Back in his village, people shouted to each other across fifty to a hundred feet. Every time he returned from the terrace, Mangasuri snapped at him. 'Can't you speak softly? The entire town is privy to your conversation. You're behaving like a savage.'

But he could never curtail his voice. Perhaps the phones that picked up lip movements were more expensive than his.

He had heard that the boys and girls who indulged the foolishness of love whispered all day and night into their phones. Some held their phones with both hands and busied their thumbs, typing pages into them. He would watch their thumbs wriggle like newborn mice. What could they be up to? Texting girls, waiting for their replies, replying to those replies ...

That was how it went, wasn't it? What were the subjects of these exchanges? Were they solving the country's economic woes? He and his wife ran out of conversation in about five minutes.

Kanakasurar often said, 'If only one snatched all phones from today's youngsters, they would collapse on the road, have a fit and die like so many worms in the sun.'

Meghas had studied in a boys' school. The girls' schools had been in a segregated zone. He could hardly have scaled the gigantic wall shielding that zone. The teachers, administrators, cooks and housekeeping staff in his school had all been men. The only women the boys saw were the mothers who came to visit their children once a month. Over the last two years, they must have forgotten what girls their age even looked like. Under such circumstances, Meghas could not have found himself a girlfriend. So why was he so obsessed with buying a phone?

One day, Meghas told his father, 'Phones are not just for calls, Appa. You can listen to music, watch movies, and take pictures and send them to someone in an instant. You can email the letters and orders that come to your office right away. There are a whole lot of other features, Appa. You don't even need to go to the bank. You can finish all your financial transactions on the phone. But not on yours. Yours was the first model to hit the market after the invention of the mobile phone.'

'Let them throw in all the features they want. Why do we need those? We have the TV to watch films, the camera to take pictures. So why have another device for the same thing?' Kumarasurar asked naively.

Meghas replied, 'Let's say you need to shop for groceries. Once upon a time, you would've had to go to a different store for condiments, a different one for vegetables and a different one for utensils. Now we have a supermarket, don't we? The big cities have malls. You can buy everything you need at one spot. This is the same thing. It's all-in-one. You don't need a whole bunch of devices, each of which can only carry out one task.'

Kumarasurar could not argue with that. But he remained firm that he would not buy his son a mobile phone. Meghas made inroads from various angles. He would need a phone once he went away to college. Why not buy it a couple of months earlier, so he could get used to it? Kumarasurar reminded him that some colleges banned the use of mobile phones, and it would all go to waste if Meghas joined one such.

Meghas answered with clarity and determination: 'I will never join a college that has banned phones.'

The only response Kumarasurar could think of was, 'Why does a student need a phone?'

Mangasuri chimed in, 'Are you going to send your only child to a college that won't even allow you to speak to him? Aren't the two years he has just suffered through enough? I can't live without speaking to my son. Buy him what he wants.'

Kumarasurar saw mobile phones as wasteful expenditure. He couldn't be sure Meghas would get into a state-run college. Even if he did, the tuition fees and hostel facilities would be formidable. Private colleges were twice as expensive. He needed to set money aside for incidental expenses too. He couldn't afford to buy Meghas a phone of his choice.

When he explained this to Meghas, the boy assured his father that he wouldn't buy an expensive phone. They went to a mobile phone showroom in town, and Meghas chose a phone that had all the facilities he wanted. It cost under three thousand rupees. Kumarasurar was pleased.

Meghas poked at the phone all day and all night. Mangasuri had to remind him to eat. As for sleep, he only indulged it when it claimed its space. He looked irritated most of the time. Then, all of a sudden, he would burst out laughing. His parents couldn't find an explanation for either. The headset that had come with the phone became a permanent fixture in his ears. Sometimes, he seemed to dance to music playing in it. He would snap his fingers and twist his way around the house. He didn't remove the earphones even when he slept.

Once, when Kumarasurar woke up in the middle of the night, he saw his son sleeping with the earphones on. He gently pulled the plugs out of his son's ears, folded the wires and kept them by the bed. Meghas didn't ask about it when he woke the next day. He must have assumed he had put the headset away himself.

Kumarasurar told him a couple of times that he had slept with the earphones on. Meghas didn't seem to think it was a big deal. All he said was 'Mm'.

'I saw you when I woke up at night and put it away,' Kumarasurar said again.

'Mm.'

After a few more attempts, Kumarasurar heard him tell Mangasuri loudly, 'What is Appa's problem, Amma? Why does he wake up in the middle of the night and go about doing all sorts of nonsense?'

Kumarasurar decided there was no point trying to speak to Meghas about his addiction. But he couldn't shake off the habit of removing the plugs from his son's ears once the boy had fallen asleep. He would wake up in the middle of the night as if to an alarm. His eyes would seek Meghas out even in the dark. He took it upon himself to relieve the boy's ears of their encumbrance every night. The wires that made their way down from Meghas's ears would be entangled around his arms and stomach. It was an onerous task to unwind them without waking him up.

One night, Kumarasurar pulled rather hard at the wires, and Meghas woke with a start. He glared, said, 'Come on, Appa!' and went right back to sleep.

Kumarasurar was worried his son would say something harsh in the morning. But Meghas seemed to have no recollection of the incident.

Meghas would take pictures on his phone all day and download them on to the computer. He took several pictures of his mother, which gave her great pleasure. The desktop wallpaper on their computer was always one of these photos.

Since he might click a picture any time of day, Mangasuri began to ensure not a hair was out of place. Her sari was perfectly tied, her face was always fresh and her hair was braided with flowers.

When he said, 'Amma', she knew why, and immediately posed for a studiedly candid photograph.

Kumarasurar did like his wife's new-found beauty, but could a housewife look pretty as a picture all day?

'As if she's about to leave for a wedding any minute,' he would mutter within her earshot. He had initially wanted to say, 'Dressed like a goddamn bride.' But that seemed rather cruel, and so he made the slight alteration.

Mangasuri ignored him. Every day, a new photograph appeared on the desktop. Most of these had her giggling shyly and glowing with pride.

The first month of Meghas's return, mother and son were thoroughly happy. He seemed to have no intention of leaving for college.

9

It struck Kumarasurar that if Meghas could estimate what his marks in the final exams would be, they could shortlist colleges that would admit him and be prepared in advance for counselling. When he told Meghas this, the boy sank into silence for a whole day. Perhaps he felt he had just broken free from the prison of his school and was in no hurry to go to another. Kumarasurar decided to let him be for a day or two.

Later that week, Meghas approached his father. He had spoken to his friends. Students who wrote the common entrance examination aspired to get into colleges run by the state. One had to score over 995 out of 1000 to hope for admission into these. Meghas was sure he wouldn't score such high marks. The cut-offs for the second tier of private colleges were around 950. Meghas thought he stood a good chance here. There were about 50 colleges in all, and Meghas said they could whittle the possibilities down to 5 or 6.

Kumarasurar's friends had told him that two colleges in a metropolis located to the west of their town had good reputations. Meghas had heard the same. Everyone said, 'Once you enrol in that college, whether you finish your degree or not, you'll leave with a job.'

In Asurapuri, it was customary for the parents of children who had finished their final examinations to go on a 'college tour' over the summer. They would prepare a detailed itinerary that allowed them to scrutinise over a hundred colleges. They would enjoy their summers doing this. The king had arranged for special buses dedicated to these tours. The regular run-down buses wore newly painted signs that read 'Special Bus' and charged higher tariffs.

Competing with them were private buses, which advertised various discounts and offers. They gave away free coupons to people who travelled in their buses. They offered 10 per cent off on purchases made during the journey, 20 per cent off on the next booking, free packets of water for the ride, a promise to stop at any spot if a passenger wanted to use a public toilet, and several similar proposals. One was tempted to go on the journey just to avail the offers.

Meghas and Kumarasurar decided to go to the metropolis and check out the two colleges. Meghas liked the idea of train journeys. He had never travelled by train. Why, Kumarasurar himself had never travelled by train. Mangasuri wanted to accompany them, but Kumarasurar said it would cost too much. He consoled her with, 'You can come along when we drop him off at the college once he joins.'

They headed for counselling at the first college.

Right outside the railway station were ushers who grabbed them by the hands and packed them into cars. Tumbled into one such, with other parents and children sitting on each other's laps, Kumarasurar and Meghas got off outside the gates of the institution.

The college was spread across about 300 to 400 acres. Its buildings were skyscrapers—you could give yourself a crick in the neck trying to see just how tall they were, but all you'd get for your pains would be sun-blindness. It couldn't have been an easy task to acquire such vast tracts of land close to a metropolis.

When they walked into the college, they saw that all students from the second to fifth years were headed to their classes. It gave the parents much joy that their wards would be made to study without the disadvantage of a summer vacation.

A part of the administrative building had been allocated for the orientation programme, with separate areas for parents and students. Kumarasurar made his way to the parents' section. The college had had a promotional film made to show prospective parents the facilities on campus—they were given a virtual tour of the classrooms, laboratories, the hostels and the students' mess.

The final words of the narration that accompanied the video were, 'Bridles fitted with blinkers will be provided free of cost to students. This is to ensure that they do not lose focus. Our motto is "Work, work, and do nothing but work". Discipline is crucial to living up to this motto. This is why we have provided bridles for our boys and girls.'

At the students' orientation, Meghas was told, 'The restrictions on campus are not for our benefit, but for yours. Remember that horses are able to keep to a straight path without distractions and reach their eventual goal because of their bridles. Don't you want to make sure you reach your goals? Don't you want to have offers of jobs at multinational companies even before you finish your courses?'

Once the counselling was done, the parents and prospective students were taken around the campus in open vans. On several walls, they could see the college motto painted in large letters: 'Work, work, and do nothing but work'. Their first stop was the factory where the bridles were manufactured.

'The fact that our bridles are given free of charge does not imply they are of low quality. We make no compromises. Our bridles provide for a direct gaze—the gaze required to "Work, work, and do nothing but work". When distractions are removed, the mind is at rest. When the mind is at rest, the body cooperates. When the body cooperates, one can study. When one studies, one will find work. This is why we make our own bridles. You can examine their quality for yourself. Each of them is built to last through all five years of college. If a student happens to lose his bridle, a free replacement will be provided the first two times. We have various colours and models of bridles. We have delicate iron bridles for our female students. Just like slippers, bridles too are gendered. You can see which ones are meant for the faces of young women. You may choose any model you like. The choice is your right. Our only rule is that it must be worn at all times.'

A gentleman stood at the entrance to the manufacturing unit, repeating this to each person who entered. It turned out he was the head of the Robotics Department. When they did not have classes to teach, professors of robotics were apparently expected to carry out such duties.

The bridles had been arranged in an enormous hall. These were not the worn and dirty bridles one saw on the faces of horses. They were, as promised, available in various models and colours. On one side were bridles in primary colours. The parents were immediately drawn to those. In another corner were bridles in hues one had not previously imagined, quite like the twilit sky.

Innovative technology allowed them to be fitted without hurting one's ears or eyes. Anyone who saw these bridles would be tempted to try one on. The parents rushed to the bridles, giggling. They fixed the bridles on themselves and saw that they did, indeed, give them the promised 'direct gaze'. One could see nothing to one's side. This thrilled the parents. They admired their appearance in the mirrored walls of the room. Some even trotted, jumped and neighed like horses, and laughed at their own exploits.

When their sons were reluctant to wear them, the parents fitted the bridles on to the boys' faces and dragged them to the mirrors to see how well these accessories suited them. Some of the boys quite willingly wore the colourful bridles and asked their parents for their opinions on which were most becoming.

Some parents approached the professor who had been tasked with explaining the features of these bridles and asked, 'They filter the noise from the students' ears, they focus their eyesight, but they don't do anything to seal their mouths. Why is that?'

'Parents have been making this request only for the last two years. The authorities have taken this into consideration. A decision is yet to be made on whether a bit must be attached to the bridle, or made separately and also supplied for free. We hope for the bits to be made available towards the middle of this academic year. Please do not worry,' the professor assured them.

There were all manner of questions. A man whose chest shone with a pendant, ears shimmered with gold studs, and fingers and toes sparkled with enormous rings, raised his head skywards and demanded with glazed eyes, 'Will bridles in gold and silver be available?'

The professor who had been forced to represent sales said, 'We have ordinary plastic bridles. We also have many varieties of brass and iron bridles. These are in high demand. There are some parents who ask for gold and silver bridles. We will make these bridles to order within a week of your placing a request. In the meanwhile, a brass bridle will be supplied for your ward's temporary use, sir.'

'What if a gold bridle is robbed in the hostel?' a parent asked cautiously.

'Sir, the hostels have complete protection, around the clock. Students can deposit their bridles in lockers in the security room as soon as they enter the hostels, sir. They can take them before leaving for college the next day. We only charge a nominal fee for the locker.' The professor's answer was a crowd-pleaser.

'But one can't trust these kids, sir,' a parent said suspiciously. 'What if they sell the bridles outside?'

'Yes, sir, you're absolutely right. Despite all the restrictions, some students do fall prey to the devas' drink—alcohol. When they run out of money, they're likely to pawn or sell their gold bridles to satisfy their addiction. We've made our arrangements. The pawn shops and jewellery showrooms in the city are in touch with the college. The moment our bridles come to their shops, they will alert us. We can prevent this.

'We refer to our students as rats. We treat them as one would treat rats. What do rats do? When you block one hole, they dig another. Every hole you block, they dig out a new one. But can we stop blocking these holes? Let the rats dig their holes. We will seal them. If you parents join hands with us, it will be easier to prevent the rats' escape. It takes two hands to clap. This is why we respect our students' parents so much. Please don't worry that your cooperation will entail your frequent presence at the college. The helping hand we need is that you pay the fees on time. That is all.' The professor's explanation thrilled the parents.

They were now thoroughly enamoured of the bridles. Kumarasurar could barely contain his excitement. He tried on some of the bridles heaped against the walls. As he wore each one, his features settled into great composure. One must count one's blessings to be able to study in an institute like this. He had never had that opportunity. But it comforted him that his son would. And he was allowed to try on the bridles for free himself. Why hesitate when he had a chance? He tried on several and studied his reflection.

The bridle ensured one's peripheral vision was cut off. Problems arose only when one's gaze wandered. The bridles saw to it that students retained their focus. If only the bridles were available to the public, it would sort out a lot of Asurapuri's problems, Kumarasurar thought.

A professor seemed to sense that this thought was running through several parents' minds, and said loudly, 'This scheme of the college has been praised by the government. The state is considering the use of bridles among the public. All problems are caused by lack of focus, lack of the direct gaze. Protests, disruption of normalcy due to protests ... you-name-it. The government is considering free distribution of bridles. It should be evident that our college has great foresight.'

Kumarasurar was enthused. The bridles were a hit. The parents sporting these walked as if they were sashaying down the ramp at a beauty pageant. They looked like strange animals cavorting about.

Kumarasurar stood before Meghas and said, 'How does this look, aiyya? Take a photo of me like this, won't you?' The photo and selfie sessions across the room had infected Kumarasurar too.

Meghas's face showed only anger and frustration. 'Come, Appa, let's go,' he said, dragging his father along.

Kumarasurar didn't realise his son hadn't tried on a single bridle. He found it hard to leave the room that housed the accessories he was so taken with.

Meghas's bridle-less face seemed to lack something. Kumarasurar scooped up a few bridles and ran back to him. 'Try a couple on, just for kicks,' he said, holding one out. 'It's free anyway. Do you know how you'll look with this on?'

'If someone gave you shit for free, would you gorge on it just for kicks too?' Meghas cried.

It was no ordinary shout; it was a thunderous yell. Everyone in the room froze and turned in the direction of the sound. It appeared no one had understood what had just happened, or had heard the exact words. In a flash, they returned to their own conversations, and the room went back to sounding like a fish market.

The security staff deployed by the college escorted Meghas and Kumarasurar outside. They didn't ask questions, but loaded them into an open van and drove them off.

One could see students of the college walking about. The girls wore bridles that matched their clothes. The boys didn't seem to have paid as much attention; they had probably grabbed the first bridle they could find as they rushed to college. Some looked at Meghas. He sensed pity in many of those glances. There was mischief in some eyes. Others even stared with inexplicable hatred.

The staff dropped them off outside the gate and stopped just short of throwing them out of the van.

Father and son did not speak. Kumarasurar was still intoxicated by the bridles. Why had Meghas got angry, what had made him yell like that? He didn't know, but it was obvious his son did not like the college. How could a boy not like this college? He would buy Meghas a new bridle every day if his son asked. But it appeared the brat would not apply here.

Kumarasurar began to worry. He wondered where they would stay. They did have some relatives in town. Staying with family would save them the cost of boarding and lodging. Would Meghas agree? He asked him gently.

'Let's go home,' Meghas said.

Kumarasurar was startled. He had planned to stay a few days and check out at least ten colleges in the vicinity. Meghas refused. He insisted on going back right away.

His father did not understand why he didn't like the bridles. If bridles were the only problem, they could forget about this college and look at others in town which did not enforce these; one couldn't simply decide that all colleges would be like the one they had toured. He tried explaining this to Meghas.

'I won't go to any college in this city,' Meghas said, adamantly.

Kumarasurar told him that it was people who went to colleges like the one they had just visited that ended up heading multinational companies and taking home lakhs of rupees in their monthly paycheques. Meghas wouldn't heed a word.

Kumarasurar was left with no option. They returned home that very day.

'Why are you back within a day?' Mangasuri asked.

'Let it go, Amma,' Meghas said.

Kumarasurar gave her a detailed account.

'Do the girls really match the bridles to their clothes?' Mangasuri asked excitedly. 'They were free, weren't they? You should have brought one along for me to try on. If it suited me, I could have worn it to weddings.'

Meghas, who had gone to the kitchen to drink water, heard her and threw something on the floor. They heard it break. Mangasuri didn't mention the bridles again. Once Meghas retired to his room and the computer, his parents went to the terrace.

The terrace had long been the site of their private conversations. Kumarasurar told her all about the college, and worried that their son had turned his back on such a wonderful institute. Thousands of students and parents visited every day. Surely not every boy behaved like this? Some had tried on the bridles with great enthusiasm. Some hadn't been as enthralled, but had tried them on to oblige their parents. Some had worn them with irritation, but had tried them on anyway. Meghas didn't fall into any of these categories. If you insisted on having your way all the time and doing only what you pleased, how could you live in this world? Sometimes, you had to do things that were necessary, even if you had no interest in them. How could they make Meghas understand this?

Mangasuri had her own theories. 'Did you have to choose the west of all directions for the first college you went to look at? That's the direction in which the sun sets. You should never have gone that way first. That was the problem.'

But as her husband gave her the low-down, she began to sense Meghas's mindset. He had refused to study medicine. They had let him be. He had joined the cram school of his choice. They had let him be. He had specialised in the subjects of his choice. They had let him be. He had insisted he would study engineering in college. They had let him be. Now, he had refused to join a brilliant college. What could they do?

The five years of his degree would go by in a flash. He had finished school. It was a school he hadn't liked. Hadn't the two years gone by in an instant? Every time they'd visited, they had found him in tears. The grounds had echoed with wails. But now it all seemed like a distant dream. If only Meghas would buckle down and get through these five years, he would have a job, and all their problems would disappear. Kumarasurar's dead-end job in government service necessitated penny-pinching. If Meghas got into a multinational corporation, their financial troubles would end. But he didn't seem to care. Why?

After a dance of dialogue and silence, the couple made their decision. He was their only child. He had been the answer to their prayers in various temples, to their longing for an heir. And so, he had been spoilt silly. His grandparents had treated him like a prince when they had been alive. Not a word had been spoken against anything he did. They had taken great pride and pleasure in his tiniest acts. No one had gone against Meghas's wishes. They had spared the rod too long. How could they change him now?

'Our son is the only thing of any importance to us,' Mangasuri said. Every time she recollected Meghas's childhood, she would veer to his side. 'Let him study where he wants. Let him study what he wants. There is a job and salary waiting for him. We have a house of our own. Let him earn what he can. The worst case scenario is that we won't be able to boast about which company he works at and how much he earns to everyone who asks. Let it go. People only ask questions when you meet them. Let's see our days out within these four walls. Then there will be no problem.'

Kumarasurar could think of no counterargument.

10

Two days later, Meghas said his friends had told him about a reputed college in another city, which he wanted to visit. Kumarasurar was relieved that his son planned to go to college after all.

This city was located towards the east from their hometown; an auspicious direction, thought Kumarasurar. The east brings us the sun and the light, Mangasuri said. Before they left for counselling at the college, she made them stand for an aarti and anointed their foreheads with vermillion—their only aim now was to get Meghas into this auspicious institution.

The college was outside the city limits. It was the rare bus that went that way. Kumarasurar and Meghas hunted throughout the terminus for a willing bus, when a voice shouted, 'Anyone who is here to visit High Praise College may approach us! College buses are waiting outside to take you there for free!' They walked towards the voice, and spotted five, perhaps six, buses with the college logo, standing in line. People crowded into the seats. Each bus left on its mission, filled to capacity.

The institute had organised an impressive welcome and orientation. A film explaining its facilities and functioning was scheduled to screen every hour. The parents and students were ushered inside the auditorium in batches. Those who had to wait were supplied hot samosas and tea.

The theatre was an enormous hall with five-star facilities. The seats were spread across a vast expanse, and the screen was dizzyingly large. Parents and students rushed in with the eagerness normally reserved for blockbuster movies. They were served snacks and juice in their seats. They watched the orientation film as they ate, and their plates were refilled even before they could be emptied.

The main campus building was made of shiny alabaster. This was the administrative block, where fees were paid, enquiries were answered and counselling was conducted. The visitors were given a virtual tour of each department—staffrooms, laboratories, computers in every nook, air-conditioned classrooms fitted with advanced technological facilities, hostels with sparkling clean toilets, mess halls that could pass for restaurants, close-circuit television cameras to monitor the campus—and the sights were accompanied by a husky voiceover.

It appeared even Meghas was impressed. Kumarasurar glanced at him, and his face shone even in the dark of the hall. Perhaps this would be The One.

The next part of the film showcased just how technologically advanced the college was. All tasks were assigned to robots constructed to look like asuras, and these robots could do just about anything instantaneously. They washed the utensils. They cleaned the hostel rooms. They swept the campus roads.

The robot asuras were also responsible for maintaining discipline. Living asuras had emotions. They were prone to fatigue and frustration. They might let a couple of errors slide. Some might be willing to accept bribes to relax the rules. They would need to be supervised by other asuras. But robot asuras had no emotions. They could be trusted to do their work as specified by commands.

These robots dressed like regular asuras and walked about the campus undetected. They were gorgeous—apparently, asura supermodels had been used as moulds to create these robots. They wore ready smiles and had an air of serenity. When a robot asura introduced himself to the audience and bowed to them, they applauded him.

There were scenes of students walking about campus. A boy called out to a female cohort who was walking ahead of him. Before she could respond, a robot asura ran to the boy and slapped him across the face. The boy, with a hand-shaped red welt and shock writ on his face, ran for his life.

Another scene: Somewhere in the crowd, a boy eyed a girl. Spotting him, a robot asura ran at him. The boy turned tail and ran away. The robot gave chase, following him through wide streets and narrow alleys, over walls and between trees, through the corridors of the college buildings, before cornering him in the toilet. The audience fell off their seats laughing. The sequence might well have been choreographed by an award-winning film director.

Next came the hostels. A robot stood by the kitchen sink in the dining hall, watching the students as they washed their plates. A student rinsed his plate with water and was about to leave, when the robot caught him by the collar, dragged him to the sink, handed him his plate and made him wash it with soap.

The camera strolled through the aisles between the tables, and the variety of foods on the students' plates made the audience salivate. Then, the students walked to the sink, their plates polished so thoroughly that one would think they had already been washed.

One of the students left a half-eaten plate by the sink. As he walked away, a robot caught him, took him to his plate, stuck a finger in his mouth and opened it wide; holding him by the cheeks, the robot fed him from his discarded plate. As the student was force-fed, his eyes bulged with despair. The audience laughed at the boy, who was neither able to eat nor resist and escape.

The female robots were no less conscientious. The next scene showed a girl walking alluringly, her hair loose over her shoulders. A female robot intercepted her, parted her hair, spun it into plaits and then let her go. Another girl's dupatta fluttered in the breeze. A robot caught her, fixed the dupatta with safety pins over her shoulders and sent her on her way.

When the film ended, opinion on the robots was divided. Half the audience was delighted with them; the other half seemed disgruntled. Murmurs of disagreement arose; some arguments and bickering voices made their way to Kumarasurar's ears.

'Come, Appa, let's go,' Meghas said and took him by the hand. Meghas led him out of the crowd towards a waiting bus and found them seats. They dismounted at the bus terminus and got on a bus headed for their home town. Meghas was silent through the journey. It was clear to Kumarasurar that his son did not like the college. The robot asuras would not attack students who followed the rules, would they? They had been programmed to enforce discipline. Why did that trouble Meghas?

At home, Kumarasurar responded to the question in Mangasuri's eyes with pursed lips. Whatever Meghas decided, Kumarasurar would console himself with the memory of laughing at the comic scenes featuring robots. He must tell Kanakasurar about this college on his morning walk.

11

Two days later, Meghas said he wanted to check out another college.

Not bad, Kumarasurar thought, his son hadn't tired of the college hunt. He did seek to further his education.

This town was to the north of theirs. Online research showed that there were thirty-five colleges in that town. Meghas chose the five which were considered premier institutions.

Kumarasurar and Mangasuri wrote the names of these five on pieces of paper, and shuffled them before the idol of Meghasura.

In a house on their street lived a little girl. They asked that she pick the chit—the college whose name was written on this piece of paper would be the first they visited. The girl's grandmother said, 'If something good comes of it, you'll praise the child. If it doesn't, you'll blame her. You draw the lots yourself.'

It was a tedious task to convince the grandmother.

'Will one's tongue allow one to fault a child? We just want to know which college we should visit first. The child represents our clan deity.' Mangasuri was hard put to bring the girl along. They fed the child lollipop and ice cream, and sweet-talked her into picking a chit.

Eventually, father and son left for the college that the representative of Meghasura had chosen.

The town wasn't a big one. The college was not far from the city. One could walk the distance from the bus terminus. Because it was within the city limits, the campus wasn't large. Although they were squeezed for space, the buildings rose high. Each was at least fifteen floors tall and equipped with a lift. One could tour the college at one's leisure.

After this, the prospective students and their parents were given counselling in separate rooms. Kumarasurar went to the fifteenth floor. The reception was teeming with people. A counsellor sat in each of several rooms. Parents' names were called in order of arrival.

When Kumarasurar's turn came, he was ushered into a room. It was a well-appointed bedsit, built for the accommodation of guests visiting the college. A professor was at the desk. All the professors doubled as counsellors. He briefed Kumarasurar on the achievements of the college. The proprietor's first foray into entrepreneurship had been the running of a buffalo farm. It had not one or two, but a thousand buffaloes. So he was used to handling crowds. He had started the college with the money he'd made from the farm.

The professor went on to explain the college's unique selling point. It gave as much importance to average performers as it did to the top scorers. Students who had done well at school could find themselves distracted and lose focus once they came to college. The institution took this into account. It was impossible to counsel students of this age, make them understand where they were going wrong, call their parents, fine them and so on. They were at an impressionable age, and their minds constantly fluctuated. So it was customary to slap or cane each student between two and four times each day on some pretext.

The college had a unique recruitment policy for professors. Only those with strong physiques were employed. In order to prove themselves fit, the candidates had to drag two buffaloes, one on each arm, by rope, for a thousand metres without tiring. The person who came first was given the job. Five professors had to work at the buffalo farm located behind the college from dawn to dusk every day, cleaning the pen and grooming the buffaloes.

When teaching staff had such qualifications, the students had to fall in line. When they were beaten, the students had to stay still, or they would be secured with ropes.

The professor brandished a sample cane. It was three feet long and made of beautiful bamboo. As he twirled it in his hand, it shone like a bronzeback tree snake.

Apparently, a few years ago, the media had played up a story about the college. Back then, there had been neem trees all over the campus. The neem branches were used for caning the students. There were complaints that the rough texture of these branches caused scarring in the students when they were beaten and that this was affecting their futures. It was especially hard for the girls to get married because the welts were conspicuous. After this, the authorities announced that they would use canes that only caused internal injuries with minimal visibility. A memorandum of understanding was signed to import bamboo canes.

The professor offered to let Kumarasurar scrutinise the canes. Kumarasurar held each by one end and caressed it along its length. A parent had once remarked that touching it felt like gliding down a waterfall. The professor showed Kumarasurar a framed wall hanging which had this parent's photograph and his quote; and another with the quote 'Cooling smoothness'; and another which read 'The feel of a cat's fur'. Having shown him several such exhibits, the professor whispered into Kumarasurar's ear, 'A parent even said it gives one the thrill of sex. We couldn't print that.'

He grinned. With no other option at hand, Kumarasurar grinned back and ran his hands along the cane once more.

The media was all praise for the initiative. A newspaper had even carried a cover story on the canes recently, complete with photographs. As he showed this to Kumarasurar, the professor said, 'It is our responsibility to ensure that your son's body doesn't have a single scar when he returns to you in five years.'

Thanks to the college's caning policy, students ensured that they had no arrears. Through the last decade, the college had achieved a 100 per cent pass rate. Several other colleges had tried replicating their policy using counterfeit canes. But none of these canes could match the quality of this college's. The professor finished his oratory with, 'A cow must be beaten to toe the line.'

Kumarasurar himself decided this institute would not suit his son.

Other parents told him all the colleges in this town had the same policy. They all sought a 100 per cent pass rate.

'If we get admission here, we don't have to worry about whether our son will clear his papers,' one parent said.

'We can be sure he will finish the course,' another said.

They appeared certain their sons would return home. That seemed enough to Kumarasurar.

He did not know what the students had been told during their counselling sessions. Meghas did not speak about this either. They must have been told they would not really be caned; it was all for show. A real caning would result in *these* scars; what we do is simply a token caning. Even the token caning is for your good, they would have been told.

Father and son were silent throughout the journey home. It appeared no college would be to Meghas's liking. Kumarasurar considered enrolling him in an arts college, where he could study literature or history. They could find a government arts college close enough for him to attend as a day scholar, so he could live at home. Kumarasurar should find the right opportunity to put this before Meghas. Mangasuri would be upset that he had become neither a doctor nor an engineer. But she would come around. Experience was the best teacher.

12

Things did not pan out as Kumarasurar expected.

Two days later, Meghas suggested they visit a college to the south of their town. They didn't need to draw lots. There was no confusion over which college to visit. There was just the one.

Kumarasurar spoke about the college to his colleagues in the office canteen. None of them had a good impression of it. Neither their children nor their relatives' or friends' had graduated from this college. Usually, everyone knew someone who had gone to any college one named. Not this one. Yet, his colleagues did have their opinions.

'I've heard it's a kachra college,' someone said.

Someone else did an internet search on his phone and showed Kumarasurar that the college didn't have a good pass percentage of students.

Mangasuri had her own worries. She wasn't enamoured of the fact that the college was located to the south of their town, the direction accorded to Yama. And why must Meghas visit a college which didn't seem to have a good reputation, whatever its location? What if he chose a college like this one?

Meghas told Kumarasurar not to accompany him. It would suffice if he liked it. If he decided to apply, both his parents could visit the college. For once, Mangasuri didn't take her son's side. Meghas wasn't used to travelling such distances alone. It was a whole night's journey. Besides, if Kumarasurar went along, he would give her a detailed account. So she insisted that Meghas be accompanied by his father.

Kumarasurar wondered if it made sense to visit a college that hadn't earned a good name. Eventually, he decided nothing was up to him; destiny would dictate their fate. He would go with his son.

As usual, the college was outside the city limits. But a town had cropped up around the college.

The first thing that worried Kumarasurar was that it was not compulsory for students to stay in the college hostel. They were allowed to find accommodation outside the campus. Second, more than half the students were internationals. The college had few restrictions.

No college buses had come to the bus terminus to escort them. No arrangements had been made for counselling sessions or a tour of the campus. Visitors were allowed to look around at their leisure.

Eateries were scattered around the campus. Students sat in groups and pairs, laughing and chatting. The boys laughed, so did the girls. The sound of laughter inside a college campus, and that too the sound of girls' laughter. The clothes they wore didn't strike Kumarasurar as clothes. Some wore trousers slung lower than their underpants. Some wore jeans slashed across the thighs. Even beggars patched their clothes. But the students hadn't. Their flesh showed through the gashes in those tight jeans like discoloration on skin. There appeared to be no regulation on clothing. Each student wore a different style.

'What is this, aiyya? They're wearing rags,' he said.

His son wasn't perturbed. 'This is "fashion" now,' he said, laughing.

A girl chased after a boy with her arm extended and whacked him. He made a show of being hurt and rolled around exaggeratedly. The two laughed together.

What on earth, this is like a scene from a film, Kumarasurar thought.

One encountered, rather often, the sight of boys and girls making actual physical contact with each other. Kumarasurar felt embarrassed. In the canteen, girls spoon-fed boys and boys spoon-fed girls. On campus, they walked with fingers intertwined, heads leaning against shoulders and with other intimate gestures that made Kumarasurar gape.

Meghas wasn't cut from the same cloth as he. The boy looked at each spot and scene with interest and joy. His face was flushed with excitement. Kumarasurar knew his son would choose this college. He felt anxious.

The boy roamed the campus, seeming loath to leave. None of the eateries offered 'meals'. Their food items had names that Kumarasurar's tongue couldn't wrap itself around. He had never eaten a meal without rice. Even if the nectar denied to asuras were offered to him, he would ask if he could have rice to go with it. And now he would have to do without rice. He learnt that there were several eateries outside the college that offered 'full meals'. Meghas refused to come along. Kumarasurar went alone.

These eateries looked like the humble shacks one came across in villages. They teemed with foreigners who sat and ate with no hesitation or embarrassment. Why didn't the fools on campus like rice when even foreigners liked it, Kumarasurar wondered. He made his way to a food joint with a thatched roof. He learnt a lot about the college over his meal. Once upon a time, the campus had been agricultural land. The villagers had sold off their farmland bit by bit, and now worked as bus drivers, cooks, cleaners and gardeners in the college. Any villager who asked for a job was immediately granted one. The entire village had forgotten to farm and had changed professions.

Since the college had so many international students, hygiene was a prime concern. There were no restrictions on intermingling of genders. And so condoms were often found in the dustbins on campus. Many doctors in the city had minted money from abortions. One found intoxicants and hallucinogens everywhere. At dusk, one could see students sprawled on the ground, high on alcohol or weed.

'You think these creatures are here to study?' the proprietor of the eatery grunted. 'This place is for everything but academia.'

'What a town this used to be,' sighed another customer. 'This college has ruined everything.'

The founder of the college was from this town. He had studied abroad and returned with the ambition of creating an educational institution like the one he had attended.

'He used to roam this place in a loincloth as a child,' someone said. 'He went abroad and came back thinking he'd do some good. He brought along people from every country he knew. And that has led to this. It's an illustration of the proverb, "He's broken the mortar and pestle while craving beaten rice."'

Kumarasurar felt afraid.

He could see students from Asurapuri too around the place. He asked a couple of students what they thought of the college. The only answer he got was, 'Fantastic college.' What else would these boys say?

This time, too, Meghas was silent on the return journey.

He plugged his earphones into his mobile phone, closed his eyes and nodded in time to the beats he heard. His happiness and satisfaction were evident from his face. He was oblivious to his father's presence by his side.

What song was he listening to? How could he hear it through that device? Kumarasurar did not know. Meghas's every gesture irritated him. When the bus stopped at an eatery on the way home, Meghas didn't get off. Kumarasurar felt annoyed.

'Plugging that stuff in your ears all the time! Come on down. Let's go to the toilet and then drink some tea,' he snapped.

It was an order. Meghas did as he was told. He seemed to enjoy the tea.

Kumarasurar felt disturbed by his son's silence. He felt worried by his joy. What was going on?

When the bus resumed its journey, Meghas reached for his earphones again.

'Why do you need this hearing aid, like a deaf man? Can't you be normal for a bit?' Kumarasurar said.

Meghas didn't react with anger. He laughed and asked, 'Do you want to try it on? Shall I fix the headset in your ears?'

Kumarasurar suspected his son was mocking him. But he said, 'All right.'

Meghas navigated to a song on his phone, inserted one of the plugs in his ear and another in his father's. Kumarasurar felt uncomfortable, as if a fly was fluttering in there. One ear felt blocked. Meghas let the song play. All of a sudden, music made its way into Kumarasurar's ear. It came as a shock. It was as if someone was singing just for him, whispering into his ear. No music entered the other ear. He looked around the bus. Clearly, no one else could hear the song. Only one ear was privy to the song. The other ached for it. A song just for him. He felt rather scared.

It was a song from an old film, one he loved dearly. Did Meghas listen to such songs too? Did he like them? Or had he found this because he knew his father liked it? But Meghas was listening to it and keeping time with the music. That must mean he liked it. He looked at his father. He laughed at the surprise and wonder on Kumarasurar's face, removed the plug from his own ear and pushed it into his father's other ear too. As soon as Meghas did this, the song filtered out all other noise. One ear heard just the background music, and the other heard the vocals and instruments. Kumarasurar had never heard a song in such a nuanced manner. His eyes closed of their own accord.

He woke with a start when the song ended. He felt embarrassed that he had got so carried away. He couldn't meet his son's eyes. Afraid Meghas would turn on another song, he pulled the plugs out of his ears and held them out to his son. He kept his face neutral, as if this had been no big deal and the experience had held little interest for him. Meghas fixed the headset into his own ears and closed his eyes again.

Kumarasurar's anxieties began to resurface. Watching Meghas bob his head to the beats, it struck him that the boy carried all the burden of a feather floating in the air. His son seemed to have decided to join this college. What would he do if Meghas insisted on it?

'What have you decided, aiyya?' he asked, as they neared home.

'Let's see, Appa,' Meghas said noncommittally.

But Kumarasurar sensed that Meghas's mind was made up. That night, he told his wife all about the college and the fears it had aroused in him.

'If he joins that college, our son won't remain our son. You can't tell what will happen to him. It's that awful,' he said.

Mangasuri didn't know what to do. She considered her son a little child. It surprised her to think he could even talk to girls. Kumarasurar told her that Meghas had spoken to some girls in the college to make enquiries, and that he had seen their son laughing with the opposite sex.

'You must have seen this from a distance and mistaken someone else for our son,' she said.

'Yeah, yeah, stick your finger in your baby's mouth. He doesn't know how to bite, does he?' Kumarasurar scoffed.

Mangasuri was sure Meghas could not have even heard of alcohol and cigarettes and drugs; even if he had, he wouldn't touch them. His face was all innocence. She knew that under any circumstances, he would always remain her child.

His wife's naivete worried Kumarasurar. She was cooped up within the four walls of the house. She didn't know much about the world outside. And so he proceeded to tell her all about the effects adolescence had on boys and how impressionable they were. As he spoke, Mangasuri began to share his terror. And then Kumarasurar added a final touch. 'When he comes back, he won't be alone. He'll bring along some girl.'

It was then that Mangasuri realised their son was of marriageable age. What if he did as Kumarasurar had predicted? Their status in society rested upon their son's shoulders. So much depended on how and whom he married. What if he ruined everything? They would be humiliated before their relatives and friends. People would whisper about them everywhere they went, they would be mocked by everyone.

'They sent off a son to some faraway place, raving about how they were making him study. And he's come back with some woman whose caste-vaste is unknown,' they would laugh.

Her husband's potion was taking effect.

13

Mangasuri sat Meghas down and said, 'I believe the kids in that college drink.'

'Who doesn't drink nowadays, Amma?' he replied.

What did that mean? He knew about alcohol. He might even be a drinker.

When he saw Mangasuri's face change, he added, 'There are very few people like me, people who don't know anything about this stuff and don't want it even if they do learn of it.'

This warmed Mangasuri's heart. Her son had only ever left home for school. Where could he possibly have learnt about these things? He was her innocent little calf.

But her suspicions had not yet been put to rest. 'You know, they say things about drugs of all kinds. Do you think those will be easily available in that college?'

He didn't answer right away. After a pause, he said, 'Appa has got himself confused, and confused you too. Everything is available everywhere. But not everyone gets into everything. Most people in our street are like Appa; they're responsible men who go to work. In the fourth house on the street, there's a drunkard. Every day, you'll find him sprawled on the road after a bout of drinking. Everyone who passes our street knows of him. You could ask anyone in town whether they know where Appa lives, and they would have no clue. Ask about the drunkard and everyone will know. Our street is known as "Drunkard Street". All based on this one guy. Does that mean everyone on the street is a drunkard?'

Mangasuri was listening with her mouth open.

'It's like this everywhere. In the school I went to, some ten kids would have aced their exams and joined medical college. They advertise that. They've even put up ads in our town. Look at those. You'll see ten photographs of students in each ad. We don't even know for sure whether those ten kids went to my school. But everyone believes their kids will become doctors if they send them to that school because of the ad.'

Mangasuri was still listening with her mouth open. This struck Meghas as an opportune moment.

'There were two thousand of us in that school. Does anyone know the other one thousand nine hundred and ninety faces? That's how it goes. Maybe there are ten students in this college who are alcoholics. Ten others who run around with girls. Ten others who do drugs. Ten others who play cards for money in hostel. But there are thousands of students in that college. Does it make sense to judge it by those groups of ten?'

Mangasuri continued to listen with her mouth open. He was inspired to add to his homily.

'Why do you assume boys are going to go do something awful? The ones who actually do horrible things are adults. If you compare the wrongdoings of people over thirty against those of people under thirty, who do you think would be doing worse? And which will be the greater number? People who take bribes, people who cheat, people who lie, people who let others down, people who siphon money, are all over thirty. If youngsters cheat, you'll find that the reason is actually someone older. Let's say I dump a girl who has trusted me, why would I do that? Because my mother will not be okay with it, my father will not be okay with it, my relatives will not be okay with it, my village will not be okay with it. Who are these people? People over thirty, right? So is it right to keep saying boys my age will go awry?'

Mangasuri was listening with her mouth open. Feeling sorry for his mother, Meghas brought his speech to a close.

'My friend's older brother studied there. Now he's got a great job abroad. I spoke to him on Skype. He says it's a wonderful college for kids who take an interest in their studies. People like us, from good families, will find the college suitable. So don't worry.'

Mangasuri had not expected that her son would talk so much. After this speech, she found she had great faith in him. He would do the right thing. When she told Kumarasurar what he had said, her husband said, 'He knows you're gullible, and he's fooled you with his glibness. But he can't fool me, you wait and watch.'

'You're always suspicious of your son. He's far more intelligent than us,' Mangasuri said.

'Far more intelligent than you. Why bring me into it?'

That was the end of their conversation. Kumarasurar wasn't able to win his wife back to his side. Their exchanges on the terrace were no longer in harmony. His wife had become his son's mouthpiece. He began to avoid these conversations on the terrace.

14

Meghas had made up his mind that he would join this college and no other. He was worried that he might not have done well enough in the final exams to qualify for a seat. Even if he couldn't get in through the 'government quota', he could speak to the administrative department of the college about a seat in the management quota. This would be more expensive. But he had decided he would apply for the management quota if his marks were not high enough. He spoke to his mother about this, arranged for some money and paid the advance to the college. He explained that even if his rank ensured he got a seat in the government quota, the advance would be deducted from his tuition fee.

His father, having decided his marks would not be sufficient for a seat in the regular intake, was caught up in calculating how much a management quota seat would cost and where he would find the money. How much did their savings amount to? What were the loans available to him from his office? Would the bank give them an education loan? He learnt that a management seat would cost ten lakh rupees more than a government seat. It would stretch their resources.

Mangasuri did not see his point. 'We have just one child. On whom or what else are we going to spend money? Take a loan-voan and do what you must,' she said. She prayed to their clan deity for Meghas to have done well in the final exam.

Once he had zeroed in on the college he would attend, Meghas was all excitement. It turned out he had a couple of friends other than the television, internet and phone. He spent an hour every evening with them. He asked Mangasuri to make his favourite dishes and ate them with relish. His father could not match him for mood.

Kumarasurar had always been a silent worker. He was not given to office banter. These days, though, he wanted to speak to everyone he met, particularly those around his age. He made use of every opportunity to start a conversation. However it began, the conversation would end on this note: 'We have to enrol our son in college. He insists on this particular one.' His interlocutor would then voice an opinion in line with either his own experience or Kumarasurar's expression. Usually, it was criticism of the college.

He hinted to Meghas that they should check out a few other colleges. He might like others which had a lower cut-off for entry, surely? But Meghas dug his heels in and wouldn't budge.

Kumarasurar began to think about ways to arrange for the money. An old friend came to mind. Thenasurar was the owner of a small business. He was a school dropout. In his teens, he had begun to work at a blacksmith's in the neighbouring town and risen in his profession bit by bit till he owned his own little workshop. Now, he had a business that brought him a monthly income of several lakh rupees.

They were both from the same town, the same street, the same caste. They had been childhood friends, playing together. They had been classmates in kindergarten. Thenasurar had had to give up his schooling after class eight. Kumarasurar occasionally called him on the phone. Thenasurar too called every now and again. Their conversation played out like a tug of war.

Kumarasurar would not call the moment he felt an urge to speak to his friend. He would wonder whether he should call or not. This internal debate could drag on for half a day. He usually decided not to call right away. If he did decide to speak, he would wonder which would be the best time.

If Thenasurar was busy at work, the conversation would end in a minute or two. If he was free, the call would not be a short one—unless Thenasurar had made the call. In that case, he would try to finish within a minute or two. When Kumarasurar called, he in his turn would seek to end the conversation quickly. But Thenasurar would have a lot to say.

They would talk about a cat that had crossed Thenasurar's path on his way to the workshop, a dog darting across the street, his wife putting too much salt in his food the previous day, his breathing patterns, gas trouble and so on. He would give Kumarasurar no window to draw the conversation to a close. Talking non-stop, stringing his words together like a chain, asking questions to which one could only provide 'yes-no' answers, were all areas of Thenasurar's expertise. Sometimes, the call would only end when Kumarasurar's phone balance ran out.

'He cleaned me out. What kind of man talks so much? He treats his own money like iron, and everyone else's like sugarcane,' Kumarasurar would whine to his wife.

He would make a resolve that the next time Thenasurar called, he would draw out the conversation until the latter ran out of balance. But Kumarasurar was no connoisseur of fine speech. He would run out of words and lose to Thenasurar in each round.

It was a businessman's telecom venture that ended up solving the problem.

Once, when Thenasurar called, he was in no hurry to end the conversation. This surprised Kumarasurar. The next time Kumarasurar called, his friend said, 'You keep the phone down. Let me call you.' Thenasurar then disconnected the call and phoned again. He spoke a long time.

What had prompted this change?

'I've no idea what this world is coming to. He talks for a long time when he calls. Even if I call, he cuts it and calls me back. I don't spend a single paisa to talk to him. How did this happen?' he marvelled to Mangasuri.

Meghas, who was listening in, said, 'He must have started using a net card. Calls are free with a net card. You can do that too. Then you can talk to whomever you want, whenever you want, till kingdom come. Shall I set it up for you?'

The only thing Kumarasurar understood was that one could make calls for free. But he felt he should give it some thought. Nothing was free, least of all at someone else's loss. What kind of businessman would be altruistic enough to manufacture a net card which allowed everyone to speak for hours on the phone without paying a dime, forgoing all the money he could make? There must be a strategy in place. What if it were a scam or a trap of some sort? He wanted to make his enquiries before allowing his son to set up the new net card.

Now, he planned to ask Thenasurar if he could help out just in case Meghas had to join the college in the management quota. He called his friend, fixed a meeting and went to his town.

On his way, he was flooded by memories of their youth.

'What a time that was,' he sighed aloud and often.

When Kumarasurar was twenty years old, he had taken the government exam and been selected for a job. Even before his appointment order arrived, he was prime property in the marriage market. A government servant, with his guaranteed pension and fixed salary, did not have to try hard to find a bride. When he was waiting for the letter, all Kumarasurar had to do through the day was eat and sleep. He woke when he felt like it. Someone would be waiting for him with water to wash his face.

He had two younger brothers. One would position himself by his bed, and the other would take charge in the bathroom. His brothers shared several chores, including bringing him a towel, fetching him his plate, serving him food, taking the empty plate back to the kitchen, and washing and ironing his clothes.

Kumarasurar did not lift a finger except to brush his teeth, wash himself after going to the toilet, and put the food from his plate into his mouth. Someone would be waiting with water for him to wash his hands after the meal. Another would be waiting with a cloth so he could wipe his hands dry.

Their father had issued an order: 'For the first time, someone from our clan has been given a job by the government. This job will wipe away our ill luck. He must be treated like a king.'

This was repeated numerous times each day.

This little dialogue spread across town, and every time Perasurar walked past, people laughed and said, 'The king's father's here.'

This gave Perasurar great pleasure. He would hold his head a little higher.

Everyone who had once addressed Kumarasurar informally and used 'da' while speaking to him, now began to use the formal plural. Kumarasuran had become Kumarasurar. He enjoyed this change, and felt he had attained the status of Indra. It was Thenasurar who helped break this illusion.

Thenasurar, who was struggling to make a living in another city, visited Kumarasurar at home to congratulate him on the job. He added, 'Man, you've become a whale. In a few days, you're going to look like a buffalo, and you'll need to be paid to move. No girl will marry you. You could offer your hand in marriage, but all one can reach will be this fat paunch of yours.'

It was a wake-up call. Kumarasurar began to do his chores himself. He played at the village school grounds to get fitter.

He would drive away anyone who tried to help him around the house, with an angry look or word. His brothers, freed from slavery, were happy.

Kumarasurar too had reason to be happy. His penis, which had been black as coal before he had got a job, now began to lighten and glow. Every day, as he showered, he would measure its lightness and admire how fair it had become. But this joy could not be shared.

However, Perasurar came to hear of it.

And so another duty loomed before him.

A queue of marriage brokers and parents of girls began to form outside their house before the first light of dawn. Since talk of marriage could only happen on an auspicious day, Wednesdays and holy days saw the queue snake up to the end of the road. As word of Kumarasurar's government employment spread, relatives from out of town arrived in the guise of guests and set up camp in their home, determined to win Kumarasurar for a son-in-law.

The crowd on the street must be credited for the growing prosperity of the petty shop owner who lived there. He began to procure items from the city and sell them in his shop.

People who had come in from out of town asked him where they could find something to eat.

The shop owner began to package tomato rice and curd rice. He was eventually able to expand the petty shop to accommodate a restaurant in its front portion. His family placed all its trust in Kumarasurar.

Perasurar spent his mornings interviewing those in line, answering their questions and discussing horoscopes. His posture, attire and manner changed during this time. He wanted the bride to be from an affluent family. He would scrutinise the applicants' clothes. He would allocate a good chunk of time for some, while driving away others. Some of the unfortunates, unwilling to give up, pleaded with him pitifully.

This also brought about great awareness among the youngsters and their parents in town.

It became the sole ambition and dream of many young men to study well, get recruited by the government and use this job to marry a woman who was beautiful and rich. Parents beseeched their sons to study well and somehow bag a government job. When older people met school dropouts who were doing menial odd jobs, they muttered, 'If only you had studied, you wouldn't have to suffer like this.'

It wouldn't be unreasonable to say Kumarasurar had raised awareness for education in his town.

Every time he stepped out of or into the house, the prospective in-laws would gawk at him. Their stares clustered around him like flies, and he felt awkward. If he happened to stumble, the hordes would descend upon him to help him up. Some even considered hiring the two-headed andaranda bird to capture him and cart him away.

Several people spoke to Perasurar about how much jewellery they would give their daughters. Some wanted to buy rings for all ten of Kumarasurar's fingers. Others were happy to throw in gold toe rings too.

One party asked, hesitantly, 'If you could tell me your son's size, we could get him a gold ferrule. We'll even get him a waistbelt made of gold to go with it.'

Perasurar wasn't sure how to broach the subject with his son. He couldn't use a conduit. If word happened to get out, it could become a subject for mockery. But he couldn't keep the news to himself either. He told his wife as delicately as he could. It gave her great pride, and the two of them whispered about this together. Kumarasurar's mother had one major concern: What if word of his size made people jealous, and they cast the Evil Eye? So they kept the news to themselves.

Kumarasurar was keen to get married too. Watching the crowd fight amongst themselves as he walked about with nothing else to do made him dream of marital bliss. He also ached to show his new-found fairness to someone else. If nothing else, an announcement of marriage would help disperse the annoying hopefuls. But his father did not arrive at a decision. It appeared he was postponing the verdict so he could prolong his lording over the supplicants.

One morning, his mother said, 'This man won't get you married, pa. He's got greedy. It's gone to his head. He won't make a compromise. So listen to me, pa. You know how much my brother has helped us. I've told you all about it. All our cattle are descended from the buffalo calf they sent with me when I got married. It is those bulls that we've sacrificed to the clan deity. Every time I went to them with financial problems, they would delve into their paltry savings to help me out. What are we going to do in return, to express our gratitude? They haven't visited us because they're not sure they'll hear a peep from us now that you've got this job. They have a girl at home, but they haven't broached the subject. They're afraid your father will dismiss them with a harsh word or two. However high we climb, can we let go of our roots? When your uncle's daughter Mangasuri is around, can you marry someone else, my darling? Give me your consent, and I'll see to the rest.'

The scales fell from Kumarasurar's eyes. He decided to follow her advice.

He accompanied his mother on a visit to his uncle's house without Perasurar's knowledge. Mangasuri wasn't the girl he remembered from a few years ago. The first blush of youth had painted a masterpiece. Having seen her, Kumarasurar was willing to lay his life down to express his family's gratitude to his uncle. His mother's work was done. He didn't know what she said to his father, but the marriage took place. His father sulked throughout the ceremony.

Later, Perasurar would often sigh, 'If only you'd listened to me, you'd truly have lived like a king. One man actually wanted to get you a golden ferrule.'

This was only whispered to Kumarasurar, but word got around. And so, Kumarasurar earned an epithet: 'The Ferrule Man'.

Even before his appointment order arrived, a lavish wedding was organised. It took ten years and the bulk of Kumarasurar's salary to pay back the loans his family had taken for the wedding. Over those years, he was accused of ignoring his brothers' and parents' financial needs.

This is the story of how Kumarasurar was married at the age of twenty-one. It took him a few years longer to be blessed with a child. Meghas was born in his twenty-fifth year.

When Thenasurar came to see the baby, he said, 'Hmm. You're lucky. Job at the right time, marriage at the right time, child at the right time.' And he didn't fail to sigh. Each time they met after, the sigh grew longer, never shorter. The sigh, which had initially signalled the end of his speech, began to punctuate the end of each sentence, and then each word. Eventually, it replaced the words. The sighs were so elaborate it was a wonder the heat they produced didn't singe Thenasurar's nose.

This was back when Thenasurar worked in the unorganised sector. No one was willing to marry off their daughter to him. Working with iron and smoke had blackened his face. His hairline had begun to recede. He was over thirty-five when he finally got married. One saw far less of him after this. His business began to prosper.

Even so, he couldn't forget that Kumarasurar had got everything at the 'right time'. He would reiterate this every chance he got.

15

Thenasurar had once seen Meghas when he was in class eleven. That day, all he could talk about was the boy.

'I saw him as a child. Look how he's grown now!

'Just four more years, and your son will begin to earn. You can sit back and eat off him.

'Father and son look like brothers!'

He left the thoughts behind the words unsaid. And so Kumarasurar took his comments at face value and laughed with pride. But Mangasuri could fathom what Thenasurar had meant. They were:

'My children are still kids.

'I can't retire even after ten years.

'When people see me with my children, they assume I'm their grandfather.'

And so, Mangasuri began to hide Meghas away every time they had a guest. If they had a relative or friend over, Mangasuri would panic and throw Meghas out of the house.

'Where should I go, Amma?' he would snap.

'Go to the market ... go somewhere ... like a boy doesn't have a place to go to!' she would say and chase him out.

If someone turned up suddenly, the terrace offered an easy alternative. Once, when he had been packed off to the terrace, Meghas had fainted in the heat. Mangasuri found a solution. She improvised a little room under the water tank by sealing off the sides with cardboard, and kept a portable fan there for his use. Meghas would squeeze himself into this space and sleep until the guests left.

'Why are you acting like this? Are our visitors kidnappers?' Kumarasurar would scold.

'They're not kidnappers. They're people who make mincemeat of children and eat it. Don't you see each eye devouring our child?' Mangasuri would reply.

All said and done, Kumarasurar had only three friends. He could share his news only with these three. He could ask favours only of these three. Where money was concerned, Kanakasurar was not an option. He would begin to wail about all the expenses that awaited him, starting with his daughters' weddings. It would have been possible to approach Adhigasurar if he'd lived in the vicinity. But he lived in a far-off metropolis. And he was a salaried man too. Who knew what expenses he had? That left Thenasurar. Kumarasurar decided to meet him at work and talk over lunch.

The room was expansive, and the air-conditioning powerful. Thenasurar was seated behind a large table. He got up and ushered Kumarasurar into a cabin shielded by a screen. Inside was a dining table with beautiful chairs. Kumarasurar was admiring these, when Thenasurar drew him into conversation.

'Do you go to the village often?' he asked.

'No, not since my parents passed away. I'm not much in touch with my brothers. I only go to the village when I have to attend relatives' weddings and funerals,' Kumarasurar replied.

'Yeah, yeah, that's right. The moment they get wind of us being well off, everyone in the village claims to be a relative and begins to badger us. "Give me a loan for that, give me money for this"—that's all you hear. Do we carry moneybags on us or what? We make just about enough to live. If we become philanthropists, we'll turn into beggars. That's why I don't go anywhere near the village,' Thenasurar said.

His words troubled Kumarasurar. Would Thenasurar think of his request as 'badgering'? It was with a lot of hesitation and after they had spoken about everything else that he brought up Meghas's studies. He didn't mention that he was short of money.

'Hmm. So he's old enough to go to college, huh? Feels like he was in a cradle just yesterday. My son's just about to start third standard. And my daughter first standard,' Thenasurar said, with a long sigh. The heat from the sigh hit Kumarasurar's face despite the air-conditioning.

With another sigh, Thenasurar continued, 'Education is useless. I've got some ten educated kids working for me. None of them knows a thing. They come here to learn how to do everything. And on the other hand, there are kids here who haven't spent a paisa on going to college, and landed up right after thirteenth class. These kids are quick on the uptake, and they progress a lot faster. What's the point of wasting money on studies? Send him here. I'll make a Big Man out of him within a year.'

'What will he do without an education?' Kumarasurar said.

'You were such a swot. And how much money do you make now? How much would the government give you anyway? You make just about enough to run your family, don't you? If you don't get your salary on the first of the month, you'll be in the weeds. But look at me. I'm a school dropout, but I pay the salaries of everyone who works for me. I've never had to ask anyone for money.'

What had happened to the 'right time' now?

'Aren't you going to educate your son?' Kumarasurar couldn't stop himself asking.

'A school education is enough for him. All he needs is enough maths to do the accounts. By the time he grows up, my business would have grown further. Isn't it enough if he runs the business? Why would he need to turn to anyone else?'

So he had divined that Kumarasurar was here to ask for money. Kumarasurar had never before felt so humiliated. Perhaps this was how businessmen spoke. He felt jaded. What had prompted him to approach Thenasurar? He ate his food without interest, didn't speak a word about money and took his leave.

This was a long friendship, and it had ended today, he told himself. Throughout the bus journey home, all manner of thoughts flooded his mind. Would Thenasurar really absorb his children into the business without an education? Surely he would educate them before handing over the reins?

Back then, Thenasurar had quit in class eight. Kumarasurar had studied further. He had got a job even before he finished his education. A man who had been jealous, even resentful, of his government job and marriage and child, had now taken a different stance. Thenasurar had found several ways to point out that despite being more qualified, Kumarasurar made less money. Kumarasurar wondered at his own naivete—in all this time, he had never noticed this aspect of Thenasurar's personality.

He gave Mangasuri a vague account of his interaction with Thenasurar. She understood that they would not get the money from him. She consoled her husband, saying there would be no need for the money because their son would do well enough in the exam. And even if they happened to need the money, they could take an education loan from the bank or mortgage their house. There was no need to humiliate themselves by asking anyone for help. She even suggested they could sell off her jewellery. His wife's words gave him great solace. But on the eve of the announcement of results, he couldn't sleep a wink.

16

It felt as if someone were sucking all the air out of his lungs. He tossed and turned for a long time. He knew his breaths would get softer and softer, and would eventually stop. He stumbled out of bed and felt about in the dark. He opened the door gently and stepped out. The streetlights blinded him. He had to look down and very slowly lift his head, degree by degree. As his eyes got used to the light, they surveyed the street. He ensured there was not a soul outside before he took his next step.

The plants that lined the road and the trees in the house across the street were still as a picture. He began to walk the lane. The stray dogs—which barked at people they saw, ensured they had made their territorial claims clear and then backed off—were nowhere to be seen. Perhaps the strays identified him as one of their own. There was one particular dog which would moan in a strange manner and rub herself up against his legs. Mangasuri would chuckle to herself whenever she saw this. Thankfully, this dog was not around either.

The street stretched out like a drain someone had dug. He considered walking to the main road, but dismissed the thought. Someone might see him and mistake him for a burglar. People looked at him suspiciously even in daylight.

If he identified himself as Kumarasurar from the street, and not a thief, it would be fodder for gossip the next day—

his neighbours would wonder what the problem was and why he'd been roaming about at night.

A man from the fourth house on the road had, after seeing him set off regularly on his morning walk, asked him a few times, 'What's happened, sir, do you have piles?'

Kumarasurar had had to snap, 'I think you wish it on me,' before the man would leave him alone.

But his neighbour's curious glance hadn't changed. Chances were, he'd gone around telling people Kumarasurar was ill. If he had his eyes on the street now, he would think Kumarasurar was seeking a companion. He would mutter that only the diseased dogs on the street would make fit company for the lone perambulator.

Kumarasurar walked along the street, but only up to where his own boundary wall ended. If someone happened to see him, his legs were ready to dart back inside. He looked at the opposite house, with its two floors, which dwarfed his own. He felt a pang of jealousy. How could anyone breathe if people blocked the air by building such tall houses, he thought, irritated. He began to take in large gulps of air. He had never found it quite so difficult to breathe before. If he walked just a little bit faster, he found he was out of breath. He opened the gate, stepped back in and locked it behind him. He climbed the steps by the side of the house to the terrace. He sat on a bench there and stared up at the sky.

A genius's line came to mind: 'We're dwarfed by the sky.' He told himself that was the truth. The thought consoled him. A gentle breeze caressed his face. Stars were spread across the sky. Phrases such as 'A breeze blows', 'The stars shine', and 'The dark engulfs me', came to him. If he ordered it thus—'The dark engulfs me/ The stars shine/ A breeze blows'—it could work as a poem. Did changing the order of phrases change the connotations? He played around with the order of these three phrases for a while. That tired him.

But it pleased him that he could compose poetry. Back in college, he used to scribble lines like everyone else. He had made great efforts to have an anthology of poetry published. The hurdle had been his lack of funds. If only he had seen it through and published a collection, he would have established himself as a poet. He had planned to save some money after getting a job, and had decided he would then publish not one, but several collections of poetry. But once he'd had enough money to spare, the poems had deserted him. He had lost the opportunity, and it would never come by again. He could not spare any money for things like this now. He retained only the title of 'Felicitation Poet'.

Long after he lay down on the terrace, sleep continued to evade him. His eyes would droop with heaviness and he would be nodding off, when someone would shake him awake. But when he looked around, there would be no one else. Who could it be? It was his mind which was restless. It had caused his breathlessness too. Was it a symptom of cardiac arrest? It couldn't be. He wasn't sweating much. He didn't feel the slightest pain. It was the anxiety about the following day that was driving him crazy. This anxiety was holding his sleep to ransom. What could he gain from staying awake and overthinking everything? Nothing was in his hands. He couldn't change a thing. So why was he suffering so much? Why couldn't he simply let things be?

The breeze was cooling his body now. Could it be dawn yet? Then, he only had to wait a few hours. His torment would end. He wouldn't be able to sleep if he went to bed anyway. He might as well while away the time walking on the terrace. He sauntered from one side of the terrace to the other. It felt pleasant to take in the air and think about nothing.

As if something had just occurred to him, he sat himself in vajrasana. About six months ago, he had seen an advertisement for free yoga training at a large maidan. There were enormous posters bearing the photograph of a godman whose chief characteristic was that he looked at the sky and wailed.

Since the course was offered for free, Kumarasurar thought he might as well give it a shot, and underwent the training.

He remembered some of what he had been taught, and practised the asanas now. He repeated the secret mantra—'Everything happens for the best'—over and over again. His fears abated and his heart felt full with the belief that only good things could happen. But he couldn't surrender himself to sleep even after his mind had cleared.

Just then, he heard footsteps on the stairs. He peeped over the parapet cautiously. Mangasuri was climbing up with all the stealth of a shadow. He was surprised it had taken her this long to come in search of him. Mangasuri had long been in the habit of monitoring his smallest movements.

If he were staring into space, she would ask, 'Why are you staring?'

If he fidgeted a bit, she would demand, 'Why are you twitching?'

He would have to answer her. If he said nothing, she would ask, 'Can't you see a woman is screaming herself hoarse here?' And then she would begin to actually scream and throw pots and pans around. He had to answer each question.

'Nothing' and 'Just felt like it' would not do for answers. He would think of some reason for each of his actions, simply to satisfy his wife. Sometimes, it struck him that if he kept up this line of thought, he might well turn into a philosopher.

He would have to speak first now. Or, she would ask, 'What are you obsessing about to such a degree that you're oblivious to someone walking up the stairs?'

Sometimes, his wife's words sank deep into his consciousness and haunted him like an otherworldly voice.

Preempting her, he called out, 'Did you check the time?'

'Yes. I check every ten minutes. The clock's hands don't seem to move,' his wife said.

It irritated him that she hadn't given him a straight answer. But he asked in a gentle voice, so she wouldn't sense this, 'So what's the time now?'

'Only a quarter past three,' she said, sounding frustrated.

'So you couldn't sleep either?' he asked.

'I was watching you toss and turn. If I asked you about it, you'd start barking at me. I decided it wasn't worth the trouble, and kept quiet. You slipped out like a thief. I thought you'd take in some air and come back, but there was no sign of you. So I came to check on you.'

He didn't make a big deal of her veiled references to him as a dog and a thief. The same thoughts had occurred to him a while earlier. But he felt compelled to retaliate.

'You crib about me, but you were tossing about too, weren't you? And now you slip up the stairs like a cat. Thank heavens I saw you. If you turn up like an apparition, won't a man be startled out of his wits?'

'Right. Call me a cat, call me a ghost. When have you ever seen me as a woman?' she snapped.

It wasn't the ideal trajectory for the first conversation of the day. He decided to steer it in a different direction.

'I can barely shut my eyes thinking about the results tomorrow. What's he up to, by the way?'

'What's anyone up to in the middle of the night? He's asleep.'

'What does he have to worry about? Sleeping like a baby! Does he care about the results? We're the ones who are up all night, worrying about whether he will score well or not.

If he were the kind of boy who wanted to make a living, he'd be worried.'

'You never miss a chance to rant about him. He's just a boy. He'll set himself straight as he grows up.'

'Humph! Yeah, right, sure he will. He doesn't have a care in the world. He doesn't even have the smidgen of concern that you do. At least you take the trouble to assure me he'll do well. But does he have a word to say for himself?'

'What can he say if you keep asking him how much he'll score? If he says he'll do well, you'll say, "Like I don't know just how much you're worth!" If he says he'll do all right, you'll snap, "Like your wonderful answers are going to get you a government quota seat!" What could he possibly say?'

'You're always on your son's side. I've poured money into his education. And what was all that for? For my happiness? I wanted to make sure that he would do well, that he wouldn't suffer like me. Shouldn't he take on the responsibility of having put his father through all this? All I want is for him to score enough to get into that stinking college.'

'Let it go. He'll do well, you'll see. You'll be all praise for him in the morning, just you wait.'

'We'll see, we'll see. Maybe he'll do well enough for us to be able to answer the people who ask.'

'Leave that aside. You said just the other day that the college was sparkling clean? And now you say it stinks?'

'Is it enough if they clean up the grounds? Shouldn't they clean up the rest? You see those boys and girls holding hands and cuddling together, and you want to throw up.'

'Our son won't do all that. He'll come back the same sweet, golden child. He'll just glow a bit brighter.'

'It's fine if he glows brighter. If he brings along someone and glows with something else, what are you going to do about it?'

'That's all you ever think about. It's so windy. How are you able to sit here? Come on down, let's sleep for a while.'

'You carry on. I like the wind.'

'Do what you want. You'll never listen to me, and then you'll whine that you've got a cold and fever. Why won't you come down when I ask you to?'

She was still muttering to herself as she walked down the stairs.

He tried to get back into poetic mode. He looked up at the sky. But the moment had passed. The universe seemed to conspire to ruin the poetic imagination. He couldn't rescue the poet from this conspiracy.

He was reminded of a poem he had once written, imagining that he was constantly surrounded by armed hitmen: *No one can kill me, I'm a poet.*

But Time was well-armed to kill a poet. The first of these arms was family.

Now, it struck him that his wife's words, 'Why won't you come on down when I ask you to?' had carried a suggestion. When one's mind was restless, one didn't even hear the call of the flesh. He couldn't stir up interest in anything right now. He lay down, staring at the sky again.

17

Only after the morning sun had bathed his body in sweat did Kumarasurar wake up. He wasn't able to open his eyes right away. It took an enormous effort to stand up. It was well into the morning. Had he slept this long? Why hadn't anyone woken him? If he had been sleeping inside the house, would they have let him carry on this way? If he slept five minutes longer than usual, his wife would make some noise to wake him. She would increase the volume of the television, on which the Meghasura Geetam would be playing. It was so unbearable he would have to get up.

He looked at the spot where he had been sleeping. It was as if all the dust from the terrace had gathered around his body. The place he had occupied showed up like a chalk outline around a corpse. Had he slept sound as a corpse? He felt a surge of anger against his wife and son. He sat back down. Had they both slept in because he hadn't gone downstairs?

Meghas never woke by himself. Someone had to go to great lengths to wake him up. Or he would sleep into the afternoon. His mother would shout to him, but he wouldn't hear. He wouldn't stir even if somebody went near him and tapped him on the back or shook his legs. Sometimes, he would sleep with one leg over the other. If he was given a tight slap, he would gently extricate a leg and continue to sleep. His ability to sleep was remarkable.

He had been in the school hostel for two years. Was this how the boys slept there? If you remarked on it, his face would fall into a sulk. When he had been a child, that face was radiant with laughter. His hands would rise up as if to catch the laughter before it could escape. Where had that laughter gone? You couldn't say a word to him now without provoking him. He hardly spoke, not even to answer a question.

It was so irritating Kumarasurar wanted to slap his son across the face. Every time he was tempted to do this, he would go into the toilet, bolt the door and slap himself on the face over and over again. Once, he had been carried away by the emotion and used more force than usual. His face began to swell and his cheeks turned red. He was worried the secret he had kept from even his wife would get out.

He told people he had been stung by a wasp while searching through some old papers. Mangasuri stroked his cheeks to find the point where he had been stung and ensure that the stinger wasn't embedded inside.

'There's nothing of the sort,' Kumarasurar said, angrily pushing her hands away.

He had to take great pains to prove it was a wasp's sting.

Mangasuri had grown up in a village. She had no faith in allopathic medicine. She prescribed herbal cures for every ailment. She claimed the leaf of the celosia plant would soothe the wasp's sting. But they wouldn't find celosia anywhere in town, and so she used fenugreek instead. She kept repeating that a drop of celosia extract would have cured the swelling at once.

Finding this unbearable, Kumarasurar said, 'Then take a bus to the village.'

Mangasuri had never travelled alone by bus. The reason for this was that she was afraid she would get off at the wrong stop. The house was her haven. She knew even the cockroaches and ants in the house individually. She had befriended two lizards in the kitchen. A tomcat and a tabby who visited from nearby were close friends of hers too. Her other companions were a crow and two yellow-billed babblers who lounged on the terrace wall. But she seemed up to date with current affairs. Kumarasurar was often surprised by how much she knew without ever venturing out. He suspected the birds she fed were the bearers of world news.

It wasn't just Mangasuri's fear of solitary bus travel that Kumarasurar had capitalised on. In the asura tradition, saying, 'Go to the village,' was the equivalent of saying, 'Go back to your mother's home.' It was a husband's banishment of his wife. Even when Kumarasurar casually suggested she visit home, Mangasuri's face would crumple. When he said the words in anger, their effect was more pronounced. He sometimes resorted to this to shut her up. As he expected, it put an end to her talk of herbal remedies.

However, he couldn't go to office with a swollen face. He had to take a couple of days off. Meghas didn't ask him what was wrong. Kumarasurar thought to himself that this boy wouldn't bother looking after him in his old age. Not that he was dependent on his son. His pension would be enough. He was annoyed with himself. He ought to have slapped himself during the weekend so he wouldn't have had to take days off.

The next time he bolted himself into the toilet for his slapping ritual, he remembered what had transpired when he had got carried away, and his raised hand froze. Once his memory reprimanded them, his hands switched strategy. They began to bang him on the head. Since his skull was stronger than his cheeks, it didn't hurt quite as much even when he hit himself for longer. His scalp felt slightly sore, and his head rather heavy. But his heart was lighter.

Since then, his hands had switched loyalties. He would hit himself only on the head. He would cry for a while too. The ache in his heart would subside.

His wife, who seemed to have eyes at the back of her head, would yell, 'What are you doing inside the toilet for so long?'

She suspected he was engaged in another activity. He had decided to let it be.

All he wanted was for Meghas to do well enough to get a regular seat without having to pay a higher fee. Then, Kumarasurar could leave him to his life and wash his hands of him.

He rose with a sigh and looked to the east. The sun was so high it might be afternoon. No one seemed to have woken yet. He couldn't hear a sound from inside the house. He came to all of a sudden, and rushed down the stairs. He felt breathless.

As soon as he reached the courtyard, he saw a beautiful kolam outside. Hibiscus flowers had been placed tastefully in the middle. Did Mangasuri really possess such creativity, he wondered.

Clearly, his wife was awake. She would have roused their son too. He could smell incense. She must have showered and done her puja. She had been doing daily pujas all month. It appeared she had outdone herself today.

He pushed the door open and went inside. His son was at the computer. Both his wife and son were fresh from their showers. He looked at the time. It was eight. Only eight. But he had never before slept so late. He felt embarrassed to speak to them. He headed straight for the bathroom.

Meghas saw him before he could get in, though.

'Where did you go, Appa?' His tone was teasing. 'Did you sleep?' he asked, looking him up and down.

'Mm,' Kumarasurar said, not wanting to engage.

His son laughed. He continued to speak, but much to Kumarasurar's relief, he turned to the screen. 'Amma said you were roaming about all night because you couldn't sleep, and you must have gone for a walk. But you look like you've just napped!'

It was the most his son had spoken in a while.

He made for the bathroom in a hurry and shouted to Mangasuri on his way, 'Why didn't you wake me?'

His wife's face appeared through the smokescreen set off by the idlis cooking on the stove. 'Yeah, right, like I thought you'd be sleeping all this while without even feeling the heat from the sun. I figured you'd have gone for your morning walk and you'd return home only after gorging on the vadais. How does a man sleep without a care in the world when his son's exam results are due? Look at the boy, he's all dressed and ready. What's the point speaking about taking responsibility when you can't set him an example? Like I have nothing to do but look for you all morning. I have to sweep and swab the courtyard, draw the kolam, cook and do a million other things before I can babysit you. Or you'll howl that you're starving and there's nothing to eat. And I'm supposed to make waking you up another one of my chores, am I?'

Thoroughly humiliated, he stepped into the shower. His wife's words followed him through the door. He opened the tap to its full capacity. The sound of falling water drowned out everything else.

The three of them sat before the computer once he was dressed.

It was no mean feat to learn Meghas's marks. Irrespective of when one woke up, it was only at ten o'clock that the results would be published online. Every house in every city must have been connected to the internet at the time. Their connection fell through every now and again. Meghas tried to revive it each time, but he was often unsuccessful. Even when the connection held, it was terribly slow. The entire country was battling to get to the website. All these lakhs of people sought one piece of news—would their child become a doctor or not? Kumarasurar was free of this worry. His son only had to do well enough to get into engineering college in the common entrance quota. But they simply could not see his marks. They underwent this torment for a quarter of an hour.

Meghas banged hard on the computer table. Kumarasurar was afraid he would throw the computer on the floor and break it next. Mangasuri rushed to bring the boy some water. The water was of little help. His eyes turned red and began to shed tears. He ground his teeth, his breath came in angry gasps, and his body seemed out of control.

'Have some patience, we'll see the results in good time, pa,' Kumarasurar tried to calm him down.

'You don't need a medical seat. So there's no hurry. Let's wait and see,' Mangasuri said.

Meghas reached some semblance of normalcy. He phoned some of his friends. They hadn't been able to check their marks either. Then who was able to access the website? Television channels had already begun to list how many students had qualified for medical seats, and were flashing the news that all these students claimed their only goal was to go to the villages and serve the people with their medical knowledge.

There was elaborate coverage of the three toppers from Asurapuri. Within minutes, news trickled through of the toppers in each district, town and village. In the next few minutes, each clan announced how many of its people had passed and who the three toppers from each clan were. Those who were going to study medicine were praised and felicitated. There were visuals of the toppers' parents feeding them sweets. Thinking how lovely it would have been if their son had topped the exam and they had been on television feeding him sweets, Kumarasurar and Mangasuri let out deep sighs.

Now, the tone of the news changed. There was a piece on a boy who had killed himself by consuming poison because he hadn't done well in the exams. Another channel telecast news of a girl's father having died of cardiac arrest because her scores were lower than he had hoped.

There were live interviews with experts from various fields. Kumarasurar liked what one of them had to say.

'They should open many more medical colleges. The duration of the degree should be halved from seven years to three and a half. Everyone who wants to become a doctor should be given a seat. Let there be more doctors. Our motto should be not simply "One doctor for every street", but "One doctor for every family". We should eventually reach a situation where each person can treat his own illnesses. We must move towards this. This is the only way suicides and sudden death from shock can be prevented.'

'What is all this unholy talk of death? Either change the channel or switch the TV off,' Mangasuri said.

Meghas had continued to sit at the computer, trying to navigate to the site which would display his results, even as his parents had gravitated towards the television.

Then, his mobile phone beeped. He received an SMS announcing his marks in each subject.

'Now do you see how useful mobile phones are?' Mangasuri turned to Kumarasurar in delight.

Kumarasurar couldn't care less. His son hadn't let him down. He had done well enough to get into the college he had chosen under the government quota. There was no need to ask anyone for alms to pay for his education.

18

They would have to go to the capital for engineering counselling. No bus or train tickets were available. Everyone seemed to have been up all day and night to book their seats quickly. It was always he who was left behind despite every effort, Kumarasurar thought to himself. How would they travel such a long distance now? He had only ever been to the capital once. He didn't like journeys. Fortunately, he had been allocated a job in his own district. His one long voyage hadn't been made by choice.

The people of his trade union had once organised a protest in the capital demanding an increase in salary. They tried to gather as many people together as possible to show their strength in numbers. They said all government employees must travel to the capital for a demonstration. Kumarasurar had never been part of a protest. He applied for leave from office on the big day. There was talk that civil servants who did not turn up at the protest in the capital would be branded 'traitors' and made outcasts.

His colleagues warned Kumarasurar that they would stop talking to him if he didn't show up. They also told him that all costs, including travel, would be borne by the union. And so he agreed to participate. They hired a bus from their town. It didn't feel like they were headed to a protest; it felt more like a picnic. His colleagues guzzled the devas' drink, played old film songs on the bus, and shouted and jumped about. They stopped on the way to eat at a grand restaurant. Kumarasurar sampled many dishes he had never seen before.

'This tastes heavenly!' he said, and everyone laughed.

'Haven't you heard the saying that heavenly food has no taste? It's vegetarian, mind you. Asura food is far better,' a friend said.

'True, true.' 'What kind of food is a meatless offering?' 'Heavenly food is bland. Asura food is the better one.' 'And amongst all asura dishes, buffalo curry is the best.' There was much support for that view.

'Oh, I just meant it tasted good. But it's true that asura food is far better,' Kumarasurar agreed.

They all had various parts of the buffalo as curry, from the legs to the brain to the entrails. Kumarasurar's stomach and mind felt sated.

He told someone who was sitting nearby, 'This feels like a picnic. Next time there's a demonstration, reserve a place for me too.'

This spread through the bus, and everyone was thrilled that Kumarasurar himself had agreed to attend protests. They determined that they should hold these more regularly.

It was a massive protest. The police stopped the bus at the gates of the capital and arrested everyone in it. Kumarasurar was afraid at the thought of being arrested. But all the protesters were detained in a large wedding hall. The time flew by as they joked and laughed.

The trade union chiefs made speeches. Each speaker traced the history of the union and listed all the protests it had undertaken. They emphasised that this one had struck terror in the heart of the government.

The slogan, 'Poraduvom, vetri peruvom'—'We'll fight, we'll win!'—rose and subsided every now and again.

Every time a leader stepped forward to speak, a few of his acolytes shouted, 'Long live, Thalaivar!' using the leader's name. Kumarasurar found all of this extremely entertaining.

When they were released in the evening, they poured out like goats that had just been let out of their pen.

Was this all a protest was? He shared his joy with his colleagues on the return journey.

Some warned him, 'Don't think all protests are like this. Sometimes, you get beaten. If they put you in jail, you'll have to eat gruel for twenty days. There have been protests where police firing has taken place too. A lot of blood has been spilt to get us the salary we're given today.'

Kumarasurar was silent.

He hadn't taken part in any more protests.

This would be his first journey to the capital after that adventure. Kumarasurar felt drained by the ordeal of trying to find a ticket for the day of counselling. Should they go to the capital a day or two earlier? Of course, they would have to spend more money on their boarding and lodging. But that was a drop in the ocean, compared to the college fees.

Meghas was unperturbed. He booked their tickets on a private bus with sleeper facilities. Kumarasurar felt anxious on the day of the journey. The bus was to leave at ten in the night. Kumarasurar wanted to be at the terminus an hour in advance.

Meghas calmly checked his phone and said, 'The bus is a hundred miles away. It will be 10.30 before the bus arrives, loads its passengers and leaves. We don't have to be there before 10.'

He showed his father the phone. One could see at which spot the bus was. Kumarasurar didn't want to look. Meghas would tease him if he tracked the bus wrong.

'Show me!' Mangasuri said and peered. 'Oh, yes, you can see the bus moving! Why do you want to go so early? It's a five-minute walk from here. It's enough if you leave home at ten.'

'And they'll round people up ten minutes before the bus leaves too,' Meghas said. 'This is not a government bus. It's a private concern that runs the service. They believe passengers are important.'

As a government servant, Kumarasurar couldn't let a slight against the government pass. 'True, the government thinks of the people. Private companies think of passengers,' he said.

Meghas didn't appear to understand what he meant. Kumarasurar was pleased something he had said had gone over his son's head.

Meghas checked his phone every five minutes and reported where the bus was. Kumarasurar wondered how one could tell on which road the bus was, which point it was passing, which it had crossed and when it would arrive somewhere, just by looking at one's phone. Should he ask Meghas for an explanation? If he asked, his son would tell him. But it would be hard to keep up with the boy's speed. If Meghas was interrupted, he would snap. Kumarasurar decided not to ask. They left for the bus terminus when Meghas saw fit. They were on time.

The bus had sleeping facilities. He had never travelled by such a bus. It was air-conditioned too. The bedding was soft. The pillows and mattresses were white as snow. They had little cabins closed off by screens. One could draw the screen, and shut out all disturbance from the light and from people moving in their sleep. Kumarasurar marvelled at the facilities time had wrought. He compared this with the town buses on which he usually journeyed.

Their seats were in the lower deck. Should he ask Meghas to sleep by the window or the aisle? If he slept by the aisle, he may roll off in his sleep. If he slept by the window, there was a bigger risk. Accidents often occurred on the highway.

The passengers at the window seats were most affected in this case. Those in the aisle got away with minor injuries.

Meghas was the only heir in the family. He would have to further their line. Kumarasurar had lived his life. Meghas was a child, a boy who had never known a woman's touch. There was much he had to learn and experience. And so, Kumarasurar decided his son must not sleep by the window, and took the seat himself. Meghas wanted the window seat so he could take in the scenery. But his father would not let him have his way.

Kumarasurar could not sleep. He was used to the insomnia. He had another problem today. Meghas was fiddling around with his phone, and the light shone in his eyes. The boy would laugh now and again. He would send a text to someone, and continue chatting for a while. What did these kids have to talk about that merited such intense exchanges?

'Don't you feel sleepy, pa?' Kumarasurar asked.

'You sleep, Appa,' Meghas replied.

But Kumarasurar couldn't sleep. He continued to observe what Meghas was doing. The boy seemed to be watching a film. How long could one watch a film on such a tiny screen? But Meghas could stare at it for hours without tiring.

Would they find a place in the college of his choice during counselling? Meghas didn't seem worried. He didn't seem to have given a thought to it, in fact. He was engrossed in the film. How could someone live like this, without a care in the world? Responsibility was all about worrying. Kumarasurar felt irritated by his son's laughter.

'We may or may not get you into that college. Aren't you worried about it at all? I'm not able to sleep because I'm so anxious,' he said.

'Hold on, Appa, let me check,' Meghas replied. He paused the film and busied himself with something else on the phone. 'Appa, not even one person has been given a seat in computer science engineering in that college yet. We'll probably be the first ones. So don't worry, there are plenty of seats and I'll be placed easily enough.'

'How do you know?'

Meghas told him about the counselling website, on which there was a daily update on the seats that were taken and those available. One could check at any time. It surprised Kumarasurar that this facility existed, but it surprised him more that his son was so clued in. How could he have learnt so much?

This generation had its various shortcomings—they didn't respect older people, they weren't polite, they couldn't make conversation, their manners were deplorable—but they knew everything about gadgets.

Their television had had a cable connection. Sometimes, it would break down and there would only be white noise. Often, Kumarasurar would not be able to find the channels he wanted. He had once seen a channel which telecast old films and songs, at Gluttony Vilas. The shopkeeper told him it was a twenty-four-hour channel, with films telecast on holidays and late at night. But he couldn't find it when he tried tuning the television at home. He had used the remote control and navigated all the channels from 1 to 100. When he was complaining about this, his son walked into the room. He said that the particular channel was not available on a cable connection. They would need a dish, and that would beam all the channels they wanted. He also told his parents how much it would cost to set it up, what the monthly fee would be and how it should be paid. He wasn't sure his father would agree to the cost, and so he didn't urge them to switch to satellite television.

Meghas had been a schoolboy then. He was constantly advised not to watch TV. He would return home from school only at eight in the evening. He would have his food and watch TV as he ate. He was allowed to watch only until he finished. He would never finish. He liked dosais most of all. He could eat dosais for all three meals. He would have dosai for breakfast, and pack dosai for lunch. And so his mother made him eat sambar, rasam and curd rice for dinner, because she believed he would sleep well if he had rice. He would eat his meal grain by grain as he sat before the TV.

He liked watching a channel on which asuras built like mountains of meat fought each other. He would know just how many asuras were involved, and had details about each. His parents thought he was picking at his food because he didn't like it. He would pretend he wasn't interested in the television. So his father was particularly surprised to find he knew all about satellite television.

'How do you know all this, da?' he had asked.

'What's the big deal, Appa? This is the stuff we talk about in school.'

'So you guys talk about everything but your studies?'

'Can one talk about studies all the time, Appa? We talk about other things every now and again,' he had said mildly.

Kumarasurar made further enquiries about satellite television on his morning walk, and bought a dish. He was able to find the channel he wanted.

How did these kids know so much about technology? Kumarasurar didn't even have the patience to listen to someone talking about it. The clerk in his office, Kumbhas, spoke about gadgets often. Kumarasurar made a show of his lack of interest. It appeared the era was their teacher. None of these things had been invented in his own youth. These children had been born into a world which was already equipped with these things. That must be the reason they knew all that they did.

But these thoughts offered little consolation. Could all the computer science engineering seats be available, as Meghas had said? He couldn't set his mind at rest trusting a phone. What if the information was wrong? What if they went to the counselling session and found all the places had been taken? How would they zero in on another college at short notice? What if Meghas refused to join any other college and asked him to arrange the money to enrol under the management quota? How would he cobble the money together?

Kumarasurar could not overcome the demons in his mind. What could he sell? Where would he get a loan? These decisions had already been made, but he revisited them now, as he had a hundred times before. When he had exhausted his brain into sleepiness, he remembered his son and checked on him. Meghas appeared to have fallen asleep long ago, his earphones still fastened in place.

Just as Meghas had said, he was the first to register for the computer science engineering course in his college of choice. They returned the same night.

He joined college, and was assigned a room in the hostel. It all went smoothly.

Students had to be in the hostel the day before term began. A week before Meghas had to leave, Kumarasurar and Mangasuri began to make an inventory of everything they had to spare, tucked away in the loft—a large iron trunk, bedding, pillows, buckets, whatever Meghas might need.

When they told Meghas about this, he laughed. He didn't want to make the same mistake he had in the school hostel. All he needed was a suitcase with wheels and a backpack, he said. He would take only the clothes he needed. Mangasuri tried convincing him he would need a lot more. If he listened to her, they would have had to hire a lorry and empty half the house. He was so firm that she had to yield. He repeated that everything he could possibly need would be available either at the college or just outside. He would buy them later.

19

Mangasuri joined them on this trip. She insisted she had to see the college and the hostel in which her son would spend the next five years. She found everything fascinating. But she was even more terrified by what she saw than her husband had been.

They had tea at the expansive canteen. Boys and girls were sitting together, chatting and eating. Some of the boys wore sleeveless T-shirts and shorts. Their armpits, chests and half their thighs were on display. Others wore tight-fitting clothes that showed off their physiques.

Mangasuri found this disgusting. She had grown up in a village where most men wandered around wearing nothing but loincloths. But she was somehow grossed out by the boys' clothes.

Several of the girls wore tops with skirts or shorts. Mangasuri looked askance at these girls who flashed their thighs, and felt embarrassed for them. How could they step out of their rooms dressed so skimpily, she thought. She unconsciously tugged at her own blouse and sari, trying to make up for their show of skin by covering more of her own. She wasn't able to look away from them either. Watching them laugh and talk easily with the boys, she felt afraid. The fear rose as she pictured Meghas sitting amongst them.

Would their son focus on his studies here? Or would his attention turn to finding himself a girlfriend? Kumarasurar's ominous words hadn't frightened her, but seeing the college for herself had. If only she had accompanied them on their recce, she would have flatly refused to let Meghas even apply for this college. But there was no help for it now.

She looked at the girls and said to Meghas, 'Look at those creatures. How do they behave like this!'

Her son laughed, but offered no response.

She liked everything else about the college—the large buildings, the hostel rooms, the enormous canteen, the pathways lined with trees.

She found various ways to advise her son over and over again on what foods could cause health problems and how he should eat so he stayed fit. Kumarasurar barely spoke to his son. He left his wife to her duties and enjoyed her distress as he walked with them.

Every now and again, Mangasuri looked carefully at her son's face and told him, 'Keep your distance from these girls, pa.' Kumarasurar almost felt sorry for her. Meghas seemed amused.

When they took their leave, he said, 'Don't worry, Amma. I'll take care.'

They returned home in silence. Mangasuri was worried she would complain too much, and then Kumarasurar would say, 'I told you so. You never listen.' He appeared to be glancing at her triumphantly every now and again, as if to say, 'I've been burdened by these worries all this while. Now you lift the burden too.'

Mangasuri lost her sleep, as her husband had. Every time she closed her eyes, she would imagine Meghas wandering about in shorts and laughing with all sorts of girls. Was her son not hers any longer? She ought to have ensured he went to an arts college in their own town, so that he could have been a day scholar. He was their only child. He was everything to her. If she were to lose him, what hold did she have on life?

A couple of days later, when Kumarasurar was in the terrace, Mangasuri approached him hesitantly. 'Nothing untoward will happen, right?' she asked. 'Our son will study, right?'

Kumarasurar was tempted to pull her leg. 'Sure, sure, he'll study. He'll study *everything*.'

Mangasuri, who had hoped to hear a word of consolation, felt a pang. 'What are you saying?' she asked in panic.

All the emotion Kumarasurar had kept to himself, now burst and flooded out of his mouth. 'I told you so much about the college. Did you listen to anything I said? No. Your son's word is final. You didn't give a fuck what I felt. Did it strike you that I was shaken by what I saw? You were beaming with the confidence that your son wouldn't do all these things. And now you turn to me. Didn't you see how the boys and girls behave there? You ask about it, and they say their students are from abroad, and this is how they'll behave. And that's not all. There's drugs, alcohol, what-have-you. We'll just have to do our best. We'll go see him once a fortnight. We'll talk to him every now and again. We should befriend one of the professors there, and make him our mole. When you've put your head on the chopping block, what choice do you have?'

'Let's go once a week to visit him,' Mangasuri said. 'Forget the cost and effort involved. He will fuss, but we'll tell him we aren't able to live without seeing his face at least once a week. We'll buy him what he needs, and talk to him for a bit. We'll feel better.'

They were on the same page now. They stayed a while longer on the terrace, talking about various things. It had been a long time since they had really opened their hearts to each other. Troubles had a way of bringing couples closer, thought Kumarasurar. When Mangasuri moved towards the stairs, Kumarasurar followed her like a cat.

20

And now, again there was a conference on the terrace. Their son wanted a new mobile phone. It had barely been six months since they'd bought him the phone he was using. It had been bought when he was cooped up at home after his school final exams. He hadn't even finished his first year of college. Yet, he had already tired of the phone. And he wanted a new one, which was far more expensive.

His wife's pleasure at his son's demand had broken Kumarasurar. He felt all alone. This wasn't new. He had often felt alone since his parents had passed away. For as long as they had been alive, he had felt his word commanded respect. Even when they hadn't entirely agreed with him, they would humour him and do as he said. If he had happened to make the wrong decision, they would console him and do their best to reverse the damage.

Their deaths had made him a lone soldier. His wife didn't think his word was law. She tended to take the opposite point of view, and when his son was involved, she always took the boy's side. That night, the loneliness was overwhelming. He lay on the terrace, hovering between sleep and wakefulness. It was an old habit of his to sit in the terrace. His wife knew this too. Her only complaint was that he did not use the broken cot on the terrace, which would be more comfortable than the floor. But he didn't feel like getting up from where he sat.

Mangasuri came up to the terrace again after several hours. She peeped silently into the darkness, to check whether he was asleep or awake. She could never sleep when he was restless. She would spend most of her waking time checking up on him, suspecting he wasn't getting his quota of sleep.

The suspicion had been of a different nature when they were newly married. Back then, they used to live in the rented quarters provided by the government. He would sometimes go missing in the middle of the night. They lived on the ground floor. There were three floors above theirs, all occupied by government employees. Each of these families had a key to access the door leading to the terrace. Hardly anyone used the terrace. Occasionally, when there was a water problem, they would go there to check their water tanks.

Kumarasurar was the only resident who saw fit to climb three floors and mount the terrace for no reason. When Mangasuri woke in the middle of the night, she would see that her husband's side of the bed was empty. She had no way of knowing where he had gone. When she woke up in the morning, he would be by her side. Mangasuri began to suspect that he waited for her to sleep and went on a clandestine jaunt in the middle of the night.

One night, she feigned sleep and followed him quietly. She saw him climb the stairs to the terrace. Her suspicions were not put to rest. What work did he have in the terrace? She pictured each woman in the building having an affair with him. It made little sense. He wasn't compatible with any of them.

Once, she slipped up to the terrace, hid behind the door and watched. He was alone. Perhaps someone would join him? If that were the case, they would see her standing by the door and leave. She moved stealthily as a cat behind one of the water tanks. She did feel it was wrong to spy on her husband, but it was hard to bury her suspicions and behave like nothing was wrong. It was just one day, she thought to herself. She would see this through.

Kumarasurar sat by another water tank for a while. Then he got up and sat on the parapet wall. Mangasuri was anxious he might nod off and fall. But he didn't stay there long. He lay on the terrace, improvised a pillow by locking his arms behind his head and stared up at the sky. She couldn't figure out whether he was asleep or awake. He was absolutely still. She would have liked to leave him to his own devices and go back home, but that would be tricky. The moon, which had stayed hidden all this while, now shone so brightly it was as if an electric lamp had been lit over the terrace.

If only it were dark, she could have moved like a shadow and disappeared. But with the moonlight, it would be hard to reach the door unseen by him. And if he saw her slipping out of the door, would he not suspect *her* of having an affair? Worse, what if he went downstairs and realised she was not at home? What would he think then? Mangasuri was in an awful dilemma, until the moon finally slipped behind a cloud. She made for the door quickly, and determined that whatever happened in future, she would never again allow such ugly suspicions to take root in her mind. Not long after, she realised this was an old habit of his. She would often go to the terrace in search of him and find him there. The only counsel she gave him back then was not to sit on the parapet.

Now, Kumarasurar pretended he was asleep so that Mangasuri wouldn't start a conversation. Chances were that she'd come up to make amends with him after having taken their son's side earlier. Kumarasurar was in no mood for this. Knowing she would figure out he was awake if he lay too still, he made a show of turning in his sleep. Mangasuri waited for a while, looking at him, and then made her way back downstairs. He couldn't sleep after she left either. It wasn't easy to lull a crazed mind to sleep.

21

Having spent two sleepless nights this way, Kumarasurar found his eyes closing in office on the third day. One could rest one's head on the table and sleep. Nobody would question it. But he avoided this because he was afraid someone would chance upon him dozing and tell on him. The clerk, Kumbhas, was reading the paper.

When Kumarasurar had just built his own house and moved in, he had subscribed to the newspaper for a while. It seemed to him a sign of prosperity to sit on the portico of his house, reading the paper. Once he had decided to subscribe to a newspaper, he had to decide which one. Everybody he asked gave him a different recommendation. Someone would tell him a particular newspaper was the best, and then someone else would inform him that it was in fact the mouthpiece of a particular political party or, at least, that it leaned towards one.

Kumarasurar had learnt the art of not leaning towards anything. There was no paper in his language that suited his needs. And so he subscribed to a paper that was printed in a different language. He took much pride in sitting before his house with this newspaper open. But one day, when he calculated the subscription cost, it struck him that it was unnecessary expenditure. And so he stopped it.

If he was ever tempted to read a paper, he would rifle through the torn pieces of newspaper he found in the office canteen. Once Kumbhas joined his team, things worked out even better.

Kumbhas entered the office with a newspaper in hand. He read it for half an hour before he started work. The clerk was initially worried that his boss would comment on his spending his first half hour at work reading the paper. Kumarasurar himself was tempted to read the news, but felt hesitant about asking his subordinate for it. Until Kumbhas found a way out.

'Sir, have you read the paper today?' he asked during lunch once. 'The Bribe Destruction Taskforce has caught an official from the income tax department red-handed.' He had figured this news would appeal to Kumarasurar.

'Really?' Kumarasurar said. 'Show me?' And he began to read Kumbhas's paper.

Once he had read it, he began a discussion with Kumbhas. 'Isn't the salary given by the government enough for these people? Must they take food from the mouths of ordinary citizens?'

Both men were haunted by their ill luck of having been assigned to a department with no scope for bribery. And so both agreed that it was wrong to accept bribes.

'Sir, someone in his office must be the whistleblower,' Kumbhas said. 'He wouldn't have divided the bribe among his staff correctly. Someone who got the wrong end of the stick would have ratted him out.'

'True,' Kumarasurar agreed. 'That's just the sort of thing they would do. Or, he must have asked for too much money. It's possible that the person who was trying to bribe him complained to the Bribe Destruction Taskforce himself.'

'That's possible, yes. One should live within one's means, sir. Desire is the root cause of all suffering,' Kumbhas replied, offering an idiom incongruous with his age.

After this little exchange, there was no hesitation on either side. It became a custom for Kumbhas to bring his boss the paper once he had finished reading it. He would place it on Kumarasurar's table and leave. Kumarasurar glanced through it when the impulse took hold. The two usually discussed a news item on which they were in agreement.

That day, Kumarasurar reached for the paper to ward off sleep. The city news was all about protests over potholes in the road or for drinking water facilities, crimes of passion, lovers seeking asylum and so on. The national news was about new schemes that the king and government had announced, inauguration ceremonies for new buildings, visits by crucial asuras and so on. The international news was more interesting. A box on this page caught Kumarasurar's eye.

'Youngster's Heartbreaking Death while Attempting Selfie,' read the headline.

This had happened in one of the countries in the central part of Asuralokam. The boy was sixteen years old. He had asked his parents for a new phone with the latest functionalities for his birthday. They had obliged. It had cost over one lakh rupees. He had celebrated his birthday by cutting a cake at home in the morning, and had then headed off on a trek through a hilly region with his friends. They had taken various pictures on their way. The phone he'd been gifted had such an advanced camera, it was even better than a DSLR one could buy for the same amount. One might well say the phone was a fantastic camera, with facilities to make calls.

Having taken various pictures on the hillside, he had wanted to pose on a rock that jutted out over a cliff. If he posted it on social media, thousands of people would 'like' it. It could even go viral. Encouraged by some of his friends, and warned by others not to get too near the edge, he took several selfies on the projection. While posing at a particular angle, he had lost his footing and fallen off the cliff.

That was all. Even his body had not been found yet. The speed at which he had fallen had caused the phone to catapult out of his hands and towards his friends. The phone was safe. There were pictures of him standing on the rock. The newspaper had published this last picture. It was a truly remarkable photograph. But the boy who had taken this photograph, the boy in the photograph, was no more. There was an old story about a scientist who had wanted to find out what concentrated poison tasted like. He had touched a drop to the tip of his tongue and died from it. The reporter had finished his piece by comparing the boy's death to the scientist's. In carrying out his own experiment, he had left behind one last, beautiful picture of himself.

The moment he finished reading the piece, Kumarasurar put the newspaper away. He went silently to the canteen. Kumbhas figured something had affected him deeply. His boss usually asked him to come along for tea. Sometimes, Kumarasurar paid for both of them. If he was preoccupied or troubled, he would walk away silently and not invite Kumbhas. The clerk now scanned the newspaper to try and zero in on the news that had had such an impact on Kumarasurar. He couldn't spot anything that merited such a reaction. Sometimes, Kumarasurar would return and speak about the news item; sometimes he would say nothing. Kumbhas decided to wait and watch what he would do that day. Kumarasurar returned after an unusually long break.

He asked Kumbhas, 'These people who take selfies, are they ready to die for these photos?'

Kumbhas now knew what had upset him.

'It's an addiction, sir. They lust after this. A lot of people die doing this. They're thrill-seekers. Didn't you see the news four days ago? I'll find it for you,' Kumbhas said and dived under the table to retrieve an old newspaper.

The incident had occurred in their own country. Another boy had celebrated his birthday by trying to take a selfie on the roof of a moving electric train.

He was a tall youth, in his second year of college. His friends and he had celebrated his birthday and were returning home by train. At the last stop, he had decided to get off the train and pose on the roof of a compartment. His hand had struck a high voltage cable and he had been electrocuted. His charred body had fallen on the tracks. The news item was accompanied by the picture. It was horribly graphic.

Thankfully, his final selfie had not been published. His phone must have perished with him. It could not have survived an electrocution. Or they would have published the picture for sure. At least the first news item had been about a boy in some strange part of the world. But this one had occurred in a city just a stone's throw away from where they lived.

22

Kumbhas was not the kind who would let an opportunity of this sort slide. He searched the internet and found more news items to show his boss. Kumarasurar, who had never sat at the computer in all this while, now faced it to read the news.

'Sir, will you read it yourself or shall I read it out for you?' Kumbhas asked. 'Or shall I print it out?'

'No, I'll read it here,' Kumarasurar said, as he unconsciously slid into the clerk's chair.

The monitor shone bright. As he looked at it, the light seemed to scorch his eyes. What would it do to the eyes of people who worked at it all day? His son had insisted on studying computer science engineering. He would have to sit before a screen all his life. How much suffering this would involve, he thought.

Kumbhas had selected seemingly hundreds of news items. As he moved the pointer, Kumarasurar read just the first four. He wasn't able to go further than that. He felt consumed by fear and panic. His hands began to tremble, and he said, 'That's enough, pa,' and got up.

These were the four news items:

News item one:

Youngster Attempts Selfie Hanging from a Train; Four Friends Attempt Rescue, Die

A Thadagaipuram native, Bhavas, was returning by train from a visit to a temple with four of his friends, when the youngster attempted to take a selfie while hanging from the train.

His friends Sumeesh, Sanjeesh, Kareesh and Sandeesh acquiesced in this dangerous pursuit, during which Bhavas lost his footing and fell off the train.

In an immediate attempt to help Bhavas, his four friends jumped off the train one after the other. In their hurry, they did not notice a train approaching from the opposite side and all four were crushed under its wheels.

Bhavas was admitted to hospital with injuries.

A witness said the four youths had failed to see the train in the dark. The victims are said to be 20 to 25 years old. This incident occurred last evening.

News item two:

Selfie Claims Student's Life, As Daredevil Stunt on Tracks Ends in Tragedy!

A student of class eleven who had attempted a selfie standing on the tracks as an electric train approached was run over at Narandagapuram.

Dinesh is the son of Sugasur, a native of the city. He studied at a local school. Since yesterday was a holiday, Dinesh and his friend had visited a nearby zoological park. They returned around 5 p.m. The boys were walking by the railway track at the station.

As an electric train approached the station, Dinesh was overtaken by the dangerous impulse to capture a selfie of the train crossing him. He rushed towards the tracks and attempted the selfie. The speeding electric train hit him with force and crushed him under its wheels. Dinesh died on the spot.

The railway police, who arrived after the incident, have retrieved Dinesh's body and sent it to the hospital for post-mortem.

There has been a spate of deaths recently, as people have attempted selfies at mountains, at sea and on railway tracks.

News item three:

Asurapuri Tops World in Selfie Death Count

The selfie facility was introduced in smartphones as a technological advancement. As the selfie obsession spread, mobile phone companies have advertised their products using the selfie as a selling point.

Selfies have now become objects of lust. Under these circumstances, most users tend to document the places they visit, the things they do and the people they meet with selfies.

Many youngsters have died attempting selfies on railway tracks. Others have fallen off cliffs while attempting selfies during treks in the mountains.

The death count from selfies has been increasing steadily, and Asurapuri has now topped the world in this statistic.

Research indicates 68 per cent of people who died taking selfies are under 24 years of age, and 75 per cent are male.

News item four:

Selfie with Wounded Bear: Youngster Dies, Dog Fights, Onlookers Stare

A youngster was mauled to death by a wounded bear at Vanasura forest of Asurapuri while attempting a selfie with it.

Prabhasur was a native of Narapuram, in the southern part of Asurapuri. He ran a travel agency. On Wednesday, he had driven a wedding party to Korapuram city and was returning to Narapuram. His passengers asked him to stop by the forest so they could relieve themselves. When the driver Prabhasur went into the forest for a drink of water, he found a wounded bear in his path.

Thinking the bear was asleep, Prabhasur attempted a selfie with it. However, the moment he went close, the bear pounced on him. Prabhasur fought hard to escape the bear, but he was mauled.

The passengers, who had heard Prabhasur's cries, rushed to the spot and tried to rescue him by throwing stones at the bear and hitting it with sticks. But Prabhasur died of his injuries on the spot, said Forest Department ranger Dhanurasurar. The department's office is located within ten kilometres of the place where the incident occurred. Officials reached the spot to retrieve Prabhasur's body and informed the police.

If only all his passengers had attacked the bear which had him in its grasp, Prabhasur would have survived. However, only a few took up stones and sticks. The others were too engrossed in video recording the incident on their phones to save a life. A dog from the area fought the bear too, but to no avail.

The Forest Department has announced Rs 30,000 as compensation to perform Prabhasur's last rites. The government will provide an ex gratia sum to the victim's family within the next fifteen days, said Dhanurasurar.

Last month, three others who had flouted warnings and entered the forest in the same fashion were also mortally attacked by a bear, while six others were left wounded.

Selfies on mountains, selfies in lakes, selfies in rivers, selfies in deserts, selfies at sea, selfies with whales, selfies with cheetahs, selfies while standing, selfies while lying down, selfies while running, selfies while drinking and eating and walking. All of these had led to accidents and deaths. Pages upon pages of news items about these deaths crowded the internet. Kumarasurar's mind was reeling.

23

'A lust of this kind?' Kumarasurar said to Kumbhas.

The word 'lust' had only carried a single connotation to Kumarasurar before that day; he had always hesitated to use the word because of this. But now it appeared to have another meaning. What would the world come to?

'It's the lust for thrill among kids,' Kumbhas said. 'No experience, and such lust. That's why they get trapped and die.'

'Four boys died trying to rescue a friend,' Kumarasurar said. 'But he survived. It should have been he who died.'

'Who knows what fate has in store for him?' Kumbhas said.

Kumarasurar walked away without answering. He shrank into himself after this. Would Meghas know about all these incidents? He himself had just learnt of them. Meghas had only ever spent time in the house or in school. What could he know of the world? What if he attempted these selfies, with no clue about what had happened to those before him? He was not the kind of boy who obeyed instructions. He would be tempted go against what he was told. Such dangerous things should not be made available to youngsters. How did the government allow such products to be marketed? These phones ought to be accompanied by a danger sign, like the ones used near high voltage wires.

He had a phone too. It was only for calls. He could make calls. He could answer them. Why hadn't mobile phone companies stopped with that innovation? Why had they felt compelled to add more features, and claim so many lives?

His mind was in such turmoil that he forgot to get off the bus at his stop. The conductor, who knew him, alerted him and made him dismount. He walked past his home too, and had to turn back. He gulped down the coffee his wife brought like it was water. He lay on his bed. He sat before the television like a zombie. He ate the food his wife brought. He lay down again. His eyes seemed to register nothing.

If he was silent, it meant he was worried. Mangasuri understood he was in his own world. Every day, she would wait for his return, hoping he would have something cheerful to say. Having been alone all day, she ached for easy conversation. But he almost always returned from work as if he had seen a ghost. She had got used to it, and given herself over to television soap operas instead.

In his sleep, Kumarasurar was haunted by all sorts of nightmares. Trains were speeding by, one after the other, one following the next even before the noise of its approach had abated. One was stacked over another, and yet another stacked on it. There were trains as far as the eye could see. A boy stood in the midst of all this. He held a mobile phone, and his arm was outstretched. He took a selfie by the train. He stood to the side of the train. He climbed over the train. He reached for the overhead electric line. He was tossed off the train, only to fall on another train. And then on another. Each train he fell on kicked him like a football. His face could not be seen. He finally fell on to an empty track. A hand turned his head to see his face. He went close to the face. It was ... It was Meghas's face. Kumarasurar sank his head into his hands and screamed. He must have screamed out loud. Mangasuri ran to him, and shook him awake, saying, 'Enga!

Enga!' He woke up blabbering and sat up. She brought him water, and it was a while before he came to.

'Why do you do this to yourself? What's wrong? This boy wants a phone. Won't he listen if you tell him he doesn't need a new one right now? He is *our* son, isn't he? Why do you ruin your health turning all this over in your head? You never get a good night's sleep. You're up through the night. Not a day or two, but several days in a row. How can your body take it? We listen to everything you say. Now you listen to me. Let's go to the hospital tomorrow and get your blood tested for pressure, cholesterol, sugar and everything else. Okay?'

She spoke to him for a long time. He listened without answering. If he told her what was on his mind, she would be in turmoil too. He usually kept things from her for this reason, and the same went today. He had considered showing her all the news items he had read, and then decided one person in the house going crazy was enough. The last thing they needed was two lunatics sharing space.

Could all the news be true? Or had Kumbhas faked it to mess with his head? He must have learnt of Kumarasurar's dilemma over buying a phone. He should not trust the clerk. Kumbhas made a show of declaring that everything could be done on the computer, on the internet. How could he have found hundreds of news items within a minute? He might know some black magic. Everyone spoke about the internet. But surely it could not be quite so amazing. How could everyone in those hundreds of articles be selfie addicts?

People indulged in all sorts of conspiracy, with some ulterior motive. Kumbhas had trapped him in a web by getting him to read the newspaper. From the next day on, he wouldn't even look at the paper. He wouldn't listen to a thing anyone said. People weren't content with conspiring against him; they had now targeted Meghas. Kanakasurar was always regarding him with jealousy. Thenasurar had determined that he should prevent Meghas from studying further. Everyone on the street had an eye on the boy. He kept all his mischief and fuss to the house. Once he stepped out, he would barely disturb the dust on which he walked. People would marvel that a boy of his generation could behave so beautifully. They were jealous of his parents. They had cast the Evil Eye.

He must protect Meghas from all these people. He must ensure the boy studied well, and then send him off to a foreign country. What could they do to him once he was away? He wouldn't tell a soul even *where* Meghas lived.

Kumarasurar recovered, went to the living room and asked, 'Did you speak to the boy today?'

'He called at nine,' Mangasuri said. 'He didn't say anything. He didn't ask about the phone. I didn't ask either. I thought it was best not to bring it up right now.'

'Call him now,' Kumarasurar said.

'Did you see the time? It's 10.45. He could be asleep. Let's call him in the morning,' Mangasuri said.

'Are you going to call him now or not?' Kumarasurar shouted.

'Why are you yelling like this? Speak softly, won't you?' Mangasuri said, frightened.

'So you've joined ranks with everyone else? You're not going to listen to me?' he shouted again.

The neighbours would never before have heard a sound from the house. If they heard him yelling at this time of the night, they could come running to see what was wrong. The thought scared Mangasuri.

The clan deity came to mind. She ran to his idol, prayed, took the jug of holy water kept before him, splashed it on her husband and said, 'May the evil spirits disappear from everyone's sight!'

He knocked the jug out of her hands and screamed, 'Damned bitch! I ask you to call our son, and you won't listen? You're trying to kill me by splashing poisoned water on me, are you?'

'Aiyayo, what will I do, whom will I call? Whom do I have to call my own?' Mangasuri wailed, as she reached for the phone and dialled her son's number.

He didn't answer her first call.

'That monkey stays up till dawn, has he actually fallen asleep today?' she mumbled, and called over and over again.

He answered the third call with a sleepy, 'What, Amma ...?'

'Your father is screaming like a madman, da. He wants to talk to you. Wake yourself up and talk to him for a bit, pa. Don't get angry with me,' Mangasuri begged, and gave her husband the phone.

'Meghas kanna, you're not in any trouble, are you?' Kumarasurar asked, taking the phone from her.

'No, Appa, I'm not in any trouble,' Meghas said.

'Look here, pa, people say all sorts of things. They don't want us to be happy. They'll try to ruin our lives. They'll drive to your college from here. They'll call to speak to you. They'll ask you to come along with them. You have to be careful. Don't pay attention to anyone. Don't be afraid of anyone. I'm here for you. Be brave. Listen to me, the whole world has gone to the dogs. You need to be alert.'

He ranted away, and Meghas responded with, 'Okay, Appa; okay, Appa,' to all that he said.

After ten more minutes of this, Kumarasurar gave the phone to Mangasuri.

'What happened, Amma?' Meghas asked. 'Has Appa started drinking?'

24

Even if he didn't sleep a wink all night, Kumarasurar never missed his morning walk. That morning, though, he did not rise at dawn. Since he appeared to be sleeping soundly and didn't have to go to work for two days, Mangasuri did not wake him. But she did look in on him several times. Once, she went close and kept her fingers by his nose to ensure he was breathing. Then she castigated herself for it. What was she thinking? Chhi.

She found herself welling up every time she looked at him. When he had got his government job, the richest families in town had offered him their daughters. But he had obeyed his mother and married her. She knew all the financial trouble he had been through since then.

He didn't have a single 'bad habit'. He didn't think of anything other than home and family. He didn't have to suffer this way; everything could be done, anything could be faced without such torment. She didn't understand why he wasn't able to take things easy. He would turn the smallest things over and over in his mind before he made a decision. In the meanwhile, he would destroy everyone else's peace of mind too. He had never had a comprehensive health check. He was over forty years old. He often said, 'Nothing will happen to me.' But given the state he was in, they ought to get a medical check-up done. What would he say if she insisted?

Mangasuri spent her morning doing her household chores and checking up on her husband. Her son called. She didn't tell him the trouble had begun because he had demanded a phone. She didn't want him to blame himself and suffer too.

It was eleven before Kumarasurar woke up. Once she had seen to his immediate needs, Mangasuri said, 'Let's go do a medical check-up.'

'Nothing's wrong with me, leave me alone,' he snapped.

Afraid he would yell as he had the previous night, Mangasuri did not pursue this. She made his favourite dishes, and thought of subjects of conversation that would not trouble him. She realised there were few, perhaps none, only when she pondered these subjects. It took her a while to figure out what to discuss with him that day, and they were:

1. Food. She listed everything she had cooked for breakfast, and said it would be enough to last them through lunch. But if he didn't want to eat the same thing two meals in a row, she would cook something for him. 'This will go to waste then,' Kumarasurar said. 'Let's finish it off.'
2. The curry leaf plant by their house had borne lots of fruit, which drew swarms of cuckoos every morning. Mangasuri mock complained that she couldn't stand the constant singing and chirping. 'Look, even curry leaf fruits have some use after all,' Kumarasurar said and laughed.
3. She complained that nothing—neither medicated powder nor repellent chalk sticks—stopped the ants from conquering the house. 'Ants must find a way to cohabit with us. Or, we must find a way to cohabit with ants,' Kumarasurar said and laughed.

4. She said it was too hot and it would be nice if they had a spell of rain. 'There are fewer good people every day, how will it rain?' he asked.
5. They had too many vessels. They ought to stow some away in the attic, she said. He didn't offer any reply, but he parted his lips into a gentle smile.

Mangasuri gave each subject of conversation careful thought that day. She used another strategy too. She ensured she didn't offer any opinion contrary to his, or anything that could extend the conversation and steer it towards debate. Each topic was dealt with succinctly. But it was hard. A conversation without raised voices, anger, irritation or contradiction was no fun. However, she did this all day. It felt good to see her husband at peace. The events of the previous night felt like a bad dream.

25

He left at dawn for his walk the next day. The air was heavy with dew. He reached the grounds wondering how it would rain if all the water condensed into dew.

Kumarasurar usually walked alone. He was not in the habit of waiting for others or setting his pace to that of the fellow walkers with whom he exchanged greetings. That morning, he saw Kanakasurar as soon as he entered the grounds. There was a crowd around him. Kumarasurar paused. Something important must have occurred.

Spying him, and realising this provided an escape route, Kanakasurar called, 'What happened, Kumar, you weren't here yesterday?' and joined him, waving goodbye to the others.

'What happened, Kanak? You've gathered a following first thing in the morning? Did you start telling them some story?' Kumarasurar asked.

'So even you're capable of joking, huh? Didn't you see the news yesterday? The television channels were all talking about our town. And that too, my area.'

Kanakasurar lived in another part of town, where residential blocks and government housing stood side by side. Three unemployed youngsters who lived in the area had made the acquaintance of a man who promised them a lot of money and bought them expensive mobile phones as well as large motorcycles. The boys, who were suddenly cash-rich, lied that they had started working in a company. Kanakasurar said it stung his tongue to even speak about what they had actually done, sighed, and promptly began his tale.

The three young men had made friends with most of the residents of their area, and got into the habit of visiting them at home on some pretext or the other. They would ask to use the toilet, hide their mobile phones in the bathroom and switch on the video cameras. Most houses in the area had toilets and bathrooms in the backyard. They didn't have pucca roofs, and had tin sheets overhead instead. The gaps between the tin sheets and the iron rollers which held them together were ideal for hiding the phones. The boys would return to these houses, ask to use the toilet again and retrieve their phones. They would sell the videos from the bathroom to people who traded in pornography. The buyers would make small edits to the recordings and upload them on the internet.

Videos of many women from the area having showers were now online. Someone who had watched one of these videos was surprised that the bathroom resembled his own, and analysed it closely. It turned out to be his own home. The woman in the video was his wife. The view was from the ceiling, and so her face could not be seen clearly. He had initially suspected his wife of being complicit, but a search revealed that videos from several of his neighbours' bathrooms were also online. He understood that there had been some sort of criminal violation. But, not knowing what to do, he had kept his suffering to himself for a few days. He had then registered a complaint at the Cyber Crime Cell of the police through someone he knew in the department. The police had arrested the three young men the previous day, after a month-long investigation. They had been taken away at night and were now lodged in the metropolitan jail. There had been a commotion in the neighbourhood over this.

People had figured out which houses the men had frequented, and had begun to look at those families mockingly. The problem was, one or other of the accused had been to each house at least once. Some of the men beat up their wives, and the boys' crime evolved into marital discord. Apparently, videos of some of the men showering had also been uploaded online. The entire area had lost its sleep. The neighbours had gone to the houses of the three youngsters and attacked members of their families.

A woman had demanded of one of their mothers, 'Why didn't you ask your son to make money by uploading naked videos of you? Why do you send him to other people's houses instead?' The mother had locked herself in a room and attempted suicide by hanging. People had rescued her by breaking down the door. All three families had left town overnight, with a police escort.

One could arrest the culprits. But what could one do about the videos that were already online? The police had said they were trying to take them all down. Other rumours had begun to spread. They had used not only mobile phones but also micro cameras. They had hidden them not only in the bathrooms but in the bedrooms too. One could only ascertain which of these rumours were true if the three criminals confessed.

In the meanwhile, neighbours who had had tiffs with each other were saying, 'Ha, everything that happens in their house is now all over the internet.'

Others said, 'One of those boys tried to enter our house with some ruse. I chased him away saying I'd slipper him,' as if to prove their homes had been spared the humiliation.

Since Kanakasurar was from the area, people had been making their enquiries of him too.

'I won't trust a single person. Every male asura who's over ten years old behaves like a dog. I won't allow any of them near my home. I sit in my verandah in the mornings and evenings. You should see how quickly people run past my house. No one must even look up. If anyone turns an eye towards my home, I'll dig it out and hand it to him. Are these creatures even boys? They're rotten pieces of trash, offering their age as their excuse. Their appearance and speech and manner and gait make them look like animals that have been dressed in asura clothes. You know how they chop off the balls of dogs at the veterinary hospital? They should do that to all these boys. I know how their brains work. That's why I don't trust a single one of them.'

Kanakasurar could say whatever he wanted to about boys; both his children were girls. Kumarasurar, who was father to a son, could neither encourage this talk nor counter it. So he remained silent. If Kanakasurar didn't trust a single one of the boys, in which city or which world would he find grooms for his daughters? He pondered the question in his head, but didn't ask Kanakasurar, who continued to rant against boys.

Another walker stopped upon seeing Kanakasurar.

'I saw the news yesterday,' he said. 'It's all over today's newspapers too. What a time we live in! Because of the things some people do, you end up suspecting every boy. My son told me about something that happened in his college. One shudders to hear it.'

Since the speaker was also father to a son, Kumarasurar stayed to listen to what he had to say.

26

The incident in the college had involved two boys working together too. They were from affluent families. Their parents had bought them expensive mobile phones. The boys would take their phones with them and pose for pictures in crowded places, both on campus and outside. But the truth was, they were not taking selfies. They were taking pictures of women they saw. And not of their faces; they would zoom in to their chests. Pretending they were taking selfies, they captured moments when women's pallus fell off, when they were adjusting their clothes or when their dupattas moved to the side. They sent these pictures along with dirty captions to their friends and various WhatsApp groups. They found fans and became quite famous in certain circles.

Once, when they were taking a picture of a girl in class, another girl saw them in action and got suspicious. She snatched the phone and ran to the dean's office. The college authorities found numerous pictures of women. The boys' parents were quietly summoned, and they were given transfer certificates and expelled from the college. Their phones were confiscated. Their parents, relieved that the police had not been involved, took their sons away.

'Some boys do this, and give all boys a bad name,' their interlocutor said and went on his way.

Though he agreed with the man's conclusion, Kumarasurar couldn't wrap his head around the news he had just heard. He wished he didn't have so much negativity around him. He didn't enjoy the rest of his walk. Kanakasurar kept up a steady chatter, but Kumarasurar heard nothing. The smell of the vadai at Gluttony Vilas didn't tempt him. He wasn't even in the mood to drink tea. But he had a glass anyway, so Kanakasurar wouldn't see how troubled he was.

Just then, representatives of the Walkers' Association approached Kanakasurar.

Kumarasurar was not a member of this group. The morning walkers had established various associations. Walkers' Association was one of them. Then, there were Walkers' Federation, Walkers' Foundation, Morning Walkers' Association, Morning Walkers' Federation, Morning Walkers' Foundation, Federation of Walkers, Walking Foundation and several more. There was no shortage of reasons for the existence of so many groups. People banded together on the basis of religion, caste, native place, street, family, office and so on. Each group had only one item on its agenda—its members would vacation together once in three months. Depending on how many members were going, they would arrange a vehicle. They would take along a live buffalo so they could have fresh curry, and a cook would accompany them. This trip lasted two or three days.

Some people had turned walkers just so they could go on these trips. Kumarasurar wasn't keen on vacations, and so he hadn't become a member of any of these outfits. Kanakasurar often said, 'Come on, join the association. You won't have to spend much. There's a monthly membership amount. They use that for the trip. It's like EMI.' But he could not persuade Kumarasurar.

They were about to go on one of these trips soon. They began to plan the itinerary. Kumarasurar signalled to his friend that he was leaving, and went on his way.

The weekend had turned into a personal hell. He was too upset to speak. He usually had a half-hour long shower once he returned from his walk. That day, he forgot all about it. He picked at his food and went to sleep. He didn't wake up for lunch. He roused himself in the afternoon, but did not eat a thing. Mangasuri was worried. She considered calling someone home for company, but she could not think of anyone to call.

They had lived here for years. But whom did she have that she could trust with her deepest anxieties, with whom could she share her burdens? She hesitated to call her son; he was far off, and would think something was terribly wrong. She could call someone from her village to stay, but they would be curious about what had happened to merit the invitation. Soon after they arrived, they would say they had to leave. They would pass snide remarks to the effect that she had no worries, since the end of the month brought the family a fixed salary. Perhaps it was her fate to suffer alone.

Kumarasurar had a measly dinner and left for the terrace. Mangasuri didn't dare check on him or talk to him, but she remained fraught. What if he did something drastic? What was troubling him so much? All their son wanted was a mobile phone. Why had her husband gone into such panic?

Mangasuri couldn't reason with him. He never gave her scope to contradict him. His word was final. When he had first got a government job, the entire town had concluded he was a genius. They would ask his opinion on everything. A crowd would gather at his house every morning for advice, as if they were waiting for the Meghasura temple priest. They would bring their little sons to him, and say humbly, 'Do teach him how to study well and find a good job.' This ritual had made him believe he was always right. And he continued to believe it. Mangasuri wasn't sure how to approach him now.

Having exhausted himself turning the same thoughts over in his head, Kumarasurar fell asleep. It was a disturbed sleep, with dreams waking him every now and again. He dreamt about the things Kanakasurar had said that day. Meghas was wandering about with a phone in the dream.

'Why else does a boy need a phone?' Kanakasurar was asking angrily.

'You should chop his jewels off and throw them to the crow,' Kanakasurar was saying.

A large mob was beating Meghas up. Mangasuri and Kumarasurar were rushing to stop them. The police were dragging Meghas away, hitting him as they did. He was crying inside a prison cell.

Scenes like this ran before him. He didn't wake up, but he stirred every now and again. Was it dream or reality? He couldn't be sure. It seemed too real to be a dream.

27

A sudden thirst snatched his throat. His entire body felt dehydrated. It was then that he first sensed the fear that something was terribly wrong with him. He got up slowly, held on to the wall and descended the stairs. He entered the house, went to the kitchen and began to gulp down water, when Mangasuri called, 'Enga.'

She came in and stopped short; the water had spilt all over him in the hurry with which he was swigging it.

'What happened?' she asked in shock.

Kumarasurar found himself welling up. He began to cry. Mangasuri hurried to his side. He held her and wept on her shoulder. She had never seen him sob like this. He hadn't been in such distress even when his parents had passed away.

When his tears subsided, she led him to bed and made him lie down. She wiped his face, switched on the fan, patted him on the chest and lulled him to sleep as if he were a baby. He seemed to need the pampering. Mangasuri lay down by his side and rested his face against herself. Kumarasurar curled his body into the foetal position.

Mangasuri held him close, and allowed him to do as he pleased. She had never seen such frenzy or fury in him before. He eventually relaxed and drifted off to sleep. Once his breath came evenly, she disentangled herself and rose.

As she adjusted her clothes and sat in the living room, she wondered how she could alleviate his suffering. Perhaps, once he had left for office the next day, she would go to meet her son and beg him to tell his father he didn't want a phone. If she pleaded with him to save his father somehow, he would not turn her down. He knew his father well. But Mangasuri had never travelled such a long distance by herself before. She would have to ask Kumarasurar's permission. He would most likely refuse.

What other options did she have? Could she suggest he take meditation classes that would help him find mental peace? All the street's other residents, including women, were in therapy of some sort. They couldn't stop talking about the benefits of yoga. Perhaps she could ask him to join?

She considered calling Adhigasurar and telling him about the situation. But how would he help? He lived too far away to make a sudden trip. Besides, how could she say, 'He's gone crazy because our son asked for a new phone'? Even a close friend would find it ridiculous that this had become such a big deal. Mangasuri weighed and re-weighed her options until she dozed off on the sofa.

Kumarasurar went to work, but found he couldn't engage himself in anything over the next couple of days. His assistant kept the newspaper on his table, but he didn't feel like even glancing through the headlines. He went out for tea and was away a long time. He stared at the trees that abounded on the office premises and the birds flying from the branches. He mentally responded to their calls with his own. It struck him that a whole world existed within the office which he had never noticed earlier.

The premises held the Asurapuri division administrative offices. There were numerous buildings. Each of these buildings had annexes, which had further annexes. The networks of annexes extended like the tail of an animal as far as the eye could see. No one knew just how many sub-offices these comprised.

When the union elections were being held, one of the candidates had gone to each of these buildings in order to canvass for votes. He had said in the canteen, 'This is a palace of illusions, holding thousands of secrets. Even a map won't let you locate a particular place. The maps are all outdated. They were prepared when the building was first erected. Since then, there have been renovations, modifications, linkages, corridors and all manner of things. It's like a maze. You can't find your way out once you get inside a place. If you want to punish someone, you should make him stand for elections and ask for votes in each office.'

Kumarasurar had been on this campus for over twenty years. But all he knew was a single path. When he walked from the bus stop to his room, he would pass certain buildings. It was a straight road. He didn't need to make any turns. His feet knew the route well enough to walk themselves to his room without any guidance. Then, he knew the way to the canteen. That was all. In the evening, he would return to the bus stop. The same path.

For the first time, he noticed that there were little alcoves and clusters of trees which contained an ecosystem devoid of humans. He could hear various kinds of birdcalls. He had lost all faith in humanity, and felt the need to wander about in these newly discovered parts of his campus.

He felt the birds were calling out to him and asking him something. He answered them, sometimes aloud. Passersby looked at him, saw him talking to himself, and walked away quickly.

He was in a daze through most of the day, unaware of what he was doing. But the night brought sleep. The dreams persisted. Meghas went on all kinds of dangerous adventures and threw Kumarasurar into terror in those dreams.

Mangasuri was frightened by the silence into which he had sunk; but she thought he would be all right in a while, because he wasn't throwing a fit.

On the third day, his mind appeared to clear. He could bring himself to look at his colleagues and exchange a word or two. Though he hadn't opened the newspaper over the last two days, Kumbhas had dutifully kept the paper on his desk again. He looked through it, and then called Kumbhas along for tea.

When Kumarasurar invited him along, it implied he was taking cognisance of Kumbhas's astute mind. The clerk wondered what he was going to ask him that day, and what he should say in reply, as he walked with his boss. When they stepped outside, he sensed that Kumarasurar wanted to ask him something, but was hesitant.

Kumarasurar beat around the bush, asking what he had had for breakfast, how he had come to work, whether he thought it would rain and various other questions before saying, 'Well ... umm ... '

'Sir, tell me,' Kumbhas said. 'Whatever's on your mind, you can tell me. I'm like a son to you.'

The last sentence made Kumarasurar hesitate further. One could speak to anybody else, but speaking to one's own son was the most difficult.

Realising this, Kumbhas added, 'Think of me as a friend, sir.'

Even if one couldn't quite confide in a friend about everything, it was an improvement on one's son. And so Kumarasurar gathered the courage to speak.

'You know these "blue films" people speak of? Apparently it's all over the computer. Do you know about these?'

Kumbhas was both relieved that this was all the matter was, and thrilled at the knowledge that however straitlaced someone seemed, he had the same inclinations as everyone else.

'Oh, there's heaps of those, sir. The kind of variety you find in those, you won't find in anything else in the world. You can find them in any language, any country, featuring any ethnicity. It's a world where everyone, everywhere, is naked. Being naked is a primal instinct, isn't it? If you want the partially covered kind, you'll find that too. You want them going hard at it, you'll get that; you'll get every kind you could imagine. However much experience you have, you'll find new perspectives when you watch these things. You always learn something!'

He had been carried away by his enthusiasm, and had spoken oblivious to the setting. Kumarasurar looked around them fearfully, and hissed, 'Softly, softly ... speak softly,' in a beseeching tone. Kumbhas realised where he was, and looked around too, wondering if anyone could have overheard. No one seemed to have listened in. And what if they'd heard anyway? Who didn't know about porn? Kumarasurar was the only one who was clueless about the world they lived in. Kumbhas set his mind at ease and opened his mouth again.

'Not now, let's talk in office,' Kumarasurar said.

Kumbhas was deflated. It felt as if his lips had been forcefully sewn together.

28

Kumarasurar was thoughtful as he drank his tea. He had heard of 'blue films', but had never watched any. There had been little opportunity when he was growing up.

During his college days, some of his hostel friends would call him to 'special shows'. Back then, television sets were rare. One could only find them in the houses of the super rich. Video cassette shops would rent out televisions, video decks and cassettes together. These were the 'special shows' to which he was invited, but he was too nervous to go.

'At least read books,' they laughed, and offered him girly magazines. He jerked his hands away as if someone had dropped shit into them. His friends teased him mercilessly.

They asked quite openly, 'Can you get it up or not?'

Wanting to share the joy, his friends ridiculed him, insulted him, enticed him, cajoled him, but nothing worked. He hadn't gone to the 'morning shows' at the cinema either. They told him about the bit movies that were slipped in during these shows, and tried to get him to go. He was so flustered that he ran away from them. His reaction became part of college folklore.

They nicknamed him 'The Virgin King'. He thought of this as a compliment.

'How do you write poetry without knowing anything about this?' they would ask.

'Poetry is imagination. He does everything in his head,' they would laugh.

His friends believed he had wasted away his years in college.

Once he had got a job and was married, he'd had to leave for a month-long training course in a remote city. During his stay, his fellow trainees suggested they go to the noon show. Adhigasurar was among the friends he had made at the time, and Kumarasurar went because the former had invited him.

It was only when they reached the venue and he saw the poster that he realised it was 'that kind' of film.

'I've never seen a film like this before. Shall we leave?' he asked Adhigasurar.

Adhigasurar laughed. 'This is no big deal. Come, let's go have a look. They'll just throw in five minutes of bit scenes after the interval, that's all,' he said, reassuringly.

Kumarasurar decided he might as well see what the fuss was about. This wasn't his hometown, he wouldn't run into friends of relatives. One could do anything among strangers. One didn't have to worry about losing one's dignity or ruining one's reputation.

As Adhigasurar had predicted, the film didn't have much to do with the poster. It was about the life of a writer. But it was interrupted with random scenes. There was some kissing. After the interval, the cinema threw in some 'bit scenes', including one of oral intercourse. Kumarasurar was shocked by this.

Once they came back to their room, he turned to Adhigasurar and said, 'What the hell was that? Putting one's *tongue* of all things, *there* ... chhi, chhi! It's disgusting. Do people actually do things like that?!'

Adhigasurar, whose first reaction to Kumarasurar's words was shock, began to laugh right after. He laughed till there were tears in his eyes and a stitch in his side. He began to roll on the floor, clutching his stomach. Kumarasurar blinked, wondering what he had said that was so funny.

'Don't you know all this?' Adhigasurar eventually asked. 'How do you know nothing about this though you're married?' He went on to explain. For a few days after, Adhigasurar would broach the subject every now and again. Kumarasurar listened with embarrassment. He made a decision.

That was the last time he had watched a film of 'that kind'. All these years later, it appeared this field had grown tremendously.

As his boss had ordered, Kumbhas was silent until they reached their office. And then he brought his phone, and said, 'They've blocked all these websites on the office internet. Some days ago, news spread that some people in this building got together and watched porn online. Since then, they've put up a firewall. But I'll show you on my phone.'

His phone was about half the size of a laptop.

'What does this cost?' Kumarasurar asked him.

'Thirty thousand. Now there are newer models with better facilities. I should change over,' he said, opening a video link.

Kumarasurar made a show of being uninterested. Kumbhas showed him video clips from each variety that he had mentioned. They were all pornographic. As Kumarasurar watched, he grew irritated. What was secret anymore? If everything was out there, what was private? Was this how today's world worked, with nothing in life hidden from anyone else?

'Do all boys watch this kind of thing nowadays?' he asked.

Laughing to himself at Kumarasurar's naivete, Kumbhas said, 'Just the boys? The entire world watches them. Asuras of all ages watch them. There's talk that some asuris watch them too. You get everything at the click of the mouse. Why would people not watch? How *can* people not watch?'

'You're not even married yet, what are you going to do watching all this?' Kumarasurar said with a sly smile, hoping to hit Kumbhas where it hurt.

He was unfazed. 'Sir, the days when you had to learn from experience are gone. You learn by sight these days. You could close your eyes, but the world will pierce through anyway. So you can't decide to watch all this only once this or that happens.'

He dug up some articles online and rattled off statistics. He even knew who the leading lights in the industry were.

He told Kumarasurar who the star of each branch of porn was, and showed him some clips from their biggest hits. He enjoyed the sight of Kumarasurar helplessly watching on, unable to extricate himself from this web. Every time Kumarasurar came to, averted his eyes, said 'Chhi!' and moved away, Kumbhas would show him another genre of porn. Kumarasurar would look to see what it was and soon be lost in it. Kumbhas wouldn't change the film until his boss tried to look away. They lost track of time as he clicked on film after film on his phone. It surprised and startled Kumarasurar that such a small gadget could do such things.

It turned out that the fastest-growing and most profitable industry in the world was pornography.

'The turnover in lucrative fields such as information technology, medicine, sport and cinema are as nothing compared to that of pornography,' an article claimed.

Kumbhas said there would soon be 3D porn flicks and that they were keenly awaited. Kumarasurar didn't understand what he meant by '3D'. Kumbhas began to explain.

'No, that's enough,' Kumarasurar said, grimacing. 'How do they let such things happen?'

'All sorts of things are going on in the world, sir,' Kumbhas said. 'There's news all the time about the damage these films have done. Do you want to see?' And he navigated to various articles without waiting for Kumarasurar's permission.

These were reports about sex crimes that had been instigated by pornography. A man had insisted his wife replicate the acts he had watched in porn films, and had bludgeoned her to death because she had refused to comply. A student who had sent a pornographic clip to a female classmate's phone had been apprehended. There were several other pieces about the effects of watching porn.

Kumbhas increased the font size so his boss could read more easily. He also taught him how to scroll down.

Once Kumarasurar had finished reading, Kumbhas clicked on another link and said, as if he had just remembered, 'This isn't something you watch, it's something you listen to. Let's say you're travelling by bus. You can't watch this stuff on your phone. So you put on headphones, let this play and listen as you ride.'

He held out his earphones. The first and last time Kumarasurar had worn earphones was when his son had plugged them into his ears on the bus ride back from college. He had listened to one of his favourite songs that time.

This was his second time. He seemed to be hearing a telephone conversation between a man and a woman. Kumarasurar believed that an ugly swearword used during a mild tiff could break off lifelong ties. But this man and woman were using these words liberally. They were speaking about every stage of foreplay and sex. They were talking blatantly about what they felt at each point. Kumarasurar listened in a stupor for a few minutes and suddenly came to his senses.

'Do people actually talk like this? Chhi! What world is this?' he said, tearing the wires out of his ears.

'It's happening right in front of us, sir. It's the world of asuras all right. You have an internet connection at home, right sir? Try keying in any word that comes to your mind and do a search, you'll find a whole lot of things,' and Kumbhas went on to explain all the genres within this branch of porn.

For those who wanted only civilised talk, there were options featuring those. For those who liked dirty talk involving the names of body parts, there were other options. Those of a literary bent, who liked double entendres, had options too. One could choose the kind of relationship, the conversation, the act and just about everything.

Kumbhas told him about a game he and his friends played.

Most of the audio erotica was scripted. Often, male voices were electronically modified to sound female. But then there were real conversations that had been taped and uploaded online. The game involved spotting which exchanges were real and which ones scripted. Kumbhas said there were ways to spot this, but did not elaborate. He thought he would wait for Kumarasurar to insist before he revealed these hacks. Kumarasurar didn't ask, because he wasn't sure what Kumbhas would think of him if he did.

But he let out heavy sighs all day.

29

When his office hours ended and he had to leave for home, Kumarasurar felt eaten up by embarrassment and shame. Kumbhas took his leave with no trace of awkwardness; he did not seem to have any qualms about the things he and his boss had discussed; his face shone with the satisfaction of having introduced Kumarasurar to a new world. Kumarasurar could not meet his eyes.

As he walked to the bus stop, Kumarasurar thought what a fool he was to have been blind to this colossal world, to have assumed everyone's life was like his own. He hadn't been able to look the peon in the face while asking him to lock up.

He walked with his head bowed. About fifty feet from his office was a large garbage heap. It regularly raised a stink. Sometimes, it would smoke for days. He crossed the heap almost without noticing it and reached the main street after walking several blocks. He did not raise his eyes. His legs knew where to go. His thoughts were focused on one thing: if Kumbhas watched these films regularly, what must his outlook be? He resolved never to invite Kumbhas home. He must not even glance at his face. He must stop talking to him so much. He would limit their conversation to official matters. He made several decisions along these lines before he reached the bus stop.

Kumbhas rode a motorcycle. He had several friends with whom he hung out after work. Certain that he could not be around, Kumarasurar finally looked up. He got a shock. Not far away, a group of women stood naked, handbags slung across their shoulders. What the hell, he thought, and swung his head around. The men and women he saw on the other side were naked too. He looked about himself in horror. The people walking on the roads were naked. The people climbing into buses were naked. The crowd before him was naked; the crowd behind him was naked. The whole world had lost its clothes.

When his bus approached, he mounted it quickly. He made sure not to look up at the conductor as he passed him the money for his ticket. He was terrified he might encounter someone he knew. He got off at his stop and made his way homewards, staring down at the road. He had about a mile to walk. It was usually a relief to step off the packed bus and take in the fresh air. When he was in a hurry, he would take a share auto. He was rarely in a hurry. He didn't have much to do at home; that was Mangasuri's domain. A leisurely walk would do him good, he thought now.

He was halfway across the road when he froze, tormented. People in passing vehicles swore at him, using the words he had heard in the audio Kumbhas had played for him; but he did not register this. Don't these people have any sense of shame, he wondered, look at them driving naked.

The mile home seemed interminably long. He decided to take an auto. He stood by the side of the road and stared at the tar, waiting for one. He would have to look up to hail an autorickshaw. When he did, he saw that the statue on the road was naked too.

A share auto passed him by. It did not stop for him. He screamed after it, begging the driver to stop. The bewildered man slowed down, and Kumarasurar ran to it. The autorickshaw driver was naked. So were the two passengers in the front seat. They were squeezed in unnaturally close together too. The whole world had turned topsy-turvy in a day. He could not bring himself to look at his fellow riders.

When he reached home, he got off with his head bowed, counted out the money and stuck out his hand without looking at the driver. He kept his head down as he hurried across his street, afraid his neighbours would stop him for a chat; he focused on the floor as he knocked, and rushed into his house as soon as his wife answered the door, without meeting her eyes. He tossed his briefcase into its usual place, and looked down at himself to change his clothes. He gasped. He was naked too. Had he travelled all that way unclothed? His body shook. He rushed into Meghas's empty room, threw himself on the bed and began to sob. When Meghas was not home, his room was placed at his father's disposal. Kumarasurar banged the door shut, covered his naked body with a blanket and lay down on the bed.

As soon as he shut the door, Mangasuri started banging on it and screaming in panic.

'Enga! Enga!' she cried, slamming her hands against the door.

Each blow fell like a hammerhead upon his heart.

Opening the door a crack, he demanded, still without looking at her, 'What are you breaking down the door for? Is your dead father going to pay for a replacement?'

'Close the door if you want, but don't bolt it,' Mangasuri said. 'Why are you wrapped up in a blanket? Are you cold?'

'Don't open the door. If you want me, call. I'll open it myself. I'm not going to kill myself. Don't create a scene,' he snapped, shut the door and lay down on the bed.

Mangasuri, who had just seen her husband throw on a blanket over his formal clothes and flop down on the bed without so much as glancing at her, decided he was out of his mind. She must go to the Meghasura temple and propitiate Him.

She made for the puja room, prayed to Meghasura to cure her husband, placed a cup of water before the idol and then carried the consecrated water carefully to Meghas's room. She sprinkled some outside the door. She gently nudged the door ajar and saw that Kumarasurar was asleep on the bed. She stepped in gingerly and sprinkled water around the bed. His eyes were closed and he was curled up in a ball.

She went out quietly and dialled Meghas's number. There was no point keeping Kumarasurar's insanity a secret from him any longer.

'Your father's acting strange,' she said. 'Can you come home? I'm scared.'

'Ask him to rest, Amma,' he said. 'He gets into a tizzy over everything. He'll be fine if he gets a good night's sleep. Make him some dinner and ask him to go to bed. Send him to office tomorrow. Or ask him to take a day off. I'm sure he's accumulated enough leave. I have a test in two days. As soon as I'm done, I'll take a bus home. I'll be there by Friday night.'

Speaking to Meghas consoled her. She did as he had advised. She made Kumarasurar's favourite sambar. She took out fresh curd. She didn't usually give him curd with his dinner. She would make an exception today.

He didn't step out. She finished cooking and then peeped into the room. He lay exactly as before. She would let him rest a while longer, she thought, and switched on the TV. She kept the volume low. All her attention was focused on Meghas's room. In the interval between one megaserial and the next, she heard a sound from within. She went to the door. He had gone into the toilet without switching on the light.

She left the door ajar so that some light from the sitting room would reach him.

'Won't you eat?' she called.

'Close the door, close the door!' he yelled. His eyes smarted from the light.

She pulled the door shut and called, 'Dinner?'

'Bring my plate to the door and call,' he said and sat down on the bed.

He felt rather hungry. He drew a stool up by the bed. His eyes had got used to the dark. He did not need light. Mangasuri arrived with two plates. He went to the door and got them. When he was done eating, he pushed the empty plates outside.

'I'm going to sleep. Don't wake me,' he said and closed the door. He bolted it.

30

When he woke the next morning, he was afraid to get off the bed. He was afraid to shrug off the blanket and look at his own body. He did not like the light. He trembled at the thought of leaving the room. He closed the windows and bolted them shut. He sat on the bed, looking around himself like a trapped mouse. When his wife knocked on the door with his breakfast, he undid the bolt and then dashed back to the bed and drew his eyes shut. As soon as she had kept his breakfast by the bed and left, he ran to bolt the door. It was then that it struck him that everything that had happened to him was because of his eyes. They were up to no good.

He would wash his eyes before he ate. He went into the bathroom and washed them, rubbing each thoroughly. With every rub, more secretions poured out of his eyes. He lathered soap into them. That seemed to clear them a tad. He stepped outside and looked at himself in the mirror. His eyes were clear. There would be no more problems. He threw off the blanket and ate. Then, he lay down on the bed and considered his situation. His eyes had become dirty because he had watched those films for a few minutes. Heaps of dirt had smuggled themselves into his eyes. If you looked at the world with dirty eyes, everything would look dirty. He would have to deep-clean his eyes. He washed his eyes again. He rubbed soap around and into them, and lathered it well. But it seemed to have little effect on the dirt inside.

He opened his eyes wide and rubbed soap into his eyeballs. It stung. He let it stay, enjoying the burning away of the dirt. Once he had let it soak long enough, he splashed water over and over again into his eyes. All the dirt must come out. He stepped out to check the mirror. His eyes were red. He could barely see his eyeballs. If he rinsed them thoroughly, just like this, a few more times, they would be cured.

He lay down. As he faded into a dreamy state between wakefulness and sleep, he jolted himself out of bed and washed his eyes again. More secretions had gathered in his eyes. All that dirt, he thought, and soaped his eyeballs again. Seeing his red eyes in the mirror gave him a sense of relief. He tossed around in the bed again.

When Mangasuri brought his lunch, he opened his eyes a crack. She was wearing a red sari. Before he could see whether she was wearing a blouse, she had moved out of his line of sight. But at least he could see a sari. The cure was working.

'I've kept drinking water in a jug,' Mangasuri called.

It was then that it struck him. He had been washing his eyes in pipe water, which was salty. Only drinking water could remove the dirt entirely. How had he not thought of this?

'Bring me some more water to drink,' he called.

There was a water problem in Asurapuri. The water in the wells had become sluggish. The residents had to depend on the water the government pumped into their pipes. This water was salty. It had to be treated before one could drink it.

When he had washed his eyes with the water Mangasuri brought, they felt clean. He sat down to eat.

He closed his burning eyes—that soothed them. He lulled himself to sleep. But he woke every few minutes. He asked for water to drink, over and over again, and washed his eyes thoroughly.

Mangasuri, confused that her husband had begun drinking so much water, asked, 'Should I bring you hot water?'

This was an even better idea, he thought.

'Yes, heat some drinking water for me,' he said.

When she brought him a jug, he tasted the water to make sure it wasn't salty. Then he washed his eyes again. The hot water felt good against his eyes. The lather from the soap had stopped burning. It was beginning to itch. He washed his eyes with hot water thrice before he went to bed.

That night, he dreamt Meghas was watching a film on his smartphone. He couldn't see which film it was. He was sure his son was watching porn. Meghas also appeared to be forwarding the video to several people.

Kumarasurar woke with a start. He went to the kitchen, felt around for the water jug without switching on the light, heated it and brought it to the room. Mangasuri did not stir. He washed his eyes with the hot water. He did this several times through the night, keeping as quiet as he could so his wife would not wake up. He wasn't sure when he finally fell asleep, but he slept unusually late into the day.

It was past nine when Mangasuri came to wake him up. He opened his eyes. She was wearing clothes. His eyes had been cured. He felt good.

But Mangasuri took one look at his eyes and screamed, 'Aiyo!'

His upper and lower lids had swollen to such an extent that his eyes were mere slits. This must be a serious infection, Mangasuri thought, and begged him to come to an ophthalmologist. He refused.

'No, no, no,' he said. 'My eyes have just become clean. You don't know how dirty they were. All of yesterday, they were positively filthy. If I go to the doctor, he'll pour some medicine into my eyes and contaminate them again. The swelling will reduce. I'll be fine.'

He looked at himself in the mirror. His eyes appeared slightly pudgy from lack of sleep.

Mangasuri brought an ice pack and began to press it against his eyes. She did this every half hour, and by evening, the swelling had abated a little.

It was only after this that she told him Meghas would be home soon. She didn't let on that she had asked him to visit. She said he had told her he was missing home and was coming down for the weekend.

Mangasuri planned to tell Meghas about the changes she had observed in his father since he had asked for a phone, and persuade him to say he didn't want one after all.

As soon as he learnt of Meghas's impending arrival, Kumarasurar got up and went off to the terrace. Mangasuri was afraid he would go back to his previous state. But what could she do? If only Meghas would say he didn't want a phone, Kumarasurar would be all right at once. She had no choice but to hold on to hope and let things be until then. She decided not to follow him upstairs; there would be little point.

Kumarasurar expected that his wife would follow him to the terrace. He listened for her footsteps on the stairs. He consoled himself saying she must have come and gone quietly after ascertaining he was fine. All he could think about was meeting Meghas face to face. If only she had told him a day earlier, he could have planned what to say to his son. Usually, Meghas didn't speak to him. If he asked a question, the boy replied in monosyllables. Over the phone, his most frequent answer to questions was 'Mm'. This time around, Meghas might want to talk to him. Or, Kumarasurar could call him aside for a chat. What did he have to say, though, except for the one thing? He had to tell the boy he couldn't buy him a phone. That was all. But how could he tell him? And how would his son react?

31

Meghas reached home at eleven that night. Mangasuri could not recognise him. When the bell rang, she opened the door hesitantly, switched on the light and asked the person who stood outside the grille, 'Who is it?'

'It's me, Ma!' he said, sounding annoyed.

It was only after hearing his voice that she realised it was Meghas. When she saw his head, she began to cry.

'What is this horror?' she asked and wailed, hitting her chest. 'I tell you there's a crisis here, and you come looking like this. Aiyo, he said back then that our son will no longer be our son, and now that has turned out to be true. Not even a madman would wear his hair like this. My mother-in-law took one look at you when you were born and said you had inherited the palmfruit-shaped head of your family. And now look at you, your head looks like a palmfruit seed that has been sucked on and spat out. Oh, my Meghappa, won't You save my family?'

Drawn by the ruckus, several of the street dogs had gathered and were barking, filling the street with the noise. Some of the dogs growled at Meghas.

Afraid they would bite him, he called, 'Let me in fast, Amma!'

In her hurry, Mangasuri now fumbled with the keys.

'Chhi, go! Go!' she chased away the dogs, as she finally opened the door.

Her son angrily kicked away his slippers and stomped into the house.

Mangasuri wondered if she had overreacted. But she couldn't stand what he had done to his head.

A lone row of hair stood like Bermuda grass on a field, in the middle of his head. Two furrows ran along either side.

When Kumarasurar was a child, his parents used to cut his hair that way—or almost. They had shaved off the rest of the hair too, except for a blob in the middle. He was teased in school—'What is this, da, looks like a coconut that's been chewed by dogs!' 'Looks like palm jaggery has been dumped on his head!'

And if he were questioned now, Meghas would say, 'This is in vogue.'

What used to be an object of ridicule in one era had become an object of admiration in another. What used to draw admiration in one era now drew ridicule. It was as if respect and contempt worked cyclically.

Meghas felt disappointed. His stay hadn't got off to a good start. The greeting he had received from his mother and the dogs had irritated him. To top it off, he had been worried about his father, but he couldn't spot anything wrong with him. It was his mother who seemed off. That explained her wailing. Could a mother fail to recognise her son because of a change in haircut? The maternal instinct was all about recognising one's child irrespective of how he looked or in what condition he was, wasn't it? It was his mother who was acting strange. Her face looked worn and tired. He wished he hadn't come home.

He went to the kitchen and asked Mangasuri softly, 'Amma, Appa seems fine. Why did you ask me to come here for no reason?'

She looked at his head and said, 'What is this, kanna? This won't do for our family, kanna. Style your hair properly.'

'Plch. Let it go. I know how to style it. Tell me what happened to Appa,' he said.

'You'll understand the song and dance he's been making only if you stay and watch. He hasn't been to office in two days. He didn't even call to inform them about this. He shut himself up in a room. I don't know what he was up to inside, but his eyes were swollen like paniyarams. I used an ice pack, and now it's somewhat better,' Mangasuri explained.

'But that's how he is, Amma. Why are you acting like this is new? Let him mind his business, and you mind yours. He gets into panic over everything. You get into panic over him. This is all the two of you do. I'm going to go talk to him,' Meghas said.

Kumarasurar had heard his son arrive, and had moved from the room to the hall, where he was pretending to watch the television. Meghas went to sit with him. Kumarasurar stared at his head too. Meghas ignored the stare. His father wouldn't react immediately, as his mother had. Meghas decided not to bother explaining unless he was asked and sat across from Kumarasurar.

There was no sign of his ever having hesitated to speak to his father. He launched into dialogue at once. 'Appa, I told you about that phone, right? Shall we order it, Appa?'

Kumarasurar, startled that his son had taken the bull by the horns right away, said, 'Why, aiyya, what happened to the mobile phone you have now?'

'That's a dabba phone, Appa. There's nothing you can do with it. I don't even have a laptop. So I need a phone with all the features and functions I want, or I can't follow the subject, Appa.'

'But your subject is computer science, isn't it?'

'Yes, Appa. But everything is clumped together these days. I'm specialising in creating apps for mobiles. I need the latest phone in the market, Appa, or I can't work on them. Our sir is insisting that we buy the newest phones immediately.'

Kumarasurar searched his son's face for signs of his having lied. But Meghas seemed earnest. He knew his father was clueless about technology. Was he trying to pull a fast one? Kumarasurar did not step back from the conversation, though.

'So the one you have is of no use?'

'That's a basic model, Appa. It has all the features, but not one is up to date. It's just *there*.'

'What does the new one have that's so fantastic?'

'Look here, Appa. Listen carefully to what I say. There are two kinds of phones: budget phones and high-end mobiles. The one we bought is a budget phone. Take the camera; many phones didn't have a front camera back then. But now even the budget phones on the market have front cameras. The thing is, you can't capture everything on those. Photos aren't just megapictures, you know. If you want to capture something in low light, budget phones are of no use. You need a high-end model. The ones you get for ten or fifteen thousand won't do. Then there's display, then there's screen size, then there's build quality, then there's finger print speed, then there's processor, then there's RAM ... '

He kept adding 'then there's'-es. Kumarasurar kept listening, his mouth open.

Was this boy really his son? It was like he had descended from the world of the devas and was talking their language. Kumarasurar couldn't understand a thing the boy said. In more than twenty years that he had written notes and read files in his office, he didn't think he had used or read a single word Meghas spoke. Where had he learnt all this? After a while, all Kumarasurar could see were his son's lips moving and all he could hear were sounds. Nothing else.

It surprised him that his son could talk so much. Words were pouring out of the mouth of the boy who would only say, 'Mm.' His appearance had changed. So had his speech. He seemed like someone from outer space.

Kumarasurar initially felt scared. Could this be an impostor? His large head, wide mouth and the sparrow-like movements of his lips were those of his son. Once he had ensured this was indeed Meghas, he felt proud too. Mangasuri, who looked in on them every now and again to make sure father and son didn't start quarrelling, saw how pleased Kumarasurar was. She herself was surprised by this new-found aspect of her son's character, but she made a point of beaming with pride to her husband, as if to gloat that this was *her* son.

Neither quite realised when he finished speaking.

All of a sudden, he rose and went to the computer room. It wasn't clear whether he was done with his homily or was about to present some sort of evidence to substantiate his assertions. Kumarasurar had lost track of what Meghas was saying. He waited for his son to return. He was afraid he would quiz him on something he had just explained. If he did, Kumarasurar would have to stare back blankly. He was reminded of his own schooldays.

Meghas returned with a printout. It was a picture of a sleek phone. All Kumarasurar could see was the price by its side: Rs 74,999. There were various specifications and explanations, which Meghas outlined. They all had to do with the phone's features and technical details.

Kumarasurar nodded along as he listened. The one thing he understood clearly was the date and time by which the phone had to be ordered.

His son highlighted two crucial reasons why he should agree to buy him the phone. A student of computer engineering needed a laptop. He had planned to buy one during his third year. Now, they could avoid that cost since the phone would do everything a laptop could. Second, he had chosen his academic specialisation—creating a mobile phone processor. He needed a high-end mobile to do this. He presented yet another argument: he had saved them a lot of money by making it to college in the regular intake, rather than the management quota. He wasn't asking them to spend the entire difference. The phone would cost only a tenth of what they had saved.

32

Through that night, Kumarasurar could hear his son's voice in his head. Whichever way he turned, the boy was sitting across from him describing the features of the phone. Meghas changed the intonation of his voice for maximum effect. He spoke of the money he had saved his parents. He insisted they should buy him a phone. It was dawn before Kumarasurar could sleep.

Meghas devoted his conversations with his father to the phone through the two days of his stay. Kumarasurar did not respond.

As he left for the bus terminus on Sunday night, he asked, 'Appa, by which date will you transfer the money to my account?'

'I'll see, aiyya,' Kumarasurar said vaguely.

That meant he would certainly transfer the money. Meghas reiterated the final date and asked him to send the money a couple of days in advance.

Kumarasurar went to office the next day. Kumbhas asked why he had taken leave all of a sudden. He spoke with an undertone of slyness, as if to ask whether the emotions the films had stirred in him had necessitated two days off. But he accorded his boss's age enough respect to refrain from spelling it out. He was happy for Kumarasurar to take days off. During his supervisor's absence, he'd felt the reins of the office had been handed to him. If the phone rang or a superior had questions about work, he had been the one who answered.

People from other offices who needed something had had to approach him. He had made a show of his power. He had bossed around the office peon, Kandasurar. For those two days, he had not gone to the canteen for tea. He would ask the peon to buy him tea, and give him a flask.

'Wash it in hot water before you get it filled,' he would say.

Kumbhas, who never fussed about taste when he went to drink tea himself, would complain when Kandasurar brought him tea.

'What is this, it's not hot?'

'Why have they dumped so much sugar into it?'

Kandasurar, whose only role in the making of the tea was to fetch it, would curse him silently as he left on his loan recovery duties.

Kumbhas would call the peon on his phone at least five times through the day and give him a task.

'I'll tell the bosses you're never in office. It's not like *he* has to come back and write to them. When I'm in charge, I'll send off a note,' he would warn.

Kandasurar wasn't daunted. He had seen several officials of this kind, and he knew their tricks. 'Write away, sir. If there's any work pending, do write. I'll answer anyone who questions me. Your years on earth are the same as the term of my service. Keep that in mind,' he would say.

Kandasurar's oft-repeated lines to the customers of his usury business about officials were famous: 'They're the sort who've got their arses full of shit, but spend all their time staring at other people's arses and yelling that they're soiled. And these guys who spew shit will stack stones in front of them and then wipe their arses on each stone and then throw it at whomever they see around them. Whichever stone you sniff, it will stink of shit.'

Kumbhas, who had mounted the throne for the two days his boss had been on leave, now sought to reassure the latter of his importance by saying the office had lost all its sheen in Kumarasurar's absence, and he hadn't known how to answer the various enquiries that had fallen upon him.

Kumarasurar had nothing to say to Kumbhas that day. He couldn't speak about his son directly. He was careful to guard his family's reputation. But he was tempted to ask him about the phone his son had mentioned. He curtailed the impulse with difficulty. He tried changing the subject on his mind.

'You went to find a bride this week, what happened?' he asked.

Kumbhas would go to check out prospective brides every week. Once upon a time, people would have given an arm and a leg to find a groom with a government job. This had changed now. The title was not enough. They asked to see a salary slip. They wrinkled their noses when they saw the figures. They said the money would barely cover expenses for one child. Kumbhas had joined at the same position Kumarasurar had all those years ago. It was pretty much that of an office assistant—perhaps one grade above. That job didn't command respect anymore. The parents of prospective brides wanted important officials for their daughters. Kumbhas came back with a sob story every week.

'As usual, sir,' he said now, and began to narrate what had happened this time.

Kumarasurar heard him out, but couldn't think of anything but his own son.

Despite everything Meghas had said, Kumarasurar could not reconcile himself to the situation. He had tried thinking of counterarguments, but realised it was impossible to come up with any good ones. He decided he must tell him, firmly, 'I can't buy you a phone right now.' But what if his son did something drastic in a rage?

Kumarasurar had to stifle the images in his head. He would cast them aside. How?

He would bundle these images and try to bury them in the sand. But anything that was buried was eventually found.

What if he threw them into the sea? But anything that sank eventually surfaced.

It was best to burn these images. He would conjure fire in his head and try to burn the images in it. His entire life seemed to revolve around the attempt.

Where his son was concerned, sometimes he knew exactly what to do; and sometimes, he was confused.

He didn't feel like meeting anyone, but wasn't able to avoid anyone either. Every day, he wished he didn't have to leave home. No one he met had any good news to share.

That day, he didn't feel like going to the canteen. Kumbhas hesitantly asked him to come along. Kumarasurar, who thought he might go mad if he sat in his chair all day, decided to go with him. Kumbhas talked his head off on the way. It irritated Kumarasurar that someone of this age had so much to say. You couldn't assume that anyone was a man of few words. They would appear to be the silent type. But once they got a chance to talk, they wouldn't shut their traps.

He found an opportunity to escape from Kumbhas on the way to the canteen: Venjurar. Venjurar, who worked in another office in the same building, was a distant relative. The two men were always glad to see each other.

Venjurar hadn't been spotted in the canteen for several weeks, a strange phenomenon. He was the kind who took his break at precisely eleven o'clock. He would spend the next forty-five minutes in the canteen. Anyone who wanted to meet him would wait in the canteen for him at this time.

Kumarasurar now approached him and said, 'What happened, Maama? I haven't seen you in ages.'

Venjurar took him aside and said, 'It's no easy task to raise a son, get him educated and make a man of him, Kumar. I'm telling you this because you're family. Keep this to yourself.' And he told him what had happened.

Venjurar had had a son after three daughters. He was in his final year of engineering now. Because he had been born after three girls, he was the apple of everyone's eye. They had got the first two daughters married off right after they had finished class eleven. The youngest daughter and the son were the only ones who had had a good education. The girl posed no problems. She had joined a women's college and was studying well. The boy was the cause of their troubles.

They had bought him phone, laptop, everything he had asked for, and were paying through their noses for a hostel that had five-star facilities. He did well through the first two years of college. But there had been a change in the third year. Apparently, there was a whole world of online games. He had begun to play these and got so addicted that he wasn't able to leave this virtual world. He would start playing the moment he woke up and would do nothing else all day. The game was like a vice, which held you in its grip so you couldn't move a muscle.

He didn't even leave his desk to eat. He would order parcels of food and keep them on the table. If he felt hungry, he would eat while playing. To avoid getting up to go to the toilet, he started wearing adult diapers. He played all night and all day. He would only sleep when he was exhausted from playing. It could be during the day. It could be during the night. He lost track of the date and time. All he cared about was the game.

He hadn't written any of his exams during the second semester of his third year and the first semester of his fourth year. He hadn't been home much in the last year and a half. He wouldn't even come home for festivals unless he was forced. How could parents who trusted that their son could do no wrong have expected that he would come to this? They understood illnesses like fever and migraine. But this addiction was a new illness, one they had never heard of.

'We know about alcoholism. There are people in our office who spend all the extra money they make on drink and lie sprawled on the roads. We've seen drug addicts. But have we ever seen anyone become a slave to games? And what games do we know of? We only know the ones people play on the field—kabaddi, volleyball, football, basketball. But here, there's no opponent, no real person. Just figures that come and go. You play by manipulating these figures. They've pulled my son like magnets. You can drive away spirits by exorcism. But this demon is impossible to exorcise. We kept getting calls from his college, asking us to come and fetch him. When we went, this is what we saw. They gave us all sorts of terms—internet phobia, internet addiction. There are doctors in that city who offer therapy for this. When we went for a counselling session, we saw a huge crowd there. We stayed there for ten days and went to the doctor twice a day.'

'Is he all right now?'

'This demon's had him in its clutches for months, for years. Will it let go in ten days? The moment he even sees a mobile phone, his hands begin to itch. His fingers tremble. His eyes shine and he stares at the phone. He doesn't even care whose phone it is. He lunges at it and takes it. He starts playing whatever game is on it. The doctor has said he shouldn't so much as look at a phone. He says we should get him involved in other things. There is therapy for all this, and he needs treatment for at least a year. So I've found a house there and made arrangements for his mother to stay with him. But I have to go there every weekend myself. He needs constant care if he's to have any hope of being cured. We need to take him out into the real world and show him real people. His brain has to understand that the figures in the games are not real. You know the proverb, "Marriage made a dog of me, children made a ghost of me"? Well, that's my life now.'

Kumarasurar didn't know how to console him. He offered the platitudes that came to mind. 'Don't worry, Maama. Everything will turn out okay.'

When he took his leave, Venjurar said, 'Don't trust your son to study just because you've got him admission in college. Go visit him every week. Make sure he's going to his classes. Speak to his professors. If your son asks for this or that, don't buy it right away unless it's something he can eat. Think carefully before you get him a phone or a computer. Why does a student need a smartphone? Isn't a regular phone good enough to call home? They don't even need that, really. There's a phone in the hostel. There are public telephones outside. Let them use those. There's just the two of you at home. Can't you live alone? You can eat gruel once a day. Or go to a hotel for your meals, there's one at every corner now. Send your wife to stay with your son. I'm telling you from experience. Prevention is better than cure.'

33

Why had he set eyes on Venjurar that day? Troubles never came singly. They brought with them kith and kin, friends and countrymen.

Meghas couldn't be left alone. He must be reined in and spied upon. When did he leave for college? When did he return to hostel? Who were his friends? Who were his professors? They had to learn everything about him. It would not do to let things run as they were doing now. The system was wrong. Yes, it was the system which was at fault. They had to change the way it operated. If they changed that, everything else would change. He would send Mangasuri along the next day, and rent a house for her and Meghas. And then he would apply for a job transfer to that city and move there himself. The transfer order wouldn't come soon. He would try, he would find people who could facilitate it, he would grease all the palms he had to, but he would ensure he was transferred.

What did he have here, anyway? A house. Just a house. They could lock it up, and check on it every now and again. Or they could rent it out. Was a house important? It was their son who was important. If only he finished his studies and found a good job, they could buy several houses like this one. Just four more years. Once he was done, he would find placement in a company and start working. They could return home, to their house and town. In the meanwhile, their house and town wouldn't run away.

Look at the sort of things these damned asuras had invented. If a game could catch you by the short hairs, what could they have thrown into it to so entrance its players? It was no game, it was poison. The internet was a venomous snake that spewed poison. Kumbhas was a porn addict. Venjurar's son was a game addict. What would happen to Meghas?

That evening, he left office determined to ask Mangasuri to pack her belongings and make arrangements for the move. His mind began to play tricks on him once he boarded the bus.

What would Meghas be up to now? What else could he be up to, he had a phone worth seventy-five thousand rupees, he would be playing on it, wouldn't he?

Meghas was cooped up in his room. He didn't even get up to go to the toilet. The new phone shimmered. It called out to him alluringly, constantly. It would not let him sleep. It would not let him eat. It would not let him talk to his friends. It wouldn't permit him to call his parents. He had no memory of classes he had to attend. He fiddled with his phone all day and all night, playing games. Sleep deprivation had drawn dark circles around his eyes, and he resembled a slender loris. Starvation had made him look chronically ill. Holding in his urine and motion had made him sickly. His face had lost its glow. He must have gone without bathing for days. No one wanted to go anywhere near him.

Their only child. The sole heir granted them by their clan deity. Could they let him destroy himself like this? Office, home, food, morning walk ... was this all there was to life? Venjurar had said, 'Maapillai, look after your son, stay by his side. Don't let him go down this path.'

His mind in turmoil over Meghas, he entered the house and hassled Mangasuri. 'What's wrong with you, di? You have no clue what's happening to your son or where he is, and you sit and watch TV all day, huh? Pack a couple of saris and leave now. You have to stay with your son from now on. I'll be there in a couple of months. I'll beg some damned dog, pay whatever I have to and move there too. Take your things, go!'

Mangasuri looked at him in alarm.

'What is wrong with *you*?' she demanded, angrily. 'I just spoke to our son. He told me he was having sundal and tea in the hostel mess. There's nothing wrong with him. He's fine. You're going to bring something upon him by ranting away like this!'

'What the hell do you know? Damned donkey that stands guard at home! It's not enough if you birth a son, di. You need to know how to raise him. He's immersed in his phone day and night. The games in there have drawn him into their trap and made him their slave. We have to break his shackles and set him free,' he said, without sitting down.

His eyeballs had rolled upward. He hadn't even taken his office bag off his shoulders.

Mangasuri reached for her phone and dialled her son's number. The moment he answered, she handed it over to Kumarasurar. 'Here, talk to him,' she said.

He took the phone, held it to his ear and said nothing.

'Appa ... Appa ... What happened, Appa?' the boy's voice reached his ears.

He asked an old question. 'Where are you, aiyya?'

'In the hostel, Appa.'

'In your room?'

'Yes, Appa.'

He gave the phone back to Mangasuri at once and yelled, 'Look, your son's sitting in his room and playing games on his phone instead of going to college!' His voice shook. His body trembled. Meghas must have heard him.

'Give the phone to Appa,' he said to his mother.

Kumarasurar refused to take the phone. He collapsed on the sofa, broken-hearted.

'Your son wants to talk to you, speak to him,' Mangasuri cajoled her husband and moved the phone close to his ear. Kumarasurar swatted the phone away like it was a mosquito trying to enter his ear.

Mangasuri began to sob. 'He's not letting me keep the phone by his ear, da,' she wept to Meghas.

'Fine, put it on speaker mode then and keep it where he can hear me,' he said.

She did as she was told and said to Kumarasurar, 'He's saying something, listen to him.'

Meghas's angry voice fell on Kumarasurar's ears. 'Who told you I'm playing games, Appa? Who said I didn't go to college? Have you come and seen for yourself? I went to college, attended lab and just got back. I had tea at the mess and then came to my room. What time is it? Just like you've come back home from office, I've come back to my room from college. Let me study, Appa. Why are you creating problems like this all the time? Why are you insulting me like this? I know what's good for me, and what's bad. I'm not an infant. Stop imagining all sorts of nonsense and troubling yourself and us!'

He went on and on.

Kumarasurar listened to everything and said, 'Okay, kanna, okay, kanna,' over and over again, tears coursing down his face. He seemed to calm down after speaking to his son.

34

That night, Mangasuri insisted that he refrain from going to the terrace. She fed him curd made from buffalo milk along with his dinner, and sent him to bed by nine. He obeyed her like a child. Despite the comforting cool of the buffalo curd, he tossed and turned for half an hour before finally falling asleep. Mangasuri realised she could not let him go on like this. A thought struck her that night.

Mangasuri knew all three of his close friends. Kanakasurar and Thenasurar were from the same village, and even related to them. Relatives and childhood friends were most jealous of each other. So both men would be delighted if they knew of Kumarasurar's condition. Even the manner of their enquiries would reveal just how much joy bubbled beneath the surface.

'What's the point of getting a great job in one's youth, he's ended up in this state,' they would say.

His third friend, Adhigasurar, would be ideal. She considered speaking to him. As she turned the thought over in her head, she began to postpone the call. She should have spoken to him earlier. He was not the kind who would have seen it as an intrusion on his time. There was no need to hesitate now either. He lived in some far-off city and called occasionally. He spoke not just to his friend, but Mangasuri too. She had only seen him a couple of times, but he commanded respect. He could be trusted to consider things calmly and carefully, with everyone's best interests at heart.

Once Kumarasurar had fallen asleep, Mangasuri went to the terrace with the phone. The moment Adhigasurar answered, she couldn't speak; she began to weep.

Adhigasurar didn't say anything. He let her cry. Once she was done, he asked, 'What happened, ma?'

Mangasuri started in frenzy and eventually slowed down, explaining her husband's situation. She wasn't sure she had made herself clear. 'He acts like a crazy person, Anna. Today, he came back from office and asked me to pack my bags. He's behaving like a crazy person, Anna,' she said, over and over again.

He heard her out and said comfortingly, 'Don't worry, ma. I'll call him in the morning. I'll get him to come stay and see to him.'

'I'll be dead if he finds out I was the one who called you,' Mangasuri said. 'Please don't let this on.'

She felt as if a heavy burden had been lifted off her shoulders.

The next morning, Kumarasurar woke to Adhigasurar's call. He was always pleased to speak to him, and so he roused himself in a hurry and asked after him.

'It's been a long time since I met you,' Adhigasurar said, after pleasantries were exchanged. 'My mind feels somewhat turbulent. I don't have close friends here. It would be nice to have a heart-to-heart with you. Do you think we could meet?'

Kumarasurar couldn't contain his pride. His friend had chosen to share his troubles with no one else but him. What an honour that was!

'Of course, we can meet. Let me know when. Would you like to come here, or shall I come there?' he asked.

Adhigasurar had his opening. 'I know our town well. I used to live there. And I've visited often. None of you has been to see me here. If you could come over and stay for a few days, I'd be happy.'

Kumarasurar agreed to visit immediately, surprising even his friend with his willingness.

He went to Mangasuri and said with some pride, 'It seems he's in trouble. Look, he called to speak to me.'

'Really, what kind of trouble is he in that merits speaking to you?' she asked.

'We're that close,' he said.

Mangasuri laughed to herself.

Adhigasurar didn't delay the visit. He booked train tickets so that Kumarasurar would leave two days later, and sent them by text.

Kumarasurar only had a day to prepare for his departure. It would be his first long-distance journey, lasting a whole day and night by train. This excited Kumarasurar, but also made him nervous. He didn't have any bags suited to a stay of four or five days. Mangasuri told him to ask Meghas for suggestions. He didn't like the idea of turning to his son. What would Meghas say anyway? He would ask him to buy an expensive bag or suitcase. He didn't want to do this.

There had been various work conferences that Kumarasurar had not attended. But he would pay the conference fee. Each time, those who had paid the fee would be given a conference goodie bag. Some of these looked ideal for the journey. It pleased him that the fees he had paid for those conferences had finally brought in a return on investment. He chose two of the bags, one for clothes and the other for miscellaneous items.

He boarded the train from his town. Adhigasurar had booked him a berth in the second class AC compartment, in which he had never travelled before. At first, this seemed unfair to him. It must have cost a lot of money. He wanted to repay Adhigasurar for it. Then, it hit him that since his friend had invited him, it made sense for his friend to pay for it. His mind was at rest, and he began to enjoy the journey.

Now, thoughts of Meghas were like a moon that slid into and surfaced from behind the clouds. His worries about his son were eventually pushed to the back of his mind, and memories of his friend made their way to the fore.

When Adhigasurar had given up a government job to study further, it had surprised everyone.

'Why would you give up a bird in hand to chase one in the bush?' Kumarasurar himself had asked.

Laughing, Adhigasurar had said, 'Let's see what the chase is like, shall we?'

He had applied for a scholarship, got it and gone abroad to finish his doctorate at a prestigious university. It had taken him five, perhaps six, years. His wife had had a job, so it wasn't hard going. Once he had returned with his doctorate, he was offered a professorship at a university. His wife had quit her job at once. They had moved with their children to stay in the city where the university was based.

One had to be impossibly courageous to make a decision of the kind Adhigasurar had, his friend thought now. He had risen in his profession and now had tenure. It surprised Kumarasurar that he still remembered him fondly, phoned him and invited him home. The man had a loving heart. What trouble could he be in that necessitated Kumarasurar's visit? Perhaps he too had problems because of his sons. But could he really not know how to solve those problems, despite being a professor? How large would his house be? Would he ask Kumarasurar to stay over, or would he have made arrangements for him to lodge elsewhere?

Kumarasurar found it hard to remain in his cubicle during the day. He had the upper berth. If he lay down and closed his eyes, Meghas made an aggressive entry among his other thoughts. His face and body laughed before his father's eyes. He changed bit by bit into a mobile phone photograph. He waved at him from inside the phone. He laughed. Kumarasurar reached for him to drag him out. He tried to drag his father in. Neither would give up. Kumarasurar had a strong grip. But his son's was stronger.

The screen of the mobile phone felt as solid as an ancient wall built from limestone and egg. When he tried to pull Meghas out through the screen, the boy's face twisted against the glass and he screamed. It appeared it would not let him go. Unable to bear the boy's torment, Kumarasurar began to weep. He sobbed his heart out.

It was only when a fellow passenger shook him awake, asking, 'Sir, sir, what happened?' that he realised he had been howling aloud. Everyone in the cubicle was staring at him. He decided he shouldn't lie down for the rest of the journey. Even if he did, he must not sleep. He went out of the cabin.

As he stood by the door, a gust of cold wind hit him. It came as a relief. He opened his mouth as if to swallow great gulps of air. Then his gaze moved outdoors. He had never seen such scenery before.

How many kinds of land there were! Parched lands that had dried out before any greenery could sprout and quench their thirst. Mystical forests with enormous trees. Rivers that swirled and danced on their way. Hills that cropped up near and far.

And how many kinds of faces there were! Children who gawked at the train, laughed and waved. Cows and goats. Old women who herded buffaloes. Posh inhabitants of large cities.

He felt ecstatic when the train crossed unpopulated lands. He longed to live in a place like this, where he wouldn't see a soul for miles.

His destination was the final stop. So there was no need to worry about missing it, and he could enjoy each vignette. They passed railway stations empty of people. They looked abandoned but for huge trees.

His journeys usually had severe limits. He walked to the bus stop every morning. It was a ten-minute ride to his office. He took the same route home. That was all. On the few expeditions he had undertaken for his son, thoughts of Meghas had haunted him and blocked out everything else. This was the first journey to have offered him a view of the world.

35

Adhigasurar was home alone. His wife and children had gone to their village for the holidays. They had the space to talk without interruption. Both Adhigasurar's children were boys, and so Kumarasurar felt no hesitation in speaking to him about his own son.

One tends to find everyone else's house more beautiful than one's home, and so it was in this case. The university had arranged for Adhigasurar's accommodation, and though it was an old structure, the house was spacious and had a large garden. Adhigasurar was delighted to see his old friend.

It turned out there were various problems at the university, and Adhigasurar was depressed. The loneliness caused by his family's absence had exacerbated this, and he had thought it might be nice to have a friend visit him. Kumarasurar was the first person who had come to mind. He said he was thrilled to see him and felt in good company, and was sure the next few days would be wonderful.

'Think of this as your own home,' he said.

As they spoke, Kumarasurar mentioned Meghas's demand for a phone and his own depression as if in passing.

'So you're saying no one can stay good these days,' Adhigasurar laughed.

'Yes, no one is allowed to stay good these days,' Kumarasurar reiterated. 'A good person is impossible to find. A demon called the Internet has been unleashed on Asuralokam. It has possessed mobile phones and computers, and is ruining the world.'

'True, true, you're right,' Adhigasurar agreed and didn't speak further.

Kumarasurar rested through the day. Adhigasurar had taken a half-day off and returned early.

At night, he sat before his computer and asked Kumarasurar to join him, drawing up a chair for him. He got some beer from the fridge. He kept the bottles on the table, opened a cabinet, surveyed various kinds of glasses and chose two identical, ornate ones that would go with the mood of the day. They had curved handles and delicate floral patterns. They stood half a cubit tall.

'You do drink, don't you?' he asked before he poured the beer.

Shaking his head emphatically, Kumarasurar said, 'No, no. I don't have that habit.'

'What! This is against the order of asura nature!' laughed Adhigasurar.

If it had been anyone else, Kumarasurar would have given him a five-minute lecture on the evils of consuming alcohol. But he didn't launch into this with Adhigasurar.

Adhigasurar poured beer into one cup and juice into another. Kumarasurar suspected it might be an alcoholic drink too.

'It's just a soft drink, don't worry,' Adhigasurar said, jovially, clinked the glasses together and said, 'Kudhookalam!'

Kumarasurar didn't know how to respond.

'Say "Kudhookalam",' Adhigasurar said. 'What a beautiful word. You get a kick just from saying it. Kudhoo … kalam. Look at the "oo" in there … When you enunciate it, it sounds like a cuckoo's call. That's the beauty of language.'

Unable to help himself, Kumarasurar too said, 'Kudhookalam!' and was about to lower his glass right away, when Adhigasurar stopped him.

'No, no. You should have at least one sip before you set it down. That's the sabha's code of conduct,' he said.

Kumarasurar looked around him.

'What, are you looking for the sabha? Does it need ten people to make a sabha? Two people are enough. Why, even one person is enough. Even if I were alone, I'd abide by the sabha's code of conduct,' Adhigasurar said.

Kumarasurar took a sip, let the juice cool his throat and said, 'There's a code of conduct even for drinking, huh?'

'Of course. Everything has a code of conduct. Drinking is an art. How can it not have its rules?' Adhigasurar laughed.

Then, he switched on the computer and showed Kumarasurar various photographs. There were numerous pictures of him and his family in different places.

Kumarasurar looked at them, but his mind wouldn't register a thing. He couldn't get over Adhigasurar's penchant for alcohol. The man drank at home. Wouldn't his wife object? Wouldn't his sons pick up this awful habit from him and ruin their lives? How had such a good man got into such a terrible habit, and why was he not able to give it up? The questions ran through Kumarasurar's mind, while his eyes stayed focused on the screen.

After a while, Adhigasurar excused himself. He sat Kumarasurar before the computer and taught him how to click the mouse to navigate from one photograph to the next before he left the room. Kumarasurar did as he had said. He was stunned at the speed with which the photographs moved at the click of a button. Adhigasurar had plenty of pictures with his family, as well as pictures they had taken of other things. Kumarasurar stared at each, fascinated. When he turned, he saw Adhigasurar smiling, beer in hand. He hadn't heard him approach.

'Tell me the names of a few songs you like,' Adhigasurar said, using the informal singular address.

Sometimes, he used the respectful formal plural address with Kumarasurar. But when he felt close to him, he switched to the informal. The smoothness with which he switched was a treat to observe.

Kumarasurar struggled to come up with the names of songs he liked. Finally, his tongue managed to wrap itself around the titles of songs he had heard long ago and remembered. They were songs from another era. Adhigasurar played them with the visuals. Kumarasurar enjoyed this greatly.

Adhigasurar taught him how to search for songs he wanted to listen to. He asked him to call out if he had any doubts, and left Kumarasurar to his own devices as he headed to the kitchen to make dinner.

Kumarasurar had no trouble. As soon as one song ended, the next followed on autoplay. The scenes he had last watched at the cinema decades ago were playing before his eyes now. He observed each song carefully. If Adhigasurar decided to quiz him, he must be sure he could answer.

The food Adhigasurar had made was delicious, and they spoke of the good old times as they ate. They watched an old comedy after. Adhigasurar laughed loudly at each scene. Kumarasurar figured he was high. He had had three beers. He had been drinking for a long time, sip by sip. The smallest joke prompted a disproportionately hearty laugh.

Kumarasurar wasn't able to laugh. But he was worried Adhigasurar would take offence, and so he forced a laugh every now and again. Soon, he began to immerse himself in the film and found himself laughing along without effort. His laugh increased in volume, like a drizzle turning into a downpour. Sometimes, when the two men laughed together, it was impossible to tell whose laugh was louder.

They spoke late into the night. Kumarasurar felt relaxed, freed of all fear and anxiety.

'You remember that poem you wrote on the last day of our training camp? The poem spoke about how all of us had changed on the first day of the camp, and how happy we were. You had lines that went "In the hills, we're peacocks; In the trees, we're koels". That is so true. Wherever we are, we should adapt to whatever suits the place best. If we could, we wouldn't have any troubles, would we?' Adhigasurar said.

Kumarasurar was touched that his friend remembered those lines. People would ask him to write poetry wherever he went, and he would scribble a verse impromptu. The fact that his words had stayed with Adhigasurar all these years stunned him. He felt a glow of pride.

They laid their beds out side by side. Adhigasurar reached for his phone and played flute music at low volume. The room filled with the gentle sound. Kumarasurar couldn't believe that a track stored in the phone had such potency that it could echo through a room. He searched for an amplifier, but it was all the phone's work. He should ask Adhigasurar about the phone's sound system the next day. He wondered whether the music would stop once the track was finished, or whether one of them would have to manually switch it off. But it seemed too stupid a question to ask. He drifted off to sleep.

They woke late the next day. Adhigasurar had some work at the university that day too. He taught Kumarasurar how to play music on the computer before he left.

'Tell me a song you like,' he said.

Kumarasurar was at a loss once again. Then he managed to remember the name of a song.

'That's a good one,' Adhigasurar said and showed him how to search for it. He asked for another one. Kumarasurar had expected this and had used the time to rack his brain for one, so he was able to answer immediately.

Adhigasurar asked him to search for it himself.

His fingers began to tremble and sweat. But he keyed in letter by letter, and various videos featuring the song appeared. When he clicked on one and it began to play, he felt he had achieved something remarkable, and laughed triumphantly to his friend.

'That's all. It's the same thing as typing on your old office typewriter. You can use all your fingers just as you do there. A gentle tap is enough.'

And with that pep talk, his friend left. Kumarasurar was keen to see if he could search for a song all by himself, and went on to try his luck.

Now that the pressure was off, he began to wonder which songs he truly liked. Some came to mind. Which was his favourite? He tried to list them in order, but every time he thought he had a favourite, it would be pushed aside by another song he remembered. The morning slipped into afternoon. He decided he would listen to all his favourite songs and then make up his mind. He searched for them and finalised a playlist. Now he had no need to worry. He could answer not just Adhigasurar, but Kumbhas or Meghas too if they asked him to name a song he liked; he had a whole list.

Having heard all these songs to his heart's content, he read the newspapers. He went for a stroll in the garden. There were several plants and trees he couldn't identify. How did Adhigasurar find the time to tend the garden?

Just then, Adhigasurar called on his phone.

'Shall I buy lunch on my way, or shall we go out to eat?' he asked.

'Come home, let's go out to eat,' Kumarasurar said. A plan had begun to form in his head.

36

What if he surprised Adhigasurar with lunch when he returned?

Kumarasurar had cooked at home in his youth. His parents would leave early for work, and he had to cook, eat and leave for school. He was used to the wood stove. Since the gas stove and cylinder had made their way to the kitchen, he had occasionally boiled water. He had no other memories from the kitchen. Even if Mangasuri went to her village for a festival, she would not stay overnight.

'Aiyo, he'll be left to starve. He doesn't even know how to pour water out of a jug. He's never been to a hotel to eat kurma or sambar, I must make it all at home,' she would say with some pride and leave her village.

If she happened to be compelled to stay somewhere, Kumarasurar would turn to his office canteen. He would eat once and skip the other meal. One meal outside cost more than three at home. Mangasuri was the only one who was privy to his reasons.

'Hotel food gives him a stomach upset,' she would say. 'He likes only my cooking.'

Today, he felt tempted to cook. He retrieved his memories of youth and headed for the kitchen. He wasn't sure in what proportion he ought to add water to the rice. He decided to ask Mangasuri and called her.

She didn't answer his question immediately. 'Why do you want to know?' she asked.

He told her hesitantly that he felt awkward sitting around until Adhigasurar returned, and so he wanted to cook. She couldn't hide her amusement.

'You don't lift a finger here. But then you go there and cook for him, huh?' she mock scolded. She was thrilled that she could show her husband off to all the women in the street with this little anecdote that day.

She said one usually added two tumblers of water per tumbler of rice; if the rice was old, one could add up to three tumblers of water. She told him how to check whether the rice was old, but immediately added, 'But why would they not have fresh rice? Add two and a half tumblers of water for each tumbler of rice, that should take care of it.' She didn't end the conversation there. 'What kuzhambu are you making?' she asked.

Kumarasurar didn't know what to say. Mangasuri told him that paruppu kadaiyal—mashed split pigeon-pea sambar—was easy to make, and went on to explain how. She had never bubbled over with excitement like this while speaking to him before. Perhaps distance had made her heart fonder. He didn't want to hang up when she sounded like this. Once he returned, he ought to cook a meal for her. If today's lunch went well, he would do that, he decided.

The rice was in two large containers. They appeared to be different varieties. He wasn't sure which to use. He called Mangasuri again. She said the rice one used for idlis would have plumper grains, and people tended to store less of it. The other one must be the rice one used for cooking with sambar. She asked what colour it was, and told him how much water he must add.

He needed her counsel several times as he cooked. He didn't think he had ever spoken to his wife as affectionately as he did that day. When he had been steeped in the arrogance of having government employment and his head was constantly turned to the skies, he had never been able to lower it to whisper an endearment to his wife. Now he had begun to deflate and stoop until he could only stare at the ground. Though such thoughts did pop into his head, he relished the renewed joy of laughing with his wife.

It struck him that everything could be given new life. As he made rasam, he cradled the phone to his ear and followed the steps his wife listed. Rice, sambar, rasam. He tasted the rasam and sambar several times. It appeared he had a knack for cooking. He was proud of what he had made. He waited for his friend to come home with the anticipation of a new bride cooking her first meal for her husband.

Adhigasurar had not expected lunch to be waiting for him.

As they ate, he made appreciative noises and praised everything Kumarasurar had made. He had the sambar for three courses and drank rasam from a cup every now and again. Kumarasurar, surprised at how well his food was received, tasted it himself to ascertain that it really was this good. Yes, it *was* delicious.

Every sip of rasam Adhigasurar took, he said, 'Wonderful. Incredible.'

Kumarasurar felt almost shy. No one had ever praised him so much. When he had got the government job, most people had treated him with respect. Others had kept their distance. Every bit of praise he got was accompanied by waves of jealousy.

He had never heard a kind word in office. Reproach would fall from the mouths of his superiors like worms breaking out of a cocoon. But they were stingy with praise. The language itself had far more words of blame than of appreciation. The asura society believed praise would go to one's head, and abuse would keep one on one's toes. Since he had always been part of this society, he neither hoped for nor gave praise. Adhigasurar didn't have a large vocabulary for praise either, but he used each word so many times that their aroma filled the house.

Was he really part of the asura species, Kumarasurar wondered. Adhigasurar was a good cook himself. And yet he was appreciative of someone else's culinary skills. It was typical for asuras to prove their expertise by nitpicking and offering tips patronisingly as part of their critique. Adhigasurar's reaction seemed to elevate his cooking so that even Kumarasurar enjoyed its taste better. He ate a few handfuls more than usual. Perhaps it was the rusticity of his cooking that Adhigasurar had liked so much, he thought.

'We're going somewhere this evening,' Adhigasurar said after lunch. 'Let's nap for a while before we leave.'

Kumarasurar couldn't sleep. Everything around him seemed bright and shiny. There appeared to be not a vestige of darkness anywhere in the world. How could this be? He walked from room to room. He looked under the cots, inside the cupboards, into every nook and cranny of the house. There was light everywhere. He opened vessels that had lids and peered inside. There was no sign of dark. He ran out to the garden and looked under the bushes. There was no shadow. The sun seemed to shine brighter under the foliage. He was enthralled. Should he wake Adhigasurar to show him this phenomenon? But they said one shouldn't disturb another's sleep.

If he closed his eyes, surely it would be dark under the lids? He tried. But the light was blinding. He lay down, drew the sheets over his eyes and closed them again. But his lids hadn't caught a whiff of darkness. He turned so he was lying on his stomach and pressed his eyes to the pillow. No, it was still bright inside.

He realised that day that appreciation could make one's world a swirl of sunshine.

As he was enjoying the play of light, he drifted off to sleep.

When he woke, he heard an amused, 'Slept well?' and saw Adhigasurar's face. 'That was good food. I slept like a log myself. But let's leave. We're going to the seashore. Let's try to make it while it's still light.'

The word 'light' reminded him of the phenomenon he had witnessed that afternoon. He looked around himself. But the light had assumed its natural properties again. When he closed his eyes, it was dark under his lids. However, he still felt the glow of the praise he had received. He got up and dressed quickly.

37

Adhigasurar drove a car out of a garage in the backyard, which had been closed earlier. Would the university have given him the car too?

'No, they don't give us cars and all that,' Adhigasurar said. 'I'm not a Big Officer, you know! I thought it might be useful to have a car for outings, so I bought it. I don't take it out often. If I have to travel a long distance, I call a driver. It's easy to buy a car these days, isn't it?'

Kumarasurar hadn't been out since his ride from the railway station. Adhigasurar told him all about the city and pointed out important buildings and landmarks that they passed. The town was spread over a little hillock, Kumarasurar realised as the car went up and down the slope.

As they were driving downhill, Adhigasurar pointed in the direction of the sea. Kumarasurar could make out the blue, but the sky and sea seemed to be of the same colour. He had to peer carefully to discern the line of the horizon.

Adhigasurar told him there were several little beaches here, and the one they were going to see that day was the most famous. Kumarasurar had only ever been to a beach once. It was after they had been detained and released on the day of the protest in the capital. The group had gone to the beach after leaving the wedding hall. He didn't remember much of it, but it had qualified him to tell people he'd been to the seashore. So this would be his second time—no, really, his first time at a beach.

Once they had got to sea level, the beach disappeared from view for about half an hour. After crossing roads and buildings and shops and the heads of asuras and dust and tree-lined avenues and plants and fields and villages, the car finally turned to the right.

Adhigasurar indicated that he should look on both sides, and laughed.

Kumarasurar turned to one side. Just fifty feet from the road on which they were travelling were waves that gushed towards them. He turned to the other side. Heading in the same direction as they were was a stream of water. Could it be the sea on both sides? The waves clashed against each other on one side. River waters flowed towards the sea on the other. Between the two was a stretch of land perhaps a hundred or a hundred and fifty feet wide. The road occupied about twenty feet of this stretch. Fishermen's huts lined the road.

Ten miles from this spot was the estuary where the river and sea met.

'It's a beautiful sight,' Adhigasurar explained. 'When I feel like I need a breath of fresh air, this is where I go.'

Kumarasurar turned from one view to the next throughout the journey.

The chaotic roar struck their ears from one side, and deafening silence hit them from the other. Calm and fury were side by side, so palpable you felt you could touch them with your hands. Perhaps the stretch of sand between the two comprised linked hands reaching out towards both the stillness and the turbulence. The poetic sensibility that had deserted him after his youth might have found him again, Kumarasurar thought.

What if the waves rose really high or the river flooded, and the two mixed together? The thought scared him. That could happen on doomsday. But the fishermen who lived on either side of the stretch had lived there for centuries. And they were safe.

Adhigasurar, who had driven silently so he wouldn't intrude on Kumarasurar's thoughts, now saw his face and said, 'Are you scared? The sight used to frighten me in the beginning too. The fear's gone now. But the sense of wonder I first felt remains with me.'

The gentle sun of the evening smiled down upon them. Adhigasurar accelerated and then parked in a corner, before a house. They got off and walked among the coconut trees. They passed the huts, climbed the rocks and reached a turn.

Water stretched as far as their eyes could see. The sea was blue, while the river swirled black and white. They clashed at the estuary. The waves rose to an asura's height and then subsided. The sand was soft as fleece, and Kumarasurar's toes tingled when they touched the grains. Adhigasurar stood still and took in the scene.

Kumarasurar came under a spell. He spread his arms wide and shook them as if he was dusting something off, and then rushed towards the sea like a child and wet his feet in its waters. He scooped up water in his hands and put it in his mouth. It was rather brackish. He went closer to the estuary and scooped up the water there. It was as sweet as honey. Then he ran further out to sea and tasted the water. It was salty. How the nature of water changed, all within a few feet of each other, he thought.

He went back to the point of confluence and stood there. The waves reared up as if to fight the river waters sneaking into them, lost the battle, absorbed the fresh water into their own bodies and left sated. The retreat and charge and union followed each other in cycles. When he stood where the waters converged, the sea licked his feet in a teasing caress, and then rose to his knees, and then flowed away. It was as if the water were tickling him playfully. He closed his eyes, laughed out loud and allowed himself to enjoy the experience. He was tempted to wade further in. He walked forward until he stood knee-deep in the sea. But his enthusiasm hadn't abated. He longed to sink his feet into the soft seabed, just a little deeper, just a little deeper.

Water could be a clever temptress, seducing one until it could swallow one whole. The sea was an endless body of water. It curled its finger and called out to him alluringly. Kumarasurar moved further in. The last rays of the sun threw spangles of diamonds on the bubbling surface. He couldn't look away. It was as if the day were sinking into the sea, the red of the gloaming giving way to the pitch of night. He wanted to follow it inside.

As the dark spread across the waters, a single beam of sunlight shimmered on the surface. The light and water and wind appeared to dance on that narrow track, and he walked further into its channel. It was as if a net had caught the beam on either side and was jiggling it. He wanted to touch the net, and stretched out a hand.

Suddenly, Adhigasurar's voice brought him back to earth: 'Don't go further than that!'

He stopped short, not knowing where he was.

'Come back ... come this way,' Adhigasurar was calling from the shore.

Drawn by the force of his voice, Kumarasurar slowly made his way to the sand.

'What are you trying to do, going further and further into the sea? You should admire it from a distance. If we give in to our emotions, the water will pull us right in. You should be watchful,' Adhigasurar said.

Kumarasurar laughed in embarrassment.

'I come here often, so I'm used to it. I sit by the shore and watch the day recede into night. When you keep a silent watch, it disappears right before your eyes, diving into the waters without you noticing. There, look ... it's over ... it's gone.'

Adhigasurar pointed in excitement, and they watched as the last smidgen of daylight sank into the sea. The sky lost its final grip on day, and the night caressed the waters. The wonder of witnessing the day breathing its last even as the night was born left them speechless. It was only when they were walled in by the darkness that they could talk again.

'Let's go,' Adhigasurar said, turning to walk ahead. 'Coming here gives your mind and body the strength to see the next ten days through.'

Kumarasurar didn't speak. He felt he had forgotten all language. His mind was blank. You needed language only to express your thoughts. He felt all his thoughts had drained away, and there was only vast space.

'People who come here once in a while feel this way. But this is no big deal to the fishermen who have been living here for aeons. The coming and going of day have no effect on them at all; it's just an ordinary sight.' Adhigasurar kept up a steady chatter on the way back.

Kumarasurar wished his friend would keep quiet and allow him to savour his joy in silence. Why was he being so annoying? He tried to reduce Adhigasurar's voice to a hum in the background. It was a new bird's call to him now. Kumarasurar could give himself in to silence again, and lost track of when the bird's chirping subsided, when they got into the car, when they reached home.

38

The next day, something drove Kumarasurar to seek out the estuary by himself. He went to the beach. The fact that he was a stranger to the town didn't daunt him. He asked for directions, took buses, walked and eventually reached the place. It was the hour before sunset, and the western sky was at its brightest.

He sat staring towards the heavens. On the one side, he could hear sounds of the union between sea and river waters, the swell of one and the sneaking of the other and their final embrace; on the other side, he could hear the waves crash against each other and break. Devoting one ear to each sound, he continued to look at the sky, unblinking.

Two eagles soared over the waves, their enormous wings still as they spread out majestically. When they wanted to fly higher, they moved their wings in a languid, decisive gesture and shot like arrows into the sky. He flew up after them. The sky had become an empty canvas, on which they turned into paintbrushes and drew arresting scenes.

He looked away for a moment, and found that one of the eagles had disappeared when he turned his attention back to them. Where could it have gone? Could it have dived into the waves and sunk? Could it have flown towards its nest in the faraway coconut tree grove that stood in the smoky distance? He searched the sky for it, but could see only a lone eagle.

He would not let this one go, he thought, and followed its every move. The light receded from around the bird, and its figure became smaller and smaller until it was just a point in the sky. Eventually, the point disappeared into nothing. He found it stunning that one could fly so high into the sky that one vanished. It stirred emotions within him that he couldn't quite articulate, even to himself.

The pink of the twilit sky climbed higher, and the band floating above the horizon turned a brilliant hue even as it shrank in width.

Every second, the shifting colours of the sky created a new work of art. His heart was heavy at not being able to retain each of those images. Not one disappeared. Each faded into the background as a different one took shape in the foreground.

The turbulence in his mind stilled as he focused on these scenes. It was as if the day was cheekily fooling his eyes, disappearing right before him but without his noticing. The magic of these moments entranced him. But he didn't care to learn the magician's secret; he wanted to savour every moment of the spectacle, and lost himself in it.

The fishermen in their faded lungis were on the beach. A few tourists roamed about too. The light gave way to shadow bit by bit until, all of a sudden, the night announced itself. Where had the light gone? Where was the day? From where had the night snuck up on them? He couldn't understand a thing.

The night brought its own sights and sounds. Lovers who arrived in pairs and sat on the beach were approached by the fishermen, who shooed the couples off with, 'Get moving, go. You have to leave now. You can't stay here after dark.'

But no one disturbed him, or a few others like him, who sat alone. Perhaps middle-aged men who watched the sunset alone were a common sight on the beach.

The night had parked itself firmly around them like a wall of darkness. For a while, it was as if nothing moved. The waves had stopped their play. The sea was frozen in the night.

Kumarasurar began to sweat with fear. He felt suffocated, as if he had been walled in. He lay back where he was sitting. The stillness lasted only a few moments. The breeze floated towards him and caressed his body. With that, the wall of darkness splintered and the night fluttered like a diaphanous sari. The spell on the sea was broken, and the waves resumed their furious roar.

The night softened and allowed the eyes to observe the space it had occupied. The breeze pulverised the wall of darkness as it skipped towards the waves. The waves now appeared to dance in shades of black, sometimes rising, sometimes falling.

He walked to the sea and let the waves lap his feet. His entire body felt cool. He walked along the waves so they could caress his feet. The sea teased him, slapping his feet, stealing the sand from under his soles and running away with it.

He walked some distance and then turned to face the sea, his feet in the water. The ocean was before him. Was it? It was, but he couldn't see it. How could something that was there not be visible? It only existed if it could be seen, surely? Another question rose in his mind all of a sudden. What was it that had caressed his feet, the water, the waves or the sea? Which was water? Which was a wave? Which was the sea? Could one separate them? If one took the water away from the equation, where would the waves be? Without the waves, where would the sea be? What did the sea mean, anyway? They were all linked together. Was it the sound of waves that we called the sea? Not every body of water is called the sea. So it must be the sound that makes the sea.

Can an ocean be sensed just from its sound? Why did one have to take the trouble to invent a word like 'sea'? Water, wave, sea, sound ... they were just words. What would a world without words and names be like? Kumarasurar was now without language.

Everything appeared fresh to him.

He lived in a world where nothing had a name. He simply observed everything around him. He didn't need to describe anything. He didn't try to identify anything. All this world had were images. He stood and watched for a long time. Then, he went to lie down on the sand. The waves splashed against his feet. Some of the waves were more adventurous. They came right up to his hips and receded. They tried to turn him over. Sleep took hold of him at some point. He slept by the seaside like a corpse that couldn't feel the cold.

It was only when his body, wet from sea, began to shiver in the breeze that he woke. He sat up. His head seemed to be empty of memories—who he was, where he was, what he had been doing all this while, where he had come from. He was the first living organism in Asuralokam. He was a sapling that had sprouted from the sand. He stretched his hands back so he could hoist himself up and stared into the dark.

As he came to, he could see the moon shining over the sea. A beam of moonlight traced a single line before his eyes on the water surface. He wanted to walk along the line, dancing over the waves. He stood up. His legs were numb from the cold of the water. He shook them to get rid of the pins and needles. He stood trembling, watching the beam. But the single line he had spotted when he was seated was no longer there; the moonlight shimmered on the waves, through the entire expanse of the sea.

The crests of the waves shone with light and their troughs swirled in darkness. As far as the eye could see, the waves seemed to rush towards him with a frightening hunger, as if they would attack and devour him. But as they approached, they slowed their pace, and by the time they touched him, they snuggled between his toes with the tameness of a contented little puppy. He was enjoying this little game.

But suddenly, it appeared the waves had arrived with an entourage and were inviting him to come in. Yes, it was an invitation. And with what courteousness the waves invited him, over and over again, almost pleading with him! Were they asking him to become part of them? Or did they want to show him the magical world they held in their depths and stun him?

He opened his eyes wide. The waves danced seductively, their expressions and movements a study in elegance. There was no one else on the beach. This was a dance choreographed just for him. As the waves raised their hands and turned their faces to the skies, the moonbeams obliged with mood lighting.

His legs had recovered now. He walked as he watched the dance.

The nature of the waves changed now. The waves turned into an asura hand that had gathered in its palm all the pleasures of the world. He stood entranced. Two asura hands. With arms. Those asura arms had spread wide to gather him up too. When arms had stretched themselves out to fold one into such a loving embrace, how could one resist? Kumarasurar ran towards the waves. His feet slipped and he fell. He got up and ran faster. All he wanted was to sink into those arms that were waiting to clasp him to their bosom.

39

It was well into the day when Adhigasurar woke him up. He had made breakfast and laid it out on the table, and had been waiting for him. Kumarasurar dressed and joined him, embarrassed. He didn't know when he had returned home from the beach. His last memory was of plunging into the waters. How and when had he got back? If only he had stayed a little longer, he could have seen the sunrise too. Why had he missed it and returned in such a hurry? He could make no sense of his decisions.

As soon as he was seated, Adhigasurar looked at him, smiled fondly and said, 'Shall we go to the beach today too?'

Kumarasurar was confused. Had he really gone to the beach the previous day, or had it been a dream? Had he spent the night there? What had he told Adhigasurar before he left? Where had he boarded the bus? He couldn't recall any of these details. He hid his bewilderment and said, 'Sure, let's go.'

They went to the beach again that evening. By the time they turned into the path that led to the beach from the main road, the light had begun to dim. Their goal was to reach the estuary. Not all goals were realised; sometimes, one had to let go; sometimes, one had to change one's goal. Or, one could decide upon a different path to the goal, depending on opportunity and circumstance. It was rarely that one felt the pleasure of achieving a goal. What would happen that day? These were Adhigasurar's thoughts on the idea of goals.

Kumarasurar felt the notion of 'goals' didn't merit so much thought or discussion. He was rather surprised by this change in his attitude. He made a show of listening with interest to what his friend had to say. His affection for Adhigasurar seemed to have waned.

Everyone lived within a set of boundaries that circumscribed one's life. When one stood within one's ambit and looked at someone else, it appeared the other person was crossing his limits. When they were circumscribed by invisible lines, how could one tell what was right and good within the boundaries?

'Today, I have something else to show you,' Adhigasurar said, and drove him to a liquor shop by the beach.

The shop was a little thatched shed among the coconut trees. A couple of customers were waiting. Kumarasurar and Adhigasurar chose one of the tables erected outside and sat across from each other. They could see the entire beach from this point. It was as if the waves were welcoming them to the shop. Kumarasurar happily folded his hands in greeting and accepted the welcome. It was rather nice to watch the sea from a distance, he thought. There was a subtle difference between the attachment kindled by proximity and the affection by distance. The joy he felt at watching the sea seemed to have communicated itself to the waves, and they skipped about as his heart did.

A man came to their table.

'Can we get it freshly tapped?' Adhigasurar asked.

The man said they could, but it would cost more than toddy that had already been brought down from the trees.

'That's fine, get us fresh toddy,' Adhigasurar said. 'There's nothing in the world that can hold a candle to coconut toddy. Would you like to taste?'

It was as if Kumarasurar had been expecting the invitation. 'Sure, might as well try it,' he said.

'Really? You'll have some?' Adhigasurar couldn't hide his surprise. He seemed quite thrilled.

Kumarasurar didn't know what had prompted his sudden decision. The sea welcomed everything that came close. All one needed was to learn how to welcome everything. He kept the thought to himself, but laughed out loud.

When they asked for freshly tapped toddy, the proprietor said he could make the arrangements as long as they would have at least two padis—about six pints—of it. Adhigasurar agreed.

A man who was at the shop began to prepare himself to tap the toddy. He tied a tapping box around his waist and armed himself with a coir rope. He went inside the coconut grove, stood under a tree, made a stirrup around his legs and climbed up the tree as if he were ascending a ladder.

'This is the real fresh toddy,' Adhigasurar said.

The man scaled the tree, reached for where the tapping pots were and emptied the toddy into a container he had carried with him. They watched as he shimmied back down.

When Kumarasurar turned back to stare at the sea, Adhigasurar looked amused. Even when he was offered other views, his mind was on the sea. But this too was a view of the sea. The sea and the views one could take of it had no bounds. Everything belonged to the sea.

In the distance, they could see the sunlight dancing on the waves.

The toddy container was brought to their table and strained before their eyes. There were beetles and bees floating on the surface. The scent of the toddy had drawn them, and they had fallen into it to become part of its flavour. Having disposed of their bodies in the bin, the man brought them jugs of fresh toddy.

Adhigasurar poured the drink into little mud tumblers and handed one to Kumarasurar, who took it with some hesitation.

'Kudhookalam!' Adhigasurar cried and brought his tumbler to Kumarasurar's.

His excitement was infectious, and Kumarasurar replied with enthusiasm: 'Kudhookalam!'

Adhigasurar closed his eyes, took a deep sniff of the tumbler and then had a few sips.

Kumarasurar hesitated with the tumbler in his hands and was about to keep it on the table, when Adhigasurar stopped him and said, laughing, 'Ahaan! You have to take at least one sip after you say "Kudhookalam" and before you set it down, remember?'

Kumarasurar's tongue tasted alcohol for the first time. It had the subtly sweet flavour of jaggery mixed in fermented rice water. It had a sharp tinge of tartness, as if a sliver of the evening's sunshine had been mixed into the liquor. Toddy was a heavenly amalgam of sweetness and tartness.

As Adhigasurar sipped his toddy, Kumarasurar glugged it down.

A platter of fried fish appeared on the table. It was the perfect pairing, toddy and fish. When Kumarasurar's attention was diverted to his food and drink, the sea had gone dark. He looked up and felt sad that he hadn't noticed. But then, the sea knew the trick of disappearing into darkness right under one's nose. Today, the gift of the sea to him was the toddy. He must relish every drop of it. He found he now craved the liquor, and drank it as he listened to Adhigasurar's chatter.

The toddy before them was being fast depleted.

At one point, Kumarasurar began to speak. 'Adhi … I'm greatly indebted to this sea. You introduced me to it. No, no … The sea introduced me to you … What do you think a sea is? The sea is …'

40

Once he returned to town, he went back to work in the office. He didn't speak much to Mangasuri, but despite his silence, he seemed happy. She observed little changes in his behaviour. He continued to shut himself up in a room, but she could hear the sound of music from inside. Sometimes it seemed he was playing a film on the computer. He once voiced his appreciation for a meal she had prepared with a single word: 'Incredible.' He hadn't looked at her—his face was turned to his food—but it thrilled Mangasuri.

He seemed to fall asleep as soon as he went to bed. His stints of meditation on the terrace had stopped.

One night, he approached Mangasuri, lay down by her side in bed and began to caress her.

Mangasuri did not let her husband in on her observations. But when she spoke to Meghas in Kumarasurar's absence, she told him joyously about these little changes. She called Adhigasurar to tell him too.

'Next time, you join him here, ma,' Adhigasurar said.

That weekend, Kumarasurar told his wife, 'I have some work in office. I won't be home until nightfall.'

He barely had work during weekdays. What work could demand his presence in the office on a weekend, and that too till nightfall, Mangasuri wondered. Kumarasurar knew his lie was transparent. But he did not want to tell her his plan. He got on a bus to Meghas's college and waited at the hostel for his son's return.

When he saw his father, Meghas stopped in surprise. What had prompted this sudden appearance? Could there be some problem between his parents? There was no chance of that. In all these years, they had let various opportunities to fight slide. Even if they began to argue, one would give in before it could escalate. Meghas had often wondered how they could lead such a deathly dull life together.

'What happened, Appa?' he asked.

'Come, let's go out,' his father said.

Meghas sat Kumarasurar at the reception and made for his room to change. His pad was in such a state of disarray it would not do to let his father see it.

There was something else he had to do, which needed privacy. He wanted to call his mother to ask about Kumarasurar's uncharacteristic visit. Mangasuri was surprised. 'If only that man would respect me enough to tell me his whereabouts. What am I going to do, lie across his path? I'd have sent along some food that you like. Why did he run off to see you without breathing a word to me?'

There would be no stopping her rant. 'All right, all right, we'll talk later, I have to go,' Meghas said hurriedly. He washed his face, dressed quickly and went down to the reception.

Kumarasurar was talking to the clerk. Meghas wondered whether he had been making enquiries about him. What would the clerk have said? The boys at the hostel had often felt he saw himself as a policeman and them as criminals in his charge. His favourite pastime was to whine about the students to their parents. Whatever the man had said, Meghas decided he could sort it out later. He called out to his father.

Kumarasurar turned and looked his son up and down. Was he going to ask him why he needed two sets of clothes a day, Meghas fretted.

'Did you buy these clothes here? You look good,' Kumarasurar smiled.

Meghas grinned back.

It had been a while since his son and he had shared a moment, Kumarasurar thought. He knew Meghas loved dosais and asked him to choose a good restaurant. The one Meghas suggested was a bus ride away. The restaurant specialised in dosai varieties, and he ate there on occasion.

As they walked towards the bus stop, Kumarasurar stopped an autorickshaw and said to Meghas, 'Let's not go by bus.' He didn't ask the driver what the fare would be. As they rode to the restaurant, he chatted with Meghas about life in college. Meghas waited for his father to launch into his regular lecture, but it didn't come. He asked questions, listened to the answers and looked contemplative, but did not voice his opinions. When they arrived, he paid the fare the driver demanded without haggling.

'Order for both of us,' Kumarasurar said. He reached for the water jug at the table and drank as if he had been thirsting for days.

As they waited for their dosais, he turned to Meghas and asked, 'How long to go?'

'For what, Appa?'

'For that mobile phone to come to the market.'

'Maybe ten to fifteen days. Why, Appa?'

Kumarasurar reached for the jug again. 'I'll put the money in your account. You order the phone.'

'No, Appa. I've decided I don't need a new phone right now,' Meghas said quickly, studying his father's face.

'Why don't you want it anymore? There's no problem. Buy it. Buy whichever one you like. There's no money crunch at home.'

'No, it's just that last semester, our lecturer spoke in such an interesting way about creating mobile apps, I thought I'd get into that field. But this semester, we have a fantastic professor who's teaching us coding. I think I want to specialise in that instead.'

'Really?'

'Really. So the phone I have is enough for now.'

'But you can buy one which is more technologically advanced, with better features. Don't worry. There's no problem.'

'No, Appa. If you think about it, you only really need a mobile phone so you can make calls. I barely have time to study. I don't want to distract myself and waste time. I only speak to you and Amma anyway. The phone I have lets me do that. I'll buy a new one when I see fit.'

'So you don't want one?'

'No.'

'You sure you don't want one?'

'I'm sure.'

'Buy it.'

'I don't want it.'

'Well ... even so ... order it anyway.'

'Why? I just told you I don't need it.'

'I'll toss out my old one and start using the new phone. Will you order it for me?'

Meghas began to choke on his dosai. Kumarasurar rose, thumped him on the back and handed him a glass of water.

Acknowledgements

The writers Gayathri Prabhu and Nikhil Govind, who work as professors in the Department of Philosophy and Humanities at Manipal University in Karnataka, hosted and supported me as I was writing this novel. My days there were brightened by the presence of the department's students and my friends, Jackson and Vivek.

Three people read the first draft of the novel. My wife, Ezhil, had positive feedback for me; my daughter, Pirai, told me she wished Kumarasurar and Mangasuri had had a girl child too; my son, Paridhi, provided much of the raw material for the novel, read it and gave me his stamp of approval.

Several dear friends read and gave me ideas to revise the second draft of the novel. Sukumaran voiced his opinion with a 'sabaash'. As always, R. Raman (Kalyanaraman) gave me a nuanced response. Isai read the work with hesitation and affection, and shared his thoughts. T. Rajan has been my touchstone.

My friend K. Kasimariyappan read the book twice and gave me detailed feedback which has greatly improved the novel.

The final draft was read by my friends Kalachuvadu Kannan, K. Mohanarangan and A.R. Venkatachalapathy. Kala Murugan ensured that the bookmaking was done with nuance, and in accordance with my wishes.

Kalachuvadu Kannan saw the novel through every stage of its progress right up to its publication.

Nandini Krishnan, who has translated this novel into English, is very familiar with my work. She has read my books thoroughly, and wrote a detailed profile of me back in 2013. It gives me great joy that a person who knows the nuances of my work has translated this novel.

I'd like to thank Westland for publishing *Poonachi, or the Story of a Black Goat* and *Amma*, the English translations of my books *Poonachi* and *Thondrathunai*, which have given me so many new readers and so much recognition. I am grateful to V.K. Karthika and Janani Ganesan in particular.

I am grateful to my friend Kalachuvadu Kannan for his efforts to have my books translated into several languages including English.

My heartfelt gratitude to everyone.

26 November 2018
Perumal Murugan
Namakkal

A Translator's Response

Nandini Krishnan

When *Estuary* was published in Tamil, it created a buzz about being Perumal Murugan's first urban novel. However, it is less an urban novel than a story of migration, the migration we often take for granted when it is intra-regional. It is not the story of the Punjabi boy who arrives without language to Canadian shores and drives trucks in the hope that his sons or grandsons will hold their own with 'real Canadians' and build the kind of mansions he passes on the boulevards. It is not the story of the Bangladeshi boys in Italy whom we met in Amitav Ghosh's *Gun Island*, nor that of Najeeb Muhammad of Benyamin's *Goat Days*, nor that of the Indian nanny who must surrender her passport to the family that has employed her in Saudi Arabia, nor that of the Ph.D. student from Ghana who arrives in London on scholarship and sweeps the streets at night because his stipend is just enough to cover his student expenses and make up for the salary he would have made back home, but not enough for his family to speak of the successful son who has 'gone abroad'. It is not even the story of the Nepali security guard who is struggling to learn Tamil. But it is all their stories, and the story, too, of the waiter who beseechingly asks the foreigner eating alone at a table whether he can practise his English with her. It is also the story Mr Biswas might have told if he had sought to build his house in the twenty-first century.

Estuary may be, in some ways, Perumal Murugan's most autobiographical novel, while also imagining a completely different life for the protagonist, Kumarasurar. Like the author, Kumarasurar is the first graduate from his family. Like the author, he speaks a single language with authority. Like the author, he gets into government service, ensuring lifelong financial security (or so he thinks). However, unlike the author, he is not a famous writer. Nor is he a professor with a posse of adoring students whom he can mentor, batch after batch—students who will look up to him and, in a way, replace the son to whom he has become increasingly irrelevant.

Perumal Murugan's remarkable insight into the life of a man whose assurance of an extraordinary life has turned into a parody of itself elevates the novel to near-allegory. Kumarasurar watches in bewilderment as his wife, who has barely seen the world outside their home, remains central to her son's life and even learns to speak his language of gadgetry and innovation, while he himself deals with the realisation of his near-impotency as he moves from being the guide to the guided.

What does it do to a man who is approaching middle age—and realising that the awe he once inspired in his village for passing a formidable examination and landing a coveted government job has long disappeared—when he is derided by his own child, the child to whom he was once a hero?

Even as he examines the devastating heartbreak that fatherhood can bring, Perumal Murugan gives us a nuanced perspective on the power of money and language. In many ways, it is Kumarasurar's lack of English that denies him a protégé at work. In her brilliant novel, *My Sister Chaos*, the Australian writer Lara Fergus says in her migrant-narrator's voice:

'Since arriving here I have gone further—expanded my vocabulary, perfected syntax, almost eliminated my accent. At interview with prospective employers I knew that if I were to falter in this official language then so too would their perception of my ability in other areas. Even children can conjugate verbs effortlessly in their mother tongue. The inability to do so infantilises the speaker in the eyes of others, in a way that is beyond both logic and justice.'

It was the very same sentiment the Tamil writer Salma expressed at the Jaipur Literature Festival 2019, at a session I was translating, while speaking of the frustration of having an opinion but not the vocabulary to express it in English. 'English is a language of access, not of intellect,' she said. 'But we tend to confuse intelligence with the knowledge of English, and that is why people lose their confidence, children who don't know English lose their confidence. When there was an attempt to impose Hindi on Tamil Nadu, there was a great protest against it because Tamilians believed the language we need in schools in order to access the world was English and not Hindi.'

This is also something I observed with Perumal Murugan himself at sessions at literature festivals, where a Tamil-to-French or Tamil-to-English translator would often sum up five minutes of erudition into two simplistic sentences. When *Estuary* was first released, in 2020, I offered to translate all the press interviews—the questions into Tamil, so he could respond to them, and his answers into English. It moved me to see the enthusiasm with which he responded to the Tamil translation of the questions, and to think that conveying the clarity of thought and nuance of expression in his responses fell to a translator.

Kumarasurar deals with this too—being monolingual in a world that is increasingly governed by knowledge of a foreign language. He is out of his depth, not only with the changing technology to which he must adapt himself, but also with the language that will enable him to do so. But 'the most unkindest cut of all' may be that among those who hold his floundering in contempt is the boy he made—his son, for whom he ensured the most sophisticated education and the highest access to the modern world that he could afford.

As I read the Tamil version, I found myself thinking of the parking assistant who once told me proudly that all his three daughters were graduates; of our electrician's son who went to a missionary school and has just got into the B.Com. programme at a prestigious college, and who must study for his exams in a two-room house in a street where loudspeakers blare all day and through most of the night; of a member of the housekeeping staff at a clinic who told me her daughter was working in a private bank. It made me wonder how these children see the parents who have worked so hard to give them a chance at a comfortable life. It made me think of Alfred J. Prufrock, as Kumarasurar wonders constantly, 'Do I dare?' and, 'Do I dare?'

Estuary is a book about language and class and aspiration and hurt. It is a book about parenting, but also a book about watching oneself, censoring oneself—at work, at home, in thought, in speech, in deed. It is a book about mental health as much as it is about societal pressure. It is a book about daring to 'disturb the universe', a book about 'decisions and revisions which a minute will reverse', a book about a man to whom the mermaids will not sing. It is a book that makes demands of the reader, who cannot sit back and nod along with a critique of social injustice, but who must scour the lines for what lies in between. It is a book unlike any Perumal Murugan has written before, and a book I feel privileged to have translated.